Copyright

The author has asserted their moral right under the Copyright, Designs and Patents Act, 1988, to be identified as the author of this work.

All Rights reserved. No part of this publication may be reproduced, copied, stored in a retrieval system, or transmitted, in any form or by any means, without the prior written consent of the copyright holder, nor be otherwise circulated in any form of binding or cover other than that in which it is published and without a similar condition being imposed on the subsequent purchaser.

NO AI TRAINING: Without in any way limiting the author's [and publisher's] exclusive rights under copyright, any use of this publication to "train" generative artificial intelligence (AI) technologies to generate text is expressly prohibited. The author reserves all rights to license uses of this work for generative AI training and development of machine learning language models.

Previously published under the pseudonym: J. M. Ruddock

A CIP catalogue record for this title is available from the British Library.
Cover design: Covergirl
Images: Inara Prusakova via Dreamstime & Richard Burchett - Sanctuary (1867) via WikimediaCommons

A Daughter of Warwick

The Story of Anne Neville Queen to Richard III

Judith Arnopp
Previously published under the pseudonym J. M. Ruddock

List of Characters

Edward Plantagenet - Yorkist King of England
Elizabeth Woodville - Yorkist Queen of England
Richard Neville, Earl of Warwick - The kingmaker (Anne's Father)
Anne Beauchamp, Countess of Warwick - (Anne's mother)
Isabel Neville, daughter of Warwick
Anne Neville, daughter of Warwick
Richard Plantagenet, Duke of Gloucester, brother to the king
George Plantagenet, Duke of Clarence, brother to the king
Cecily Neville, Dowager Duchess of York, King's mother
Henry VI (deposed) Lancastrian King of England
Marguerite of Anjou, Lancastrian Queen of Henry VI (deposed)
Edward of Lancaster, Lancastrian Prince, son of Margaret of Anjou and Henry VI
Edward Plantagenet, son of Richard and Anne of Gloucester
Edward, Prince of Wales, son of Edward IV
Richard, Duke of York, son of Edward IV
Henry Stafford, Duke of Buckingham, cousin to Richard
Francis Lovell, friend of Richard of Gloucester
Elizabeth of York, daughter of Edward IV
Cecily of York, daughter of Edward IV
Characters not mentioned here are probably fictional.

PART ONE
'Girl'

Middleham-1461

It was the end of a bright October afternoon. A lone hawk soared above the Yorkshire Dale. Far below, the red, saffron and gold robes of three figures splashed against the purpling moor and caught the eye of the bird of prey. As their voices spiralled upward, the hawk's shadow passed over a running dog.

A small girl wept piteously. While her female attendant, Jayne, offered her comfort, the elder child protested that it was long past time to return to the castle.

'No, Isabel,' replied Jayne. 'I will not leave him; he can't be far. You go back if you like; I would rather face your father's anger than lie awake all night thinking of Troy out here alone. It's all right, Anne, we'll find him, don't worry.'

Anne dried her eyes and scrambled to her feet, a hand to her brow as she scanned the horizon for a sign of her pup. He had disappeared quite suddenly, initiating a frantic search. Anne's face was tear-streaked, and her dress torn and stained. Her elder sister, Isabel, fretted to return to the castle, reluctant to risk the wrath of their father. As they circled, and peered across the rolling hills, calling and calling, Anne's hopes were fading as quickly as the light.

'We have to go back now. I'm sorry, Anne.'

Reluctantly, Jayne ushered her weeping charges back to the castle. Anne lingered behind, her head drooping, her tears falling but, as they neared the gate, she stopped and cocked her head, drawing her sleeve across her cheek to dry her tears.

'Listen.'

They all froze, scarcely breathing. At first, all they could hear was the whistling wind as it raced across the moor but then the sound came again. Anne raced toward the twisted bole of a tree growing beneath the castle walls.

'Troy!' she cried, scooping the whimpering pup into her arms and burying her face in his fur. His body wriggled in her grasp. She looked up at her sister, her face filthy with tears.

'I told you we'd find him, Isabel. All it needed was a little faith.'

'Yes but look how late we are. We will be lucky to escape a whipping.'

Isabel grabbed her sister's hand and dragged her toward the safety of the great hall.

Most days it was easy to sneak unobserved through the large gateway that led into the stable yard but today as they entered a clarion of trumpets announced the arrival of a troop of horse. At the sound, the castle keep shattered into confusion. Voices shouted and servants appeared as if from nowhere to attend the cavalcade that clattered across the drawbridge, filling the bailey with horses, fluttering pennants showing the bear and the ragged staff, and the Warwick coat of arms. The Earl of Warwick was home from court, bringing with him the king's brothers, the young Dukes of Gloucester and Clarence, the younger of which had come to make his home at Middleham.

Anne cowered close to the wall, fearing to move lest she be noticed and risk her father's wrath. She watched a groom take the bridle of her father's horse while he dismounted; he drew off his gauntlets, slapped his mount's rump as he passed. The great beast sidestepped, tossed his head with a jangle of harness. Warwick's companions also dismounted, and she was surprised at the friendly manner in which her father flung an arm about the neck of a dark-haired boy. A taller, fairer boy joined them, one hand on his sword.

Anne knew who they were and, her interest piqued, she wondered which of the king's brothers were which. Is the boy which her father was speaking to George or Richard?

It was a great honour for Warwick to be chosen to oversee the military training of the king's young brother, and a feast had been prepared to mark the occasion before the harsh schedule began. Warwick was gesturing about the bailey, showing off his home to his companions. The hard ride had whipped colour into his cheeks, and he looked healthy and self-satisfied, his laughter ringing out across the castle at something the older boy had said. Sensing he was in good spirits, Anne sighed in relief but did not go forward to greet him.

Clutching the dog to her muddy bodice, she strained her ears to hear but they were too far off, and she could only make out the tone of his voice. And then, as he turned to guide his guests to the great hall, he noticed her and stopped in his tracks. He glared at her, withdrawing his friendly arm, and interrupting the young duke's tale, his eyes bulged with suppressed rage.

'Well, this is a fine greeting. You look more like a kitchen drab than a daughter of mine. Get out of my sight, before I lose my good temper.'

Anne thrust the puppy into the arms of a nearby groom.

'Please can you bathe him and have him brought to me later?' she begged before she fled.

To reach the hall it was necessary to pass close to her father and his companions, and as she scurried by, her father cuffed her lightly about the head. She ducked away, shamed, and as she fled she was aware of the boys watching; the dark-haired boy flashed her a look that might have been pity but, as she scurried by, the laughter of the tow-headed boy drifted after her.

The nurse was in a fluster.

'Where have you been?' she cried as soon as Anne appeared. Without waiting for an explanation, she tugged at the laces of her gown, rubbing her face with a rough cloth before hastening her into fresher, more formal clothes. As the comb dragged through her hair, Anne reflected that it was not the luxurious toilette they had planned. All afternoon the kitchen scullions had laboured up and down the twisting stairs with slopping buckets of water for the bath, but now the tub of water was unused and rapidly cooling. Soft towels were warming before the fire; she had looked forward to wrapping her freshly bathed body in them, relaxing by the fire before she was dressed but it was too late now. The nurse tossed her a pair of slippers, barely waiting for her to slip her feet into them, before thrusting her toward the door.

'Hurry up, child, everyone will be waiting.'

The girls were seldom invited to dine formally in the presence of their father but, as the honoured guests were of a similar age to Isabel and Anne, he had deemed it appropriate that they be present. Warwick was not one to miss a lucrative opportunity.

By the time they reached the hall it was already filling with revellers. Isabel and Anne peeped from behind the arras, absorbing the gaiety of the torch-lit scene. The hall was full of people, shouting to be heard above their neighbour. Fires raged, and as the warm air mingled with the cold, the wall tapestries swayed, the torches guttered, casting devilish shadows on the walls.

The tables were clothed in white damask tablecloths and strewn with wreaths of dried poppies and roses; the top table adorned with the best plate. Beneath the table, her father's wolfhounds waited strategically for scraps and bones. High above the hall, the minstrels were warming up in the gallery and the discordant sound of tuning harps, pipes and lutes mingled with the hubbub of voices.

As Warwick and his guests took their seats, pipes of hypocras and malmsey were borne in on silver trays and servants darted between the diners, their hasty feet crushing the dried gillyflowers that had been strewn through the rushes to permeate and freshen the heavy air.

The music had begun in earnest by the time the girls sidled into the room and slid as imperceptibly as possible into their places. They sat tall in their seats, trying not to be noticed while they absorbed the proceedings with wide eyes. It was a heady atmosphere. The flickering light of many torches softened the contours of Warwick's great hall, the strains of music from above conflicting with the roar of conversation, growling dogs and clattering flagons.

While striving not to notice them, Isabel and Anne took special interest in the king's brothers. While she was making note of their noble bearing and elegant manners, Anne jumped visibly when the dark-haired boy caught her looking and raised his cup in her direction. This one, she decided, must be Richard of Gloucester, the younger of the two, the other must be George of Clarence. Anne ducked her head in confusion and pretended to pay attention to her trencher.

As she worked her way through the many courses, she wondered how the boys could be so calm when their father and brother had only met their deaths in December last. Their ignoble treatment at the hands of Lancaster must still be painful. After the battle at Wakefield, the Duke of York and his son, Edmund had been beheaded, the duke mocked with a paper crown before their heads were placed above Micklegate bar in York. After Towton, the battle in which York was again victorious, the heads were replaced by those of Lancaster but even so, the boys must surely still feel the loss. Anne couldn't imagine ever coming to terms with such a thing.

The struggle for the crown between the houses of York and Lancaster had been going on for so long, Anne was uncertain of the cause. The two houses were of the same blood but sprung from different branches. Both houses traced their lineage to the sons of Edward III, but Lancaster had been in power until the previous king, Henry VI had fallen to some strange malady that made him unable to talk or govern. Nobody wanted his wife, the French woman, Marguerite to have the regency until her son came of age to rule, so Richard's father had been given the role of protector. Adherents of Lancaster however, continually undermined and challenged him until ultimately civil war had broken out. Anne greatly disliked talk of war, yet it was a conversation that so dominated her father's house that she could not help but be aware, even if she didn't fully understand. She just instinctively placed her allegiance with her father, whom people named Kingmaker, since he placed the present king,

Edward IV on the throne. Isabel also informed Anne that father's plan was to tighten the links between the Nevilles and the king's family but marriage.

Picking with delicate fingers at the baked capon and sipping the green soup of almonds from a silver spoon, she raised her eyes again. Finding Richard's still upon her, she immediately lowered them. Gloucester laughed gently, and the next time she looked up, he raised his glass. She fumbled for her own and lifted it in response, trying to drink from it before realising it was empty. Blushing, she beckoned for her cup to be refilled.

Richard was interesting and nice looking. She liked the way his hair covered his skull like a dark cap, his eyes were dark and his expression sad, but he seemed friendlier than his brother. The next time their gaze met, Anne smiled shyly before turning to speak to Isabel.

Warwick's daughters were not the only ones to be excited by the arrival of the king's brothers. The younger household squires craned their necks to catch a glimpse of their new peers, vying for their attention. As the initial shyness wore off and lips and fingers became greasy from the feast, the boys began to spar verbally with their new companions, making them welcome.

At nine years old, Richard seemed quite grown up to five-year-old Anne who had seldom left the shelter of her father's castle, but she looked forward to knowing him all the same. His brother, George was twelve and as such, considered almost a man. He was more alarming than Richard and all through dinner she was aware of his loud voice, the rough jokes he shared with the other young men. Many of them were beyond her understanding but she laughed with the rest of the company, even when her sister blushed and turned her face away. George's golden good looks and bluff humour seemed to make him a favourite among his peers, and he made free with the watered-down wine. He belched loudly, and often and Anne noticed that between mouthfuls, he wiped his lips on the sleeve of his rich doublet.

From the corner of her eye, Anne saw him raise his goblet to Isabel, who blushed and smiled before averting her gaze. Before supper was done it was clear, even to the girls, that George of Clarence enjoyed a spree; something he would find lacking when normality returned to Middleham. Usually, the meals were far less ostentatious; the fare wholesome but plain, the emphasis placed on quality rather than quantity. The young men who found themselves part of Warwick's household quickly discovered that life was stark under his rule. He expected them to be up at dawn, eager to learn to shoot straight, to ride and behave like knights of the realm, to command armies. Life at Middleham was relentless, so perhaps it was just as well that George, who clearly favoured the easy life, would not be staying long.

From his place at table, Warwick observed the young dukes interacting with his daughters. He stroked his moustache thoughtfully, pleased at the early signs of attachment. He hoped the boys would form solid bonds with the other squires for he had high hopes for the likes of Francis Lovell and Robert Percy who were rapidly learning to master the crafts of knighthood and chivalry beneath his tutelage. He turned his attention to Gloucester, who despite his slight frame and physical challenges was the most promising boy in his charge. He was determined and Warwick knew that determination went a long way. The boy had already proved loyal to his family, to the realm and his friendship with either daughter was a thing Warwick intended to encourage.

The primary trenchers were removed and replaced while the next course was ushered in. Eagerly, the diners rinsed their fingers into the rose scented water and soon the table was groaning beneath the weight of woodcock smothered with saffron, a spicy compote of vegetables coloured with sandalwood powder, and a vast pie filled with small birds, served with scallions and mushrooms. In the torchlight, the juices of a huge loin of pork glistened alongside a pottage of spiced lamb, green salad, steamed peas and fresh grapes. As the dishes were laid out, the company fell silent as they savoured the sight of the delicacies and when the first mouthfuls were taken, the cries of appreciation drowned out the sound of the lutes.

Anne leaned back in her seat, her stomach protesting at the unaccustomed richness and quantity of food she had eaten. She rubbed her eye and, stifling a small groan, tilted her head back, her eye travelling up to the vaulted roof where swirling blue wood smoke sought an exit into the night. The idea of fresh air was enticing, and she lacked the appetite or room for more food. Even the thought of the sweet honey-laced pears and almond custards that were to follow sickened her and, in an attempt to shift some of what she had already eaten, she assumed a more upright position and belched quietly into her kerchief.

Her mother, Anne Beauchamp, the countess of Warwick leaned closer, and quietly suggested she retire to the close stool before the onset of the next course. Anne obediently slid from the room and found Jayne was waiting to attend to her comfort. By the time she slid back into her seat and picked up a napkin, the jester, accompanied by a piper were taking up their position before the high table.

The smaller man balanced on the shoulders of his companion and juggled four pomegranates while the taller man continued to pipe, and without causing the man on his shoulder to fall, cut a ridiculous caper. His long limbs, clad in red and blue hose were like those of a spider, and the points to his shoes were long enough to stretch halfway across the hall.

The clown was well known to both the girls; he was not as spry as he had once been but still managed to find the energy to chase a shrieking Anne and Isabel around the garden. Often, he entranced the girls by discovering coins and sweetmeats in their ears.

The antics of the clown helped the company digest the surfeit of food, filling the time before the trenchers were replaced for the final time, and the sweetest course of all was brought in. As the diners picked up their spoons, the Earl of Warwick rose somewhat unsteadily to his feet and silence fell upon the gathering.

Richard Neville was accustomed to public speaking and savoured his audience. Every sweating face in the hall was tilted to his as they waited for his wisdom. He wet his lips, enjoying the manner in which they hung upon his words. He scanned the hall and, more than a little drunk, swayed dangerously before raising his flagon.

'My Lord, Duke of Clarence, My Lord, Duke of Gloucester. In this household we teach boys to be men, train them to be honest knights of the king, true subjects of God. It is with great pleasure that I welcome you both to Middleham Castle.'

Middleham – 1464

Anne spun in circles on the dale, the world spinning so fast it blurred, the muted moorland colours merging and embedding deeply into her soul. The colours of home, the colours of childhood, the mulberry hues of adolescent love. It had happened so subtly yet so thoroughly, she could not remember when Richard hadn't been part of her, and George hadn't been part of Isabel. That both sisters had fallen so deeply in love with the boys their father intended for them was nothing short of miraculous. In most similar cases, girls were married off to strangers of their father's choosing, and often those men were old, many times married, and more suitable to the grave than the marriage bed. Although nothing had been formally decided, there was an understanding that when they were older, Anne and Isabel would wed the brothers of the king.

Anne jumped, jabbing her needle into her finger as her father burst into the solar where she was sewing with her mother and sister. A tiny red bead of blood bloomed upon her white skin, and she popped her finger into her mouth and sucked it, looking on with alarm as her father paced furiously about the floor.

His Countess, well-accustomed to the vagaries of her husband's temper, placed her needlework on the settle and rose, her gown trailing elegantly across the Flemish carpet.

She poured him a cup of wine but when she offered it, he struck it from her hand and sent the vessel spinning to the floor. The girls watched open-mouthed as it came to rest at Isabel's feet, dribbling a pool of ruby wine onto the hem of her gown.

While their father's shadow leapt in mummery of his incomprehensible rage, Anne pulled a face at Isabel. He was often angry, always curt and seldom bluff, but this fit of ire was unprecedented in its ferocity. His eyes bulged and his face was very red. Anne didn't want to watch but couldn't take her eyes off the vein that pulsed ominously in his temple as he strode about the room, kicking out at the dogs, knocking over a stool.

Eventually he paused near the fireplace and struck the stone mantle with his fist.

'What an arrogant, self-seeking cur. I would never have believed this of him, never! To treat me in this way, it's outrageous. Where would he be today if it were not for me? Exiled that's where, or dead. He has made me look a fool. Me; the Great Warwick, a fool.'

In his agitation he had neglected to notice the presence of his daughters. The girls sat stock still, wide-eyed at the scene they were witnessing. The countess clasped her husband's arm.

'Who has dear? What has happened? Her voice was soothing. 'Do tell me what has happened.'

Warwick turned and stared intently into his wife's gentle eyes, the concern he found tempering his rage, just a little. The next time he spoke, his voice wavered slightly.

'Edward. Edward has betrayed me. All the time I've been forming an alliance with France, he has been mocking me; making me a fool. He announced today, quite casually, when we were at counsel, that he cannot honour the alliance I've spent months arranging with Bona of Savoy BECAUSE HE IS ALREADY MARRIED!'

The women's mouths fell open. Anne and Isabel let their stitching fall to their laps.

Warwick inhaled, swallowing audibly before continuing more quietly. 'It seems that he was married months ago to a Lancastrian widow, one of the Woodville clan. I have no doubt, they've been mocking me the whole time.'

His sorrow hardened again into anger. 'WELL, I WON'T STAND FOR IT. I'm the one who put him where he is, and if this is how I'm to be repaid, well, we'll see who wields the real power in this country. I'll make him regret not heeding my counsel.'

The countess patted the sleeve of his travel-stained surcoat. He stopped pacing, his head drooped.

'Richard, you mustn't do anything hasty; he is the king after all. Why don't you sit down and tell me whom has he married? I'm sure she can't be as bad as you say. I might be able to think of a remedy. Come, come along, sit here.'

She patted the settle and Warwick obeyed, running his fingers through his wiry grey hair.

'Elizabeth Grey,' he snarled, jumping to his feet again. 'The widow of Sir John Grey, whom we slaughtered at St Albans. She's an ambitious witch, years older than Edward with a couple of Lancastrian brats in tow, as well as an enormous family, every one of them as self-seeking as herself. I never thought I could hate a woman more than I hate that Bitch of Anjou, but this one comes very close. Why the hell couldn't he have just bedded the woman and have done with it?'

Isabel gasped at this indelicacy, and Warwick turned, finding a welcome vent for his fury.

'Why are you two still here? Get out and stay out,' he roared. The two girls, followed by a pack of small dogs fled from the chamber in a flurry of gowns and fur. As they sped down the spiral stair, their father's anger bounded after them until they emerged gratefully into the late September afternoon.

In the garden, the girls, seeking the sanctuary of the rose arbour, perched on a seat of camomile. Troy turned in tight circles on the golden gravel path, searching for just the right position in which to resume his slumber. The garden had declined with the passing of high summer, and the once fragrant rose-covered walks were now jewelled with rose hips, and the grass sprawled in clumps of decaying hay. Yellowing leaves and seed heads clogged the fountain, and the turf seats were muddied and unpleasant to sit upon. Anne, feeling the wet seeping through her skirts, got up and went to dip her sore finger into the water. Half-decayed leaves floated on the surface, and she began to fish them out and drop them onto the ground with a splat.

'What do you think Father will do now?' she asked. 'I don't think I've ever seen him that angry before.'

'How do I know what he'll do? It's none of our business, after all, and it will hardly affect us will it?'

Idly, Isabel stroked Troy's coat with the toe of her slipper.

'But what if father falls out with the king?' Anne persisted. 'It will affect us then. We won't be able to go to court when it is time. And what about Richard and George, they may have to go away, and we should never see them. I would miss Richard, and I know how fond you are of George ... even if you will never admit it.'

Isabel lowered her chin and smiled a secret smile.

'Mother will calm Father down, don't worry. Once he's recovered from the shock he'll return to court and our lives will settle down again. And as for George,' she confided archly. 'I do like him, but not enough to break my heart should he go away. I'm quite confident he'll come back.'

The three years that Richard had spent at Middleham Castle had been happy. He had proved a willing pupil and matured into a competent soldier although his battle skills were yet to be put to a real test. To Anne's secret pride, he excelled in the tiltyard, and everyone agreed he was almost ready to take his place in the world. It was not secret that the Earl, eager for an alliance between his daughters and the royal house of York, fostered the natural friendship that developed between them. It was easy for Richard and Anne to meet often but George wasn't always at Middleham; he split his time between his brother's court and Yorkshire, but the relationship between him and Warwick had blossomed. Just that afternoon George had arrived from court and, having sought out his brother, was eager to discover the whereabouts of the girls.

As soon as George was refreshed after the hard ride, the brothers sought the girls out in the garden. Richard, ignoring the autumnal damp that began to seep through his clothes, lounged at Anne's feet, while George plucked a shiny, red rose hip from the bush and began to dissect it, piling the white powder that he found within onto the gravel.

'Of course, I've known about the wedding all along,' he bragged, 'but Edward dared me to speak of it.' He glanced at Isabel to see if his lie impressed her and found himself distracted by her pretty face. 'The Woodville woman is comely enough, if you like that sort of thing, but she's rather haughty and quite old. I prefer someone younger myself, and of course, I would never wed a Lancastrian. If I were King, my wife would necessarily be of York.'

Isabel looked at George through her lashes. Straightening her back and pushing back her shoulders she displayed herself to the best advantage. George, letting his appreciation show, leaned a little closer.

'Of course, your father has every right to be angry at the manner in which Edward treated him. If it were me, I'd be seeking some sort of public apology.'

Richard shifted his position on the cold ground and, after a glance in Anne's direction, cleared his throat before offering a contradiction.

'You may seek it, but you'd not get it, George. Edward is King; it is not for the likes of us or Warwick to question his authority. We owe him loyalty, both as our monarch, and as our elder brother. I am not overly familiar with the Woodvilles, but I am confident Elizabeth must have some merit if Edward has chosen her as his wife. I think we should withhold our judgement until we know the facts.'

George regarded his brother steadily.

'You haven't seen how angry Warwick is, Richard. I don't think he'll ever forgive Edward for this; he may be forced to make the best of it, but I don't think things between them will ever be the same.'

Richard got up and brushed away the blades of grass that clung to his hose, he held out a hand to Anne and she took hold, allowing him to assist her to her feet. As he led Anne away with her dogs leaping around them, Richard paused and turned to address his brother who now lounged beside Isabel on the turf seat.

'I sincerely hope you are wrong, George, because I rather think that Edward and Warwick need each other. In fact, I think the country needs them both.'

Middleham - 1465

Middleham Castle was somehow colder and bleaker when Richard and George were away. Both Anne and Isabel found themselves with too much time on their hands, idle hours in which to quarrel over trivialities. They had spent the rainy afternoon in the solar with their mother's women, where the conversation was dull and the line of green stitches that Anne was working seemed interminable and worryingly crooked. She was sure to have to unpick them and start again.

Isabel sighed so loudly, so long and so often that, at last, their Mother's patience ran out and she sent them from her presence. Glad to be free of their mother's jurisdiction, they retired to their bedchamber where the nurse snored before a sulky fire. Anne threw herself upon the bed and plucked at the coverlet.

'How many days does it take to ride from Westminster?' she asked for the hundredth time.

'For goodness' sake, Anne, it depends on how hard you ride your horse. How should I know? Maybe they'll stay and visit with the king or Lady Cecily for a few days, or maybe they'll join Father in France. Just stop dwelling on the subject, you're driving me mad. They'll be here when they are here, and not before.'

Sometimes it seemed to Anne that Richard was the only person she actually liked. He was the only one who never became impatient with her incessant questions, never lost his temper or threw cushions at her. When they played chess, he had a trick of slowly stroking his left eyebrow if she were about to make an unwise decision which gave her time to rethink her move before she made it. He was very clever, and she thought him far better looking than George. He was never overdressed but he kept his dark hair tidy without being over-concerned about his appearance. George was far too fond of fine clothes, and vain about his polished blond hair and startling blue eyes. He strutted about as though it was his right that all eyes should be upon him. There was something indefinably unsettling about George, and something indefinably comfortable about Richard. Anne missed his companionship when he was away. She sat up and stuck her legs straight out on the counterpane and waggled her feet, admiring the twinkling gems upon her slippers.

She sighed. 'I wonder when they'll be back.'

'Anne,' screamed Isabel, and hurled a cushion from the wooden settle. Anne, anticipating a battle, stood on the bed and prepared to return fire but their nurse awoke with a snort, and sat up in her chair, wiping drool from her chin.

'What are you two up to? Sit down, Anne; you are not a hoyden.'

Obediently, Anne lowered her pillow and rudely poked out her tongue, silently promising Isabel that the fray was merely postponed, not terminated.

'Oh look, who's that riding in?' The nurse hobbled over to the window. 'Ouch, my feet have gone to sleep. Oh, it's young Gloucester and his men.'

With a squeal, Anne rushed to the window, pushing her elder sister out of the way.

'Oh, it is Richard, it is! How wonderful! But George isn't with him, Isabel. I can see Lovell and Percy, but no George.'

Isabel sat down again, scowled into the fire while Anne rushed from the chamber and down the stairs. She skidded to a halt before entering the hall, taking several deep breaths to compose herself. When she opened the door she found the men gathered about a table. Richard was holding a cup of ale and just about to bite into a capon.

'Oh' she said, feigning surprise. 'I didn't know you were back.'

Richard turned, put down his food.

'You'll not go to Heaven, Anne,' he laughed. 'I heard you thundering down the stairs just now but I'm glad you're pleased to see me, so don't try to pretend you're not.'

'You are right Richard,' she said, embracing him. 'I am pleased; it is so very, very dull here when you are gone. Come, let's retire to the solar. Mother and Isabel will want to hear all about the new Queen. Where is George, by the way?'

'George was ... erm, busy when I left but he said he'll be here in a day or two.'

The companions laughed and as Richard collected his flagon and whistled to the dogs, Isabel emerged from the stairwell, her dour expression making it clear she had heard Richard's reply.

The countess and her ladies were still assembled in the solar and welcomed Richard readily, offering him wine and wafers although he'd only just eaten. While he held his hands out to the fire, Anne bombarded him with questions.

'Tell us, Richard,' she begged. 'Is the Queen as handsome as they say?

The smile on Richard's face faded as he recalled the ostentation of the Queen's coronation. While Warwick was sent on a diplomatic errand to Burgundy and France, Richard and George had attended the ceremony at the king's request. As he recalled the events of the day and tried to make his descriptions as pleasing to the ladies as possible, Richard's eyes narrowed.

'The morning of the wedding was wet, and the skies lowering for May. I heard the queen complain afterward that her gown became so heavy with rain, she could barely stand up in it. She seemed to take the bad weather as a personal affront, and her disappointment showed on her face, which rather marred her good looks. Her fine gown was splashed by mud, and her fair hair was darkened by the rain but, damp and bedraggled or not, I have to say, she is very beautiful… in a brittle sort of way.'

Richard looked down into the plump face of his favourite Neville sister and smiled.

'So yes, Anne, the queen is very, very beautiful. She wore a wine velvet gown and splendid jewels. Her hair is as fair as they say, so fair that it shines almost white, and her teeth are straight and her figure shapely as a woman's should be but,' he added confidentially. 'In my opinion, she isn't a patch on you.'

Anne' mouth fell open, and she turned pink before covering her face with her hands. The countess and her ladies laughed indulgently. Momentarily confused, Anne allowed Isabel to take over as chief interrogator and the elder girl leant forward, her long dark hair peeping from beneath her veil.

'What role did you and George have? Were you introduced to her? Did you kiss her hand? Did she speak to you? What did she say?'

Richard took a deep breath before attempting to answer so many questions.

'George and I were expected to be present but nothing much was expected of me. George led her into the church, but I don't think they conversed very much. I'm not sure if she is haughty or if she were just savouring her moment. When we were presented to her afterwards she was not overly friendly, but Edward was as bluff as ever. I would have liked more time with him, but he was surrounded by the Queen's family for most of the time. There are certainly enough of them.'

The news from court was so welcome, the women failed to notice how carefully Richard selected his words. Anne, overcoming her former confusion, clasped her hands to her chest.

'It must be so frightening to be a queen. Everyone looking at you and waiting for you to trip over your train or let the crown slip from your head. But at least Elizabeth is beautiful and doesn't have to worry that the people might not like her, if she looks the part nobody will care what she is like inside. Imagine how awful it would be to be a plain queen and know that the people are thinking how dull your hair is, or how small, or how stout you are. I'm glad no king will ever want to marry me, for I should hate very much to be queen.'

The company tittered and the countess shook her head over the simple ways of her daughter. She sometimes worried that Anne lacked the suitable material to be moulded and trained in the role that noble women were destined to play. With a pang of anxiety, she considered the future, her thoughts turning from Anne to her elder daughter.

At fourteen, Isabel was already beautiful and almost ripe to be a bride. She had a certain poise that was totally lacking in Anne and was far more suited to her future role as a duchess than her younger sister. The Countess of Warwick sighed and, putting the matter from her mind, signalled to one of her ladies to order refreshments.

The following years were fraught with troubles centred around the queen's family. Elizabeth made little secret of her dislike for Warwick whom she thought Edward allowed far too much power. She also resented his brothers, particularly George, who made no attempt to conceal his dislike for his brother's wife. George and Warwick begrudged the favours Edward heaped upon the queen's family, the advantageous marriages, the most fertile lands and richest properties. Most of all Warwick resented her interference with matters of state, something no queen should be allowed to meddle in. The last straw for Warwick was Edward's refusal that George and Isabel should marry and as the breach between the king and Warwick widened, Richard of Gloucester was caught in the middle.

With rebellion in the north under the banner of one Robin of Redesdale whom many whispered was brokered by Warwick, Edward's patience began to thin. Anne's peace of mind was fragmenting, Isabel was distraught over the loss of

George and Warwick began to wish he'd placed another of York's sons on the throne.

In the dead of night, Anne and Isabel were roused from bed and bundled into a litter with their mother, the horses directed toward the port of Calais.

Calais – 1469

Anne wiped her eyes on the hem of her sleeve and crossed to the window that looked across the bustling port of Calais. It was an unfamiliar scene, and she missed the lonely Yorkshire dales where there was so much space between the earth and sky that she often wondered what it would be like to fly.

Usually, she didn't mind being alone but today she missed the comfort of her sister and mother, or even her woman, Jayne. With his customary roughshod ways, Warwick had neglected to inform his family of their imminent journey, making their departure from Middleham both abrupt and unexpected. Among the many treasures Anne had been forced to leave behind, were her maid, Jayne, and her dog. She hoped they were being cared for in her absence.

The channel crossing in the company of her father, mother, sister and George of Clarence had been choppy and unpleasant. She had spent most of her time retching over a leather bucket. It was her first time at sea and if it were not for her longing to return to Yorkshire, she'd wish it were her last. Never in her life had she felt so sick.

She had no idea why they were here, and the unfamiliar chamber offered little in the way of comfort. She missed her dog and her friends and her things. She hadn't even thought to grab her embroidery to bring with her. It wasn't so bad for Isabel who at least had George for company, but Anne despaired of ever seeing Richard again. As the scene of Calais blurred behind her tears, she wondered where he was and what he was doing. She missed his steady friendship as much as she missed and pined for the familiar sounds and smells of Middleham.

It was obvious something was very wrong, but nobody would tell her what. It had something to do with the king and she prayed her father would soon just kiss and make up with him. Warwick had been simmering with rage since they left Yorkshire and nobody had dared speak to him during the crossing, not even to ask their direction. Although Anne questioned her, Mother just shook her head and maintained a stolid, obedient silence. As for Isabel, she thought and spoke of nothing but her imminent nuptials.

'I cannot wait to be George's wife,' she said, while Anne rolled her eyes and bit back an uncharitable reply.

Anne's uncle George, the Archbishop of York, had travelled with them, and to Anne's confusion, was to marry Isabel and George this morning. Once, Anne would have welcomed the wedding and felt joy for her sister, but now she only wanted to stop it.

Any marriage taken against the express wishes of the king was something to be feared and dreaded.

Isabel had been provided with a fine new gown, but Anne was to make do with her best blue velvet. As they made hasty preparations for the journey, it had been hurriedly and inexpertly packed, but she smoothed the crumpled fabric as best she could. Nobody seemed to be bothering with her and no maid had come to help her dress, so she struggled into her clothes, dabbed her red-rimmed eyes, and waited to be summoned to the hall.

It was a small assembly, and a dour one. The only members of the wedding party to look pleased were George and his bride. As she took her place at his side, Isabel tossed back her long, dark hair that was left loose and uncovered to illustrate her virginal state. The sight of it reminded Anne of happier times. She closed her eyes and pictured their shared bedchamber at Middleham where she had seen it crackle beneath the brush as the nurse briskly applied the one hundred strokes. Anne sighed for the days that she had always taken so much for granted.

Isabel had no reservations about the union with George, and as her father gave her into his keeping, she smiled brilliantly at the gathering. As Anne watched her childhood friends exchange vows, a lump rose in her throat. The day could and should have been so very different.

If Father hadn't fallen foul of the king they would have been married in Westminster Abbey where English crowds would have gathered to cheer the happy couple and sprinkle the bride's path with blossoms. Richard would have been present, and he would have hinted to Anne that their own wedding would soon follow. All the cousins would have celebrated under the affectionate eye of their affable cousin, King Edward. Instead, it was a rushed, clandestine and illegal ceremony, with only the presence of Uncle George, the Archbishop of York, making it legal in the eyes of the church.

If only things were different. Anne knew her father had tried very hard to remain loyal after the king's unpopular marriage. He had tried very hard, she was sure, to maintain the peace, and had even ushered Elizabeth into the abbey chapel at Reading for her ceremonial recognition as Queen of England. And he had stood as Godfather when her first child, a daughter whom they named Eliabeth, was born. For the sake of the king, Warwick had quashed his real opinions and donned a fixed smile while he officiated at the marriage between Edward's sister, Margaret, to Charles of Burgundy. He'd made quite sure that nobody suspected his opposition to it.

But, despite his efforts, the rapine presence of the Woodville faction at court had slowly eaten away at her father's forbearance and alienated many other Yorkist supporters too. How was he expected to stand by and say nothing when the Woodvilles were given titles and lands that should have gone to their betters?

The final straw for Warwick came when his brother, the Chancellor, George Neville, was replaced with Robert Stillington, the Bishop of Bath and Wells. This insult, quickly followed by Edward's refusal to consider an alliance between George and Isabel had caused the final breach.

It had been hard for Anne to see Richard torn between loyalty to his brother, and loyalty to Warwick. She had watched him agonise over every decision, every word. He never once spoke against either Edward or her father, but it was clear that if ever a young man were torn, it was Richard. His inner battle had eaten away his peace until he was finally forced to choose sides.

When Warwick begged Richard to join him on the day he dragged his family over the sea to Calais in direct opposition to the wishes of the king, Richard did all in his power to persuade him to stay. And while Warwick poured a deluge of recrimination upon his head, Richard looked into Anne's tortured eyes and elected to stand with his brother, the king.

Her heart was broken, and it was difficult not to resent Isabel as all her dreams were realised.

I won't marry anyone else, Anne thought. If I can't have Richard, I will refuse all other suitors, go into a nunnery and live a chaste life of contemplation.

Pontefract Castle- August 1469

It was good to be back in England. As Anne fell across the threshold and the familiar scents of Yorkshire engulfed her, Jayne held out her arms for a welcoming embrace. Beside himself with joy, her dog leapt up, barking his high-pitched bark and leaving muddy footprints on her gown before tearing around the chamber. When the chaos of his welcome faded and she was rested and refreshed, she was escorted to the chamber set aside for her use.

'I've missed this,' she said, as she allowed Jayne to cosset and pamper her. 'I hope to never leave England again, there is no place like the country you are born in.'

While Jayne recounted all the news and the little brindle greyhound curled his small, trembling body in her lap, some of Anne's joy faded. Every so often, her dog licked Anne's hand as though to reassure himself she was really there for he sensed she was very close to tears.

The last few weeks had been confusing and lonely, denied information about her father's movements, and bereft of her sister's companionship, she'd no idea what was happening. She wished things could be as they were before but that could never be. She and Richard were now on opposing sides in a civil war and if they did meet again, it wouldn't be as friends.

Jayne, seeing Anne's pinched and worried frown, clucked around her, ordering a posset and slipping off her shoes, chattering all the while.

'Oh, Mistress Anne, I've been so worried. I had no idea where you were, or if you were coming back. Nobody has known what to think and we've seen no visitors since you left, and since none of us retainers ever travel, we have had no real news, just rumour after vicious rumour. Tell me, has Isabel really married George? Oh, it seems just five minutes since she was a little girl running round beneath my feet. Was the wedding very splendid? I'll wager she looked fine. I am sorry I missed it. We've been so very quiet here, so you can imagine our surprise when your father turned up unexpectedly with the king.'

Jayne's babbling voice floated around somewhere just outside the range of Anne's consciousness, but the last sentence registered, and she sat up abruptly.

'The king? Here? What are you talking about, Jayne?'

'Didn't you know, Mistress Anne? There was a battle, somewhere near Banbury, between your father and the king and Warwick was victorious. The king is being held here ...as a prisoner so they say, in the North tower. I'm told that your father is refusing to let him go until he agrees to certain conditions.'

Anne rose from the bed and peered from the chamber window across the bailey to the tower opposite where a dim flicker of light was showing. If what Jayne said was true, it explained why her father had chosen to bring the king to Pontefract rather than Warwick.

Warwick castle was far too close to London, and London was far too loyal to the king. Here, they were safer from attack. She turned from the window, aware that her father's actions were nothing short of treason. She frowned and gripped Jayne's wrist.

'What of Richard, Jayne? Where is the Duke of Gloucester?'

'I don't know, but he isn't here. I think your father let him go free but not before he executed the queen's father and her brother … as I understand it.'

'Oh my God, but Richard is safe, you are sure of that.'

'As sure as I can be in these uncertain days.'

'God be praised. Try and find out where he is, ask among the household.'

A frown marred her face as she contemplated the hopelessness of her future. What would Richard do now? She knew him too well to assume he would do nothing, but also acknowledged that any action he took on his brother's behalf would forever alienate him from Warwick.

Bile rose to her throat as she faced the realisation that Richard was lost to her forever, and all her exhaustion forgotten, she paced the room with a fury of restlessness, deaf to Jayne's pleas to lie down. At length, she stopped pacing and pulled off her veil.

'Brush my hair, Jayne, and fetch me a fresh gown. I will attend supper in the hall, after all.'

As she slipped into the overheated feasting hall, she was reminded of that long ago celebration when Richard first arrived at Middleham. But tonight, the atmosphere was very different. Tension hung in the air; the servants creeping around as if they'd just received a whipping. The most obvious cause of the discomfiture was the huge figure of King Edward lounging in her father's chair.

Outwardly, he was relaxed but, with Warwick whispering rapidly into his ear, his eyes remained hooded and watchful. The earl, having succeeded in temporarily separating the king from the Woodvilles was losing no opportunity to air his views. The countess, catching sight of her daughter, beckoned her forward with a tight smile.

'Well, Anne. How nice of you to join us. Come, dear, let me introduce you to the king.'

Anne's heart quailed as she approached King Edward for the first time. *It is alright. He is Richard's brother,* she reassured herself. *Richard worships him. He cannot be that bad.* On reaching the dais, Anne hesitated and essayed a curtsey as she had been taught. Warwick looked up, as surprised as his wife to see her there.

'My Liege. May I introduce my youngest daughter, Anne.'

At that moment, the minstrels struck up in the gallery and Edward stood up. He towered over her, but she found she couldn't resist returning his smile. The king took Anne's hand and raised her from her knees, looking deeply into her eyes before spending over-long kissing her fingers. When he straighten up, Anne noticed a trace of royal saliva glistening on her skin.

Knowing her face was scarlet, Anne held her breath while his appraising eye ran over her. He held out his arm, and astounding them all, tucked her hand into his elbow and led her away so that no-one could, in courtesy, follow. She felt diminutive, like a child beside him and her discomfort increased when he halted beneath a flaring candle sconce. Then he turned and bent slightly to accommodate her lack of stature.

'So, you are Richard's Anne? Now we've met, I can see what all the fuss was about. He is eager to wed you when you are of age, did you know that?'

Her blushes were answer enough and the king didn't wait for her reply. 'I have, so far, refused my permission and his displeasure was very apparent, although he said naught. I take it his tender feelings are mutual'

Anne stuttered unattractively, while the king laughed, his easy manner encouraging her to shake off her fear. Summoning all her courage, she swallowed and asked the question she'd longed to.

'How is Richard, My Liege? Have you any news? I have not heard from him at all since ...'

'Haven't you?' questioned the king. 'Well, that's good news for me. I haven't seen him either but at least I now know he isn't in league with your father. His loyalty will be well-rewarded. What of George, my dear, do you happen to have seen him?'

The flush that stained Anne's cheek confirmed that she had. She fumbled to explain.

'G-George accompanied us to Calais, Your Grace. I don't believe he meant to betray you, but my father promised him great rewards, among them the hand of my sister, Isabel. She was his- his …'

'Prize?' The king offered, obligingly.

Anne was torn between duty to her father, loyalty to her king and love for Richard. She had no wish to betray her family but, oh, how she wished things could return to normal.

Apart from the tightening of his jaw, Edward revealed no emotion. He straightened up and even the closest of his acquaintance would not have known his devastation at the news of George's marriage to Warwick's daughter. Warwick would use George against him. It was clear that Warwick's intention was to depose Edward and put the crown on George's head.

***

Anne and Isabel stood on the battlements and watched a seemingly endless line of troops approach. They counted at least eight different banners. The Dukes of Suffolk and Arundel were the first to arrive, closely followed by Lord Howard and the Duke of Buckingham and the Duke of Hastings; Lord Dacre and the Earl of Essex had just been spied approaching from the south. Anne's heart leapt when she finally spied the banner of the White Boar of Gloucester, and it continued to beat uncomfortably loud as he drew nearer.

Richard is here. Richard is here. Richard is here.

Certain of George's imminent death, Isabel wept inconsolably and clung to Anne as though her life depended upon it. Unaware of the new life that stirred gently in Isabel's womb, Anne shook off her sister's hand and peered cautiously over the battlements at the milling horse. If a battle was to ensue how could she hope for a victor? The triumph of the king meant the demise of her father, just as victory for Warwick meant certain death for Richard.

He would come and find her soon; he would explain it all. Perhaps he would ask her to go with him and beg the king for her hand.

Her attention was taken by a clamour on the steps of the hall and the men in the bailey fell silent as Warwick and George emerged under armed guard and were led toward their horses. A surge of activity as men remounted and formed into positions. On the steps, the hand of the countess wavered slightly as she bid her husband a last farewell.

Edward, in charge of the realm once more, wheeled his horse, signalled to his men to follow and galloped off to make his triumphant re-entry into the City of London. Slowly the gathered troops followed the king's wake and when the castle compound was all but empty, and the usual peace resumed, Anne turned away. She had placed her foot on the first step, when the sound of a fast horse approaching urged her to turn again. She rushed to the battlement and with both hands resting on warm stone, she strained to see over the parapet.

Richard!

He hauled his mount to a halt so abruptly that sparks flew from the horse's hooves.

'Hey, you there,' he yelled to a passing boy. 'Where will I find the Lady Anne?'

As fear stabbed her heart, Anne sank to her knees, cowering behind the crenulated wall, and prayed he would not see her. The man below seemed so different to the Richard she knew; he was so alien, so mature and commanding. He was a man now, and she wasn't ready to face him, in fact, she was so profoundly ashamed of all that had happened, she didn't feel she could ever see him again. She was afraid. What could she say? And what could he want from her, a traitor's daughter?

She breathed more easily when the voice of the stable boy floated up, denying any knowledge of her whereabouts. But, as Richard wheeled his horse about the yard she could not resist one more peep over the parapet.

'Anne, Anne,' Richard yelled, but although hot tears flooded from her eyes, she would not answer. She thrust her fingers into her ears, stopping his beloved voice but still, through her heartbreak, she heard him call,

'I have to leave now. I must follow Edward, but I'll be back, don't worry Anne, I will be back.'

Then, dragging his horse around, he galloped off in pursuit of his king.

***

The executioner's axe cast its long shadow all the way to Yorkshire where Warwick's family waited to learn his fate. They did not expect their men to return, the king would not be so magnanimous, not after the execution of the queen's father and brother on Warwick's order. That single action sealed his fate, condemning him as a traitor and ensuring Queen Elizabeth's hatred. She would want vengeance, and Edward, who denied her nothing, would let her have it.

Almost as soon as the king and his prisoners had departed, Isabel had taken to her bed and now, as her pregnancy made itself felt, she spent her time either weeping or vomiting into a bowl. Anne, still a maid, felt detached from Isabel; a world of experience lay between the sisters now.

The women reassured one another that all would be well. After all, the king and Warwick were old friends, and surely Edward could find it in his heart to forgive him. And how could the king execute George, his younger brother, his mother would never forgive him. Surely the years Warwick had devoted to the king would not be forgotten; all the years he'd been his loyal henchman must amount to something.

Isabel was convinced she would never lay eyes on George again. She refused to eat, and soon the weight began to fall from her bones. The countess fought for composure but was inwardly quailing. She continued to run the household as efficiently and concealed her inner turmoil from her daughters and servants. After the day he was taken into the king's custody, she didn't weep again.

And neither did Anne.

After Richard's departure, once the dust had settled, she went quietly about her everyday business as she waited miserably for news. Only those that knew her well realised that the girl who had once skipped, now only walked.

But, to everyone's astonishment, one afternoon a few weeks after the king pardoned them, the two men rode calmly into the castle, demanding wine and dinner. The countess and Isabel were boundless in their thanks to God, but Anne, although grateful for her father's reprieve, remained subdued.

She knew, pardon or no pardon, she had lost Richard and would never be happy again. She just hoped that life would regain some semblance of normality. The coming birth of Isabel's baby would mark a new beginning.

The king had not let Warwick off completely free. He had lost some important revenues as well as his position as Constable of England. That honour was bestowed instead upon Richard of Gloucester for his unwavering loyalty.

It was a weighty mantle for one so young and many eyebrows were raised at the king's decision, but Edward was grateful to his brother and determined to reward him well. As expected, George sneered at the honours but, unknown to him, it was Richard whom George had to thank for his freedom. Gloucester had worked hard to convince Edward that their brother had acted entirely under Warwick's influence, and that George was sincerely repentant. His position, Richard argued, had been made impossible by the fact that Warwick was his father-in-law. In the end, Edward conceded the victory and let Richard have his way.

The Queen and her family were livid when they heard of the king's leniency, but Edward argued that forgiveness was often the best policy and people loved a merciful monarch. His efforts to reassure his Queen of that fell on deaf ears, even though he insisted that forgiving them didn't mean he would ever be foolish enough to trust them again. Her impotent rage that the murderer of her father and brother should go unpunished injected the first rancour into the marriage.

Edward trusted that Warwick, having been shown mercy, would come to heel, and that George would be kept out of trouble by Isabel's imminent confinement. And so, while the traitors, Clarence and his father-in-law, returned to their comfortable homes and their comfortable wives, Richard was kept busy in Wales, quelling uprisings at Carmarthen and Cardigan. And when she learned of it, Anne was left in limbo waiting impotently for news. But it wasn't long before Warwick and Clarence were once again intriguing against the king.

The English Channel - March-1470

Anne was plunged back into the nightmare as once more she found herself with her family aboard a fleeing vessel heading for the sanctuary of Calais. A single lantern swung above her head as, green-faced and sweating, she hung over the leather bucket that was clenched between her knees.

She had long since lost the contents of her stomach and now only retched weakly and helplessly with each new surge of the ship. Her hair was scraped from her face and secured with a piece of twine, wet patches showed beneath her armpits, and her soiled gown clung damply to her legs. The roaring wind and battering rain echoed terrifyingly to the women huddled below deck. They were all going to die.

Mercifully, Jayne was with them this time and applied herself to the task of caring for her young charges.

'You'll be well enough, once we reach land, but I'm not sure about Isabel.' She yelled over the raging storm.

Anne lifted her head, peered queasily at her sister and realised it was not mere seasickness that assailed Isabel.

She writhed on the single low bunk, her long hair matted, and her gown vomit splashed. When Jayne took a damp cloth to wipe the sheen of sweat from Isabel's face, it came away bloodstained where she had bitten through her lower lip.

Isabel panted like an animal, trying to conserve her strength for the next onslaught. Jayne, rising above the numbing cold and the constant rolling of the ship, did the best she could, clinging to a rope to stop herself from sprawling on top of Isabel in the bunk.

Isabel stirred suddenly and kicked off the confining blanket to retch again. An ungodly stench emanated from the bucket but there was no time to empty it. The vomiting was followed almost immediately by another birth pang, stronger and longer than the last. Her bellow of pain roused Anne from her self-pity and, pressing a kerchief to her mouth, she crawled across the surging floor to her sister's side.

'Bella,' she groaned with the ghost of a whisper. 'Is your time nearer now? Try to hold on, we'll be in Calais soon; it can't be very much longer. It seems we've been at sea for days.' She stroked her sister's hair away from her face and took her hand. 'Hold onto my hand, Bella, and if it gets too bad, give it a good squeeze, as hard as you need to. I'll not leave you again, do you hear, I'll be here by your side.' Then, turning to Jayne she whispered, 'Fetch Mother, Jayne, we can't do this alone. God knows, she must know more about birthing than either of us. I'll sit with Isabel while you're gone, but hurry for God's sake. I don't know what to do.'

Thankfully, now preoccupied with Isabel's greater need, Anne's own agonies subsided. She sat in a daze, humming an old tune and, at intervals, mopped Isabel's brow. It was as if she was trapped in some terrible never-ending dream. The ship lurched and the lamp swung crazily overhead. When the door opened admitting a wild gust of night air, the flame almost went out altogether. Jayne lurched back into the cabin.

'Your Mother's on her way, Anne, but I have some other news.' She dropped her voice so that Isabel couldn't hear. 'The crew are saying the French are refusing to let us land and are forcing us to put back out to sea. We may not now be docked in time for the birthing.'

Anne's face grew paler. Women died in childbirth. It happened every day, and those women were giving birth on dry land, with hot water and an experienced midwife at hand. Anne knew, without having to be told, that Isabel's chances of survival were slim, and she was inexpressibly grateful when her mother staggered through the door.

Now she could let go, Mother would make everything right.

The countess pushed back a strand of damp and bedraggled hair and pushed past Anne to attend her eldest daughter. She shook her head, angry at the plight of women. Isable is scarcely out of childhood yet here she is about to become a mother. She made the sign off the cross and sent up a hasty prayer before placing her hand upon her daughter's stomach. After a few seconds she turned, her expression fierce.

'Why was I not summoned sooner?' she spat. 'The birth is imminent, and there is no time for proper preparation. Anne, fetch a bucket of fresh water and some twine from somewhere. Hurry up, girl.'

The countess, however, was wrong. There was time, plenty of it in which to watch as Isabel's pains grew stronger and her strength weaker. She writhed and screamed, thrashed uncontrollably as the babe fought to be born. Her screams were so loud, they rose above the sounds of the wind. On deck, the sailors crossed themselves and mumbled about the curse of having women aboard.

The countess pulled off her soiled veil and, twisting it into a rope, gave it to her daughter to bite down upon. Anne was unused to seeing her mother with her head uncovered and noticed for the first time that her hair was streaked with grey. Isabel clung to her sister's hand, and Anne held on even when her fingers cramped. Her own seasickness overlooked, Anne sweated now for Isabel who, forced by ungovernable urges, sat up and strained with all her worth.

She bore no resemblance to the Isabel Anne knew. There was no hint of gentility about her now. Her face grew crimson, a vein on her forehead pulsing, her eyes wild and wide as she fought to eject the babe from her narrow frame. As her delicate tissue tore to accommodate the child's head, Isabel sat bolt upright, opened her mouth and bellowed like a heifer in calf.

'I will never be a mother.' Anne vowed. 'Not if it means suffering like this.'

Isabel fell back suddenly, limp and lifeless on the bunk. At first, Anne thought her sister was dead, she turned to her mother, her lips parted, her breath coming short and fast. Then slowly, her eyes strayed toward the blue-skinned rabbit that her sister had birthed.

'What is it?' she gasped.

The countess said nothing as she worked quickly at the lifeless infant that sprawled between Isabel's legs. Her usually spotless hands were smeared red, and globules of blood spattered the bedding and pooled on the floor of the cabin. Blood, it seemed, was everywhere. In silence, Anne's mother wrapped the baby in a bloodstained sheet and handed it to Jayne.

'Where is she going?' Anne clung to a rope to stop herself from falling and Jayne turned to her, shook her head once.

'Mother?'

Wiping her brow with her forearm, the exhausted Countess, stared bleakly at Anne. 'I'm sorry, but the child did not live ...' Her voice ended on a sob.

'But where is Jayne taking him?'

'Away from Isabel. He will be disposed of at sea.'

'For the fish to eat? Why can't we take him home, bury him properly?'

'We can't, child, we can't ...we simply can't.'

Anne wanted to scream, to lay blame upon her father for subjecting them all to this but she knew better than to speak against him. She turned to Isabel who still did not move.

'Poor, poor Isabel,' she whispered.

Anne leaned closer, looked into her ravaged face. She was breathing but quite unconscious. Taking a sponge from the half empty bucket she gently dabbed her sister's face while, in tortured silence, her mother sponged Isabel's torn female parts. As they drew a rough blanket up to Isabel's chin and left her to sleep, they heard a sailor call that the port of Normandy was in sight.

Amboise France – April - June 1470

Isabel made a slow recovery. She had watched from her chamber window as the springtime blossomed into Summer. First came the rain, then a watery sunshine flooded the room with the smell of wet, fertile flowers. As the light grew stronger, crawled up the castle walls and in through the casement window, advertising the official advent of spring, Isabel improved, but only in body. Not in mind.

She answered when spoken too but made no voluntary conversation. When Anne announced the arrival of Spring she showed no sign of enthusiasm. She ate what she was given without relish and without repletion, and often vomited afterwards. Each morning, her mother came to sit with her for several hours, chatting as she held her hand. They had no clear idea if Isabel understood about the loss of her child, or anything else that was happening.

'You will have another child, Isabel,' Anne had said, as if she was wise in such matters. 'You are young yet, and more children will erase the grief you are now feeling.' Isabel nodded but since she agreed to everything, it was unclear if she really understood.

She didn't even respond when George visited, and she scarcely seemed to notice when he left a farewell kiss on her brow. She was indifferent to everything. Anne was not sure if she was grieving or gone mad. Her breasts that had been bound to deter the production of milk has shrunk now, and the bruises on her limbs had faded. While her body made a slow recovery she waited for hour after hour and did nothing but look from the window. Anne, beset with problems of her own, knelt at her feet.

'I need you, Isabel. I wish you'd wake up and help me. They are making plans that concern me, they are forcing my hand. I don't know what to do." Anne whispered, shaking her sister gently by the arm but Isabel made no response.

King Louis of France had earned the name of *Spider King* because he constantly spun webs of political intrigue. He was currently in league with Marguerite of Anjou, undertaking not just the expense of her household now she was in exile but also now safeguarding Warwick's womenfolk.

Having promised to assist Marguerite and Warwick to reinstate Marguerite's husband, Henry VI on the English throne, Louis demanded their help with his quest to thwart Charles of Burgundy.

On the afternoon that Marguerite introduced her son Edward, the Lancastrian heir, to Anne and her family, the atmosphere was abrasive. The conversation was stilted and uncomfortable and only Isabel, lost in her private grief, was oblivious to the inappropriate company in which they found themselves.

Enemies make uncomfortable bed fellows, and it was uncomfortable to converse with the woman whom Anne had been raised to regard as her father's greatest foe '*The Bitch of Anjou*' he used to call her, and they had never questioned their father's opinion. Marguerite put down her cup and stood up. When she crossed the room and came to a halt in front of her, Anne didn't know where to look. Marguerite folded her arms and tapped a well-shod foot impatiently on the floor. Anne cringed beneath her undisguised loathing.

Whatever have I done wrong? Anne thought, but as the conversation between her father and Marguerite unfolded, her situation became clear.

They expect me to wed Marguerite's son! But, he is of Lancaster, Anne thought, *Father must have run mad.*

'Just think, one day you will queen of England, and probably won't have long to wait.'

While Marguerite looked down her long nose, Anne's mind searched for a way to escape it.

I don't want to be Queen of England; I want to marry Richard of Gloucester! But of course, she said nothing of this aloud.

They spoke as if the deal was already signed and sealed, as if she had no say in the matter at all. She tried to catch her mother's eye, but the countess just looked coldly away. Anne knew her father well, she was well aware that any protest she made would be thrust aside. Her eyes pricked with unshed tears, her throat ached to scream, her heart filled with rage.

Like a rat stuck in a drain, Anne was lost in a nightmare from which she couldn't wake. She sat bolt upright on the settle, nervously dissecting a lace kerchief into her lap while, beside her, the seventeen-year-old Prince of Lancaster made little attempt to disguise his own reaction which seemed to be in accord with Anne's.

Under orders from his mother to make himself pleasant, he barked out,

'Do you like dogs?'

Anne leapt nervously. *Dogs?* She thought, desperately searching for the right answer. *Do I like dogs?*

'Yes, yes I do,' she stammered. 'We have several at home ... in Yorkshire.'

The thought of her puppy's tiny body and comforting tongue brought fresh tears to her eyes. She may never see him again.

'I prefer mastiffs,' the boy continued. 'One of mine killed a bear once; the old flea-bitten beast didn't stand a chance and was ripped to pieces in no time.'

As he spoke, Anne glimpsed at his face and quailed inwardly at what she found there. He was sitting upright, a hand placed on each knee, and a bloodthirsty smile was slashed across his strong jaw while his blue eyes blazed with remembered blood lust.

She swallowed audibly. 'I like Italian greyhounds.'

Edward looked startled.

'Italian greyhounds?' he exclaimed. 'They aren't proper dogs. We must find you a more fitting companion when we are wed. I won't tolerate small dogs in my household. My mother and I breed Alaunts; perhaps we can find a pup for you.'

Anne remembered her father's huge shaggy hunting dogs, and hoped it were an empty promise. The reality of her forthcoming marriage appalled her. There was not a single aspect of the arrogant prince with his copper gold hair and energetic eyes that she found appealing. Her gaze drifted to the window where Isabel was still locked in temporary madness. Anne closed her eyes and envied her sister's oblivion.

PART TWO
'Bride'

<u>Amboise, France - 13 December 1470</u>

The morning of the wedding dawned frigid and grey, and it was bone-achingly cold in the chamber where Jayne bathed and anointed Anne with scented oils before lacing her into the wedding gown.

A glimpse in the polished pier glass showed how the luxurious gown completely overshadowed her. Above the diminutive jewel-encrusted torso, her eyes were darkened and dilated by fear. Her hair was brushed to a silken sheen and, in testament to her innocence, left to hang loose to her waist. On her wedding day she should be joyful, but instead she was miserable and there was nothing she could do to conceal it.

When she descended to the hall, she was paid the expected compliments, but the words had no meaning. It was as if all the warmth had gone from her world. As she was marched toward the awaiting carriage she wanted to wrench herself away and run.

The cathedral towered over the city, the spires seeming to reach directly up to heaven. Inside, the wedding party were dwarfed by vast pillars, and intimidated by the saintly silence. Daylight shone through coloured glass windows to stain everyone with a rosy hue, but within her sumptuous gown the bride shivered.

The cold stone walls were interspersed with recesses, shadowed in inky darkness but the aisle along which Anne was escorted was illuminated by scores of expensive wax candles. Beneath her feet, the black marble floor was as slippery as ice and, to prevent herself from fleeing, she focussed upon the kindly face of the bishop.

Isabel and the countess waited near the altar, but Marguerite paced the tiled floor of the nave, her footsteps violating the ethereal silence of God's house. She needed to have the matter over and done with and urged Anne to a relentless pace toward the altar.

As she was traded into the hands of her former enemy, Anne moistened her lips, swallowed with a dry painful throat while the sickening smell of incense made her want to vomit. She needed to run. She longed to snatch back her hand, lift her skirts and flee. But some exterior control made her stay, the ceremony passing in a haze as thick and as depressing as fog.

As she made the required vow, the reality began to dawn on her. She belonged to Edward now, and by association to Marguerite, to *Lancaster*.

What on earth would Richard say? When he heard, would he think she welcomed it?

She somehow found herself ushered outside into the pale December day, and as the bells rang out, all she could think was that Richard was lost to her now forever.

Already, the day was drawing in, and little time was lost returning to the castle for the festivities. They sat at the high table, like a pair of effigies, and accepted the toasts and offerings that came their way. A sumptuous meal followed where the health of the bride and groom was drunk, over and over, and people began to quip about the night to come. Throughout, Marguerite remained tight-lipped, unsmiling but Somerset, who people whispered was Marguerite's lover, was more benevolent, going so far as to bestow his blessing on them.

Everything about the day was a trial for Anne, especially the feast. Each time her husband reached for something on the board, he took the opportunity to touch her thigh beneath the table. She wanted to slap his hands away, hating the false cheer of the ceremony but at the same time, she dreaded its ending. Anne took refuge in her wine, drinking cup after cup, not caring if she was labelled a toper. She was tired, miserable unto death, and haunted by the coming night. If only it was Richard beside her, she would have been elated; she would have danced and laughed and looked forward to the bedding. But now, it was wrong to even think of him and the what-might-have-been.

It was much later when Edward swaggered into the bedchamber with a goblet of wine in his hand and with an arrogant wave, dismissed Anne's attendants. As he swayed unsteadily into the room, his hound at his heels, Anne stood staring into the fire and tried to pretend she was somewhere else. Clad only in a white linen bed gown, her hair tightly braided into snakes that swung down her back, her appearance belied her fourteen years.

She looked no more than twelve.

'Come here, wife,' Edward slumped into a seat but, when she tried to obey, one of his dogs growled menacingly. She froze in fear. Her husband laughed and put down his wine cup and scrutinised her. Anne closed her eyes, disgusted by his regard and thought of Middleham, of the high wide dale, where she belonged.

After a few moments, that seemed like hours, Edward heaved himself from his chair and pulled the ribbon from her hair, loosened the braids to let it fall about her shoulders. He grunted appreciatively before fumbling with the tie at the neck of her gown. Her throat was long and white, a tiny racing pulse at the base betraying her fear. When he placed his wet lips against it and his tongue squirmed like a worm against her skin, she tensed, every muscle in her body resisting his touch.

His arm snaked around her, and he clenched her bottom, pulling her close against him. She gasped, needing to stop him, somehow. If she could just have some time in which to adjust, time to school her body into acceptance. Time to breathe and gather herself.

'No wait, Edward please, wait.' She tried to wriggle from his grasp. 'Could we just talk for a while first?'

'The time for talking is past, madam,' he growled, tugging at her shift. Anne stood naked and trembling with his eyes upon her. She dropped her chin, crossed one arm over her breasts and sought with the other to conceal her quaint.

Edward laughed. But not for long, grasping both wrists, he pulled her arms away, affording himself a better view. Keeping her eyes tightly closed, she let her head fall back, denying his greedy eyes.

'You're very skinny,' he said. Then, twisting her wrist in his firm grip, he forced her to turn around to afford him a view of her rear. 'Too skinny.' He slapped her buttocks hard and thrust her forward onto the bed.

Anne scrambled to the top of the bed, curled into a ball, and buried her face in the pillow. She dare not watch as he shrugged out of his tunic and unlaced his hose. Edward surveyed his skinny prize.

'You could have made this easier,' he said before taking her by the ankle and dragging her to the foot of the bed. Anne was determined to be brave, determined to accept what she must but the moment Edward's fingers touched her skin, she knew she could not. She wriggled, and twisted, biting and slapping in an attempt to escape.

Impatiently, Edward struck her on the jaw.

She did not fight him after that. There was no point. Instead, she lay still and even when the pain was almost more than she could bear, she made no response. She forced her body to relax, craned her head away from him, bit her lip and prayed it would soon be over.

But Edward was a young man, and the night candles were burnt low before he finally rolled away and fell into a noisy slumber. Anne lay stiffly upon pillows embroidered with the hated red Lancastrian rose, not daring to move for fear of waking him and encouraging him to begin all over again.

After a while, realising she needed the close stool, she attempted to slide from the bed but, the moment her foot touched the floor, Edward's dog raised its ugly head and growled, showing her his huge teeth.

Hastily, she withdrew her foot.

She lay awake, uncomfortable and unhappy, until the light of dawn began to creep into the chamber. The only sounds that disturbed the silence were Anne's stifled sobs. She rocked gently upon the pillow, hugging her knees to her chest, until she heard the bell for *prime.*

It was a white-faced bride that entered the solar the next morning. Thankfully the chamber was empty, apart from Isabel, who was in her habitual chair. Anne hurried to her sister and put a hand to her head, stroking her hair as she circled the chair. With a rueful smile, she remembered how the Isabel of old used to put Anne's fears firmly into perspective.

Where was that girl? Was she lost forever?

Anne sank to her knees and laid her head in Isabel's lap allowing the tears to fall again.

She had never realised it was possible to weep so much, but soon her face was wet, dampening Isabel's skirts. She clutched her limbs, writhing and twisting against the horrible future she now faced. After a while, Isabel's breathing altered, and she reached out gingerly to touch Anne's hair.

'Anne?' she questioned. 'What is wrong, dear? Are you ill?'

Anne's sobs ceased. She looked up at her sister, and when she saw Isabel display awareness of something external to her own grief, she smiled.

April 1471

The past few months had been hard. Abandoned in France with Marguerite and Edward, while their father and Clarence crossed the channel to renew their challenge for Edward's crown, the days were long and miserable. Isabel bid George a tearful goodbye, clinging to his doublet when he left a perfunctory kiss on her brow. He scowled as he pulled away. Still smarting from Warwick passing him over as the next king, George's hopes of ascending to the English throne were dashed by this new alliance with Lancaster. Behind his father-in-law's back, he seethed with discontent.

Warwick assured him that should Edward meet an untimely death, then George would be next in line to the throne, but George wasn't content with that. Lancaster was young and, if the nightly attention he paid his wife was anything to go by, Anne was bound to present him with an heir very soon. Fearful of that, George watched Anne intently for signs of pregnancy, and cursed beneath his breath each time the newlyweds retired early to their bed.

George knew his status, and his future was in jeopardy. It was with a heavy heart that he set off with Warwick to depose his own brother. Not for the first time he began to regret the choices he'd made.

As the Duke of Clarence, George was among the richest and most powerful lords in England, and he cursed himself for not having been content with that. Too late, he had come to realise that Warwick's plans put him in a bad position. He would have been far better off as a favoured brother of King Edward than brother-in-law to a Queen consort. His brother, Richard's fortunes were testament to that, and George envied his sibling's power and influence with the king. Isabel was probably as disappointed as he in the direction their lives had taken.

But, as things stood, there was little he could do about it, and so he continued to follow Warwick. With a heavy heart, he set his army against his brother's and watched with regret as Warwick forced Edward and Richard from the country to seek sanctuary at the Burgundian court.

Never one to let his true feelings show, the letters he sent to Isabel boasted of the ease with which the task was undertaken. He said nothing of his real feelings about the reinstatement of half-witted Henry upon his uncomfortable throne.

Six years after being knocked from power, the bewildered Henry VI was restored to power. Freedom sat uneasily upon his shoulders now, and he was thankful for the comforting presence of Warwick who, so obligingly, made all his decisions for him. He yearned for the tranquillity of his Tower apartments where he had been content with devotion and study. Now, seated upon a docile mare while they paraded him before the citizens of London, he raised a feeble hand in response to the half-hearted cheers.

Now that the scales of war had tipped again, and the royal palace thronged with reinstated Lancastrians, the Tower dungeons steadily filled with the supporters of York. But Warwick had underestimated the citizens of London. They had loved Edward and soon grew restless beneath the helm of Warwick. Men were defecting daily to Edward's cause and to make matters worse, news arrived from Westminster, where the queen had taken sanctuary that considerably strengthened the York cause.

Elizabeth Woodville had given birth to a lusty son. Edward of York now had a male heir.

The arrival of the new prince increased the likelihood of Edward's IV's reinstatement, and Charles of Burgundy, uneasy at the thought of Marguerite and Warwick's alliance with France, agreed to assist Edward in his efforts to regain his throne.

Isabel and George's hopes sank even further, and Marguerite railed at her son, accusing him of tardiness in his quest to plant a Lancastrian heir in Anne. This, in turn, urged him to attack the project with renewed vigour. Anne, given little respite from the husband she despised, grew thinner and paler under the pressure of his nightly attention.

Warwick, still maintaining a firm grip over Marguerite's husband, decided it was time to act, and persuaded her it was safe for her son to set foot upon English soil. Taking the Neville women with her, she embarked for England on the early tide to join Warwick, Clarence and the feeble-minded King.

There was something familiar in the breeze, and indefinably English. Anne and Isabel inhaled gratefully as they stepped onto the wharf at Weymouth. Calling for her son to follow, Marguerite pushed past them and strode toward the waiting horses. She set a relentless pace across country to Cerne Abbey in Dorset, where they rested for a day or two before resuming their journey.

It was good to be in England again and Anne found her spirits rising, just a little. But, once they were settled into the Abbey guest house, Edward lost no time in resuming his attempts to conceive an heir.

Unknown to Marguerite, the Lancastrian cause was not riding as highly as she had been led to believe. The dethroned King Edward and Richard of Gloucester, together with a Burgundian army had landed at Ravenspur. They marched unopposed across country toward Coventry where Warwick maintained a fortified position. When he learned of Edward and Richard's approach, he ordered Clarence to ride out and confront them.

The two small forces met in a small woodland clearing. King Edward raised his hand and halted their men. The three brothers rode forward to the halfway mark where George, Richard and Edward faced each other for the first time in many months; months in which everything had changed. They stared unsmiling. The horses were restive, requiring all their skill to hold them steady. For long moments, with the sunlight glinting on their armour, the brothers did not speak. Edward threw up his visor.

Facing his brother after such betrayal was hard for George. He wished he could turn it all into a joke, pass it off as a prank but he lacked the courage. Screwing up his eyes against the sunshine, he squinted into the face of the king and, to his great relief, took comfort from what he saw there. Edward gave him no greeting but waited as a myriad of thoughts ran through George's mind: Warwick, Isabel, his passionate longing for power. *Was power worth the loss of family, the loss of honour?* His horse threw back its head, pawed the woodland floor, and George reached a decision. Gathering up the reins, he dismounted and fell to his knees before his King.

As if they had been waiting for such a move, Edward and Richard also dismounted. The brothers strode forward and heartily embraced, welcoming George back into the fold.

The allegiance of George of Clarence had shifted again.

Marguerite burst furiously into the girl's chamber, her obscenities an assault to their ears.

'Out,' she yelled, grabbing Isabel's arm and dragging her from the room.

'What are you doing? What are you doing?' Anne yelled as Marguerite propelled Isabel into the rush-strewn passageway, thrust her onto the floor. Isabel gaped, raised her arms as the enraged Marguerite bore down upon her again.

'No,' she cried and, scrambling to her feet, Isabel turned tail and fled. Anne tried to follow but strong arms prevented her and threw her into Edward's chamber. Marguerite was strong, and dangerous even in a good mood. Terrified by what was happening and having no idea what Isabel had done wrong, Anne threw open the door to follow but there were guards outside. All she could do was watch from the window as her sister was ejected from the Abbey precinct.

Anne gnawed at her thumbnail. She paced the floor, oblivious now to the menacing growls emitting from the hound by the hearth. Knowing herself alone in a friendless place, after many hours of thought, she realised that she had no choice but to attempt to win the support of her loathsome husband.

Much later, when the fire had almost burned itself out, Lancaster entered. Surprised to see Anne awake, he strode over to the fire and agitated it so that flames shot up the chimney. He added a few fresh logs before sitting down, turning to his wife who, to his great surprise, smiled at him. He was even more astounded when she approached and placed a hand upon his shoulder.

'Have some wine, my lord,' she said, joining him on the settle. 'Please tell me what is happening, Edward. I know it's something bad and I'm frightened. I'm so glad you are here now.'

Warily, Edward's brow furrowed and, to convince him further, she moved a little closer and smiled again. Mistaking the look in her eye as genuine, he put his arm around her, as if they were as companionable as any married couple. Slowly, he inched his fingers beneath her bodice and, when she did not stiffen or move away, he ventured further. Swallowing her disgust, Anne closed her eyes, responding with what she hoped were convincing murmurs. If she could buy the information she needed, it would be a worthy sacrifice.

Afterwards, as they lay naked beneath a sheet, Anne put her head on his chest in feigned affection. Then, quelling her self-disgust, she turned over onto her stomach and kissed him before raising her face to his.

'Please tell me why your mother is so angry, Edward? What has Isabel done?'

Edward looked down and smiled, pleased to see her so rosy. He smoothed a stray strand of hair from her eyes.

'George has betrayed your father and gone back to Edward; so, since she is now the wife of a traitor, Mother has ejected Isabel from her household. Don't worry too much though, I have sent a groom after her to ensure her safety.'

Anne turned as rigid as stone and repeated his words.

'Ejected Isabel from the household? She's gone, without a farewell. Oh God, I'm alone here now. Will I ever see her again?'

Tears spouted from her eyes and her nose began to run.

'Hush Anne, you can write her a letter and I'll smuggle it out for you. Come here, sweet, let me comfort you again.'

But Anne, distracted by the imminent danger to her sister, forgot that she needed Edward's alliance. She slapped his hand away.

'Don't touch me.'

And Edward, knowing he'd been duped, lost no time in quitting her chamber, slamming the door behind him.

April 1471

As the war ripped across the kingdom, Anne was left completely in the dark as to the fortunes of those she loved. She had always upheld the adage that 'no news was good news' but now any news would be better than the tortuous uncertainty in which she passed her days. After failing to seduce her husband onto her side, she was more alone than ever. A prisoner in her chamber, she saw only the acerbic servant who brought her food three times a day and the sour-faced woman who helped her to dress. And Edward, of course, who, under orders from his mother, continued to pay his conjugal addresses.

Having no idea as to the whereabouts of her mother or Isabel, she knew she'd been sacrificed to her father's lust for power and, with the family torn apart by war, they may never be reunited again. For hours, she paced back and forth across the chamber floor, pausing only to peer from her high up window in hopes of some miraculous reprieve. Sometimes, unbidden thoughts of Richard soothed her with a taste of the days before, when her father was the king's friend and Richard set to become her future husband. Now, sullied and betrayed, she pushed the thoughts away and wished she was dead.

Anne was dreaming. She walked barefoot on a grassy ridge in a land of swirling mists and shifting rain. Her vision was hampered, and the hill she must climb was thickly wooded, the barbs on the undergrowth vicious. She rubbed repeatedly at her eyes, but her vision remained misted and as she began to mount the maiden slopes, her wet night-gown tangled about her legs, hampering her ascent. Falling over exposed roots and into sharp-thorned bushes, she scrambled on through undergrowth and across rocky streambeds. Blind and cold, the distant clash of steel drew her on until, at last, she entered a small clearing and came upon a knight. He was standing, sword in hand, with his back toward her.

She crept closer, containing her fear to ask him what direction she should take but when he turned, she realised it was her father. He was mired and bloodstained, with rents in his surcoat and great gashes in his chest, a terrible gaping wound on his temple.

Anne's words emerged slurred and slow.

Silently, her father pointed upward, and she knew she must continue to wend her weary way to the top. But no matter how fast she climbed, the hilltop grew no closer and her vision remained obscured. It was so much effort, she despaired of ever reaching her destination.

But, at long last, she reached the top, and stepped into a glade with a small church at the centre. Seeking the safety of the inner sanctum, she hurried toward the door but as she grew near, the door flew open, and a huge shaggy bear emerged. He knocked her down as he fled, and she saw he carried a staff and was pursued by an angry boar. Anne screamed soundlessly, but the beasts proceeded to fight and, when they blundered back inside, she peeked around the door, into the church.

The bear seemed older than the boar and he lumbered in a ragged circle, gasping and bleeding but all the while keeping eye contact with his adversary. Their rank animal stench assaulted Anne's nose and their hot breath steamed like a dragon's. She noticed the bear's foreleg hung uselessly and realised he was injured.

She wanted to do something, say something to divert them from their murderous intent but when she called out, her voice made no sound, and she was paralysed, unable to move. The animals eyed one another, their breath audible, their intent uncontainable. Anne raised her hands to cover her face, watching through her fingers as the boar made one last, lethal charge, impaling the bear upon his murderous tusks. This time when she cried out, her despair mingled with the dying bellow of the great bear. Their shared lament echoing around the transept.

Anne flattened her body against the wall, the chill damp seeping through her linen shift. Trapped between the wall and the boar she knew she was doomed. As the boar turned its thick set head toward her, she prayed to St Brigid but after blinking its bloodshot eyes, it snorted and trotted briskly from the church.

Anne slid down to a stone floor so penetratingly cold it roused her from sleep. She found herself in the welcome warmth of her bed and her maid, still in her night-gown, was limping across the room to answer the summons of whoever was knocking so loudly. Anne sat up, bewildered by the lingering dream and shook her head to dispel the alarming figure that was looming over her bed.

Marguerite's unprecedented visit to her chamber could only herald bad news but, refusing to give the woman the satisfaction of seeing her fear, Anne set her jaw and returned her glare. Marguerite folded her arms and tapped her foot, her pale face twisting as she considered how best to relay her news. She detested Anne. As she surveyed the undernourished body and plain face she hated her, and it seemed the ingrate returned the feeling full measure.

'Well Madam,' Anne whispered, at length. 'Why don't you give me your news?'

A muscle in Marguerite's cheek twitched as she savoured the fear in Anne's face. She took such comfort from it that she momentarily forgot the tidings were as damaging to herself as to Anne.

'Your father is dead, your uncle too and our cause is subsequently on the verge of being lost. There was a battle, at Barnet on Easter Day.'

Anne did not move. Marguerite stopped speaking and turned abruptly to the window, seeming to battle with some alien presence in her throat. When she turned she made no attempt to disguise her loathing. 'Your sister's husband dealt us a sore blow when he defected to York, and your father's inadequacies as a soldier has dealt us another. So much for an alliance with the great House of Warwick. While we were disembarking at Weymouth, it seems your father was being hacked to death by Richard of Gloucester. Somerset is preparing for one final battle and this time we will finish York for good, make no mistake. Prepare yourself for a journey and be quick about it.'

Stunned and alone in the chamber, Anne grieved for her father, not as he had been the last time she saw him but, as he had been when she was a child - bluff and blond and brave.

A father to be proud of.

Why then had he betrayed them all? Why did he turn on the king and sacrifice his daughter's happiness for his own desires? How could he have sold her virginity and future happiness? Why must life be so cruel?

As she threw her clothes haphazardly into a trunk, she reflected that her father had really been lost long ago. Despite his death, she couldn't be completely sorry for the defeat when, in her heart, she remained, as she would always remain, a supporter of York. *How is Richard faring?* She wondered for the hundredth time. He would be broken after killing Warwick. Falling to her knees, she prayed to God to send Richard strength, long before she remembered to pray for her father's soul.

May 1471

The long, exhausting journey finally ended at Malvern, close to the town of Tewkesbury and the battle took place nearby. As safe as she could be in a small priory, Anne strained to hear the distant cries of strife, the clash of steel, the scream of a dying horse, imagining the horrors taking place there. She paced the floor, hoping against hope for a York victory without stopping to consider that she was now firmly entrenched on the opposite side. If York won the battle, the Lancastrians would be put to death, as Edward of Lancaster's wife, the most she could expect was lifelong incarceration in the Tower.

The wait was torturous. She could not eat, could not drink, could not sleep, could settle to nothing and her companion, seeking to ease her own torment, fired embittered barbs at Anne that grew more wounding as the day progressed. The day was almost at an end when a messenger limped into their presence.

Ignoring his bloodied coat, the missing badge of Lancaster that had emblazoned on his breast that morning, Marguerite demanded news. The boy fell to his knees and turned a deathly pale face up to his mistress.

'All is lost,' he wailed. 'They are dead ...' He broke off into sobs, the terror he had witnessed draining his sanity. Margaret stepped closer, her fists clenched, spittle on her lips.

'Who is dead?'

'All those who mattered. Somerset, Tresham, Clifton, Audley, Gower, the Earl of Devon, all dead, either on the field, or slaughtered by the king's men afterwards. I hid and watched, unseen. The remnant of our army took refuge in the abbey but when Edward of York arrived, he ignored the law of sanctuary and instructed that they be dragged out. He slaughtered them all in the market square.'

'Oh, Holy Mother ...' Anne whispered and fell to her knees to pray for the souls lost. She prayed for both York and Lancaster, for all the good English blood that had drained into Tewkesbury soil that day. But her prayer was short lived. A scream shattered the silence, Anne looked up in time to see Marguerite cast herself to her knees and begin to beat her head against the wall.

'Marguerite!' Momentarily her mother-in-law paused, for a brief moment, she looked up at Anne through her bloodied hair, her lunatic eyes before beginning to scream again. The messenger shook his head from side to side as he backed from the room.

'I will fetch help,' he said as he fled.

Unrecognisable now as the spiritually undefeated Queen, Marguerite sprawled like one demented on the chamber floor. Each time Anne tried to approach her, she was assailed with missiles as Marguerite hurled whatever came to hand. Shielding herself with a cushion, Anne dodged a water jug and an ink pot.

'Marguerite,' she yelled, made brave by terror. 'Do you really want them to see you like this? Is this how you want to be remembered? Do not give York the satisfaction of falling into madness.'

A brief silence, hiccupping muffled sobs, Marguerite cleared her throat. Anne peeped from behind the cushion. Marguerite sat in the pool of her torn skirts, her shoulders slumped, great handfuls of hair clinging to her clothes. The great warrior queen of Anjou, the strongest woman Anne had ever encountered brought low by loss. And she hadn't even enquired after the fate of her son.

Unsure if she were wed or widowed, Anne crept forward and with great daring took Marguerite's arm, hauled her to her feet.

'Come,' she said. 'Let us find your women to put you to bed. Things will be better in the morning, perhaps we can re-group …'

Marguerite pulled her arm away and hurled Anne a look of disgust.

'I don't need your help.'

It was not until the morning that news arrived of Edward of Lancaster's death, his body discovered not among his comrades in the town or on the battlefield but some way off as if he had been taking flight from the conflict. Anne, still shocked from the sound defeat of the day before did not react to the news she was no longer a wife, her concern was for the woman she detested. The cold hearted, cruel mother-in-law who had done her best to make Anne's life hell. But this time Marguerite's grief was too deep for tears. Instead, she cocooned herself in her defeat.

Somehow Anne managed to coax, persuade, shame and provoke Marguerite into concealing her anguish from her enemy. When the Yorkists arrived to take her into custody they found her calm but no less bitter. The next morning, with her wrists bound like a felon, Marguerite rode amidst the triumphant Yorkist army into London. She ignored the cat calls, the insults and even managed to raise her head and return the stares of the populace who had come to witness her entry into the Tower of London where she was to be held, with her husband, Henry.

Anne, left alone at Malvern priory, was slow to realise that she was now a widow and free of Edward. She even spared some pity for her nineteen-year-old husband lying, butchered and bloody, beneath a shroud.

PART THREE
'Servant'

<u>Erber House London - June 1471</u>

Anne barely gave her creamy coloured mare time to halt before she slid from its back and fell into Isabel's waiting arms. The girls hugged tightly for a long moment before disappearing into the hall to sup on hot frumenty and share the events of the last few months.

So much had happened in the time they had been apart; they had lost their father, lost an uncle, and Anne had been widowed. And now they learned of the death of poor old King Henry VI. Rumour whispered he had been executed in the Tower.

Both women understood the king's motives in ending the Lancastrian threat, but it was hard to think of violence being used against the kindly, pious man. It was clear to Anne that the days of bluff King Edward were over. Treason had a way of brutalising kings.

There was so much death, so much sorrow, that it lay upon her like a shroud, suffocating all memory of happiness. She was rudderless and could not see clearly into the future and longed only for the past. The blissful childhood at Middleham castle seemed like a dream, like an illustration on the pages of a once-read story. The past was an unreachable place of fantasy.

Although widowhood had not touched her heart, she mourned for the might-have-been, and was all too aware of the unbreachable door between the dead and the living. It was a fragile door, so easily opened but once entered, there was no return. Now free from Marguerite and Edward, free from her father's jurisdiction, she should have been happy but instead she was vulnerable. For the first time she appreciated how much harder it was to live than it was to die.

Often, she woke in the night, unconvinced that Edward could no longer hurt her, his wine-laden breath now stilled forever. The worries of the last years remained with her, engraving dark thumbprints beneath her eyes.

Now, reunited with her sister she was safe at last. And began to properly unburden herself. In the safety of the chamber, Isabel held Anne's trembling hand as she related the sordid details of her marriage bed. She swung her head sadly from side to side.

'I will never remarry Bella; I will never suffer that indignity again.'

'It doesn't have to be like it was with Edward. Why, Anne, it can be wonderful with the right man, a magical thing.'

Seeing Anne's doubtful expression, Isabel laughed gently and whispered, 'Truly sister, I do not jest. George and I, well,' she blushed, elaborating her words with expressive eyes. 'There's nothing nicer, truly.'

Anne crossed the room and stood at the window.

'Perhaps we are made differently, Bella. I'm happy for you and George, and I know you will soon be rewarded with a healthy child, but I have been thinking, and I believe I would prefer to enter a religious house. Marriage is not for me.'

Isabel nodded absently as she considered George's likely response to this news. After Tewkesbury, he had become obsessed with finding Anne and having her brought into their home. At first, Isabel had been grateful, mistaking his interest for brotherly concern, but over the course of a few weeks, it became clear his main concern was whether or not she carried the Lancastrian heir.

She also suspected he had designs on Anne's share of the inheritance, both from Warwick's estate and their mother's. King Edward had decreed that since her husband died a traitor, the Countess of Warwick's estates were forfeit and to be divided between her daughters as though she were dead. George was determined that he alone benefit and was keen to prevent Anne from remarrying..

As Anne's guardian, he meant to oversee any future marriage very carefully and before Anne's arrival he had made it quite clear that Isabel was to keep a sharp eye upon her sister. He had ordered that her linen be checked for signs of her monthly flux and that she was to be allowed absolutely no visitors.

Isabel glanced toward Anne who was staring out the window. There was little sign left of the child who had danced her way through Middleham's darkest winters. She decided that until she recovered from her ordeal, it would be politic to delay informing Anne of George's stipulations.

The weeks passed. They received few visitors but were content to live quietly as they renewed their former intimacy. George was often away, and in his absence the household relaxed, and life became easier. On his return however, his drunken remarks monopolising the conversation, Anne was uncomfortably aware of his eyes upon her. More often than not, long before her usual time to retire, she made excuses and escaped to the solace of her chamber. She prayed, she sewed, she read, and the weeks passed uneventfully.

She had been at George's house at Herber for a few months when she woke to the sound of a small company of horse arriving in the bailey. She rose from the bed and peeked from the window, her breath catching in her throat when she recognised the white boar banner and saw Richard dismounting from his horse. He approached the hall, mounting the steps two at a time and hammered on the door. It was early in the day for a social call, Anne wondered if there were fresh trouble.

Before he could bang again, George appeared on the threshold and barred his entry. The brothers regarded one another, Richard stiffening and taking a step back from George's hostility. Their words were muffled but Richard seemed to be conciliatory and seeking admission to the house while George was bent on preventing it. Insidiously, he inched closer to Richard, forcing his retreat down the steps.

Knowing him as well as she did, Anne could tell that Richard was clinging to his temper; his face was red, and his jaw tightly clenched as he continued in his mission to persuade Clarence to allow him access. But it was George, ever highly strung, who was the first to lose control.

'How many times do I have to say it, Richard? She is not here, she was here for a few days but then she left, I don't know where. Perhaps she is visiting her mother at Beaulieu.'

Anne's chin dropped, astounded at his blatant lie.

'Very unlikely, George. This is Anne we are speaking of; she would never just leave without telling you her direction. Where is Isabel then? Let me speak to her.'

While George fumbled for an answer, Richard looked at the ground, letting his dark hair flop forward over his face, and then he struck at his thigh with his gauntlet, his tone clipped. 'I'm waiting, George.'

'Isabel is not well. You can't see her. I shall speak to her on your behalf and send you word later.'

Richard leaned closer to his brother, his stance angry, his voice abrasive with rage.

'You're a bad liar George, you always have been. Have the past few years taught you nothing? Have you forgotten how I spoke out in your defence after your betrayal? Have you forgotten how I protected you from the stain of treason? You betrayed our brother, never mind the king, and now you are betraying my loyalty by denying my right to speak to Anne. You, George, are a blemish upon the name Plantagenet.'

Richard turned but before he remounted his horse he called across the bailey. 'I mean to see Anne, George. She is my friend, and I will find her. In the meantime, see that she is well cared for or you will answer to me.'

At his words, a leap of hope surged in Anne's breast. She climbed onto the window seat, threw open the casement but she was too late and the sound of hooves on the cobbles betokened Richard's departure. But, before he rode away, she heard him shout.

'I won't give up, George. I do mean to make her my wife.'

Still in her night clothes, Anne hurried to her sister's chamber, bursting in unannounced.

'Why won't George let Richard see me, Isabel? What is happening? I don't understand.'

Isabel sat up, yawning and stretching, frowning against the morning light.

'You are not well enough to receive visitors, Anne; you've been through a great deal.'

Isabel didn't meet her eye as she swung her legs from the bed and stood uncertainly before her younger sister, raising her brows at the fact her hair was still in its night bands and her feet naked.

Anne frowned. The truth suddenly as transparent as Isabel's thin bed gown.

'I am a prisoner here, am I not, Isabel? George is keeping me prisoner.'

'No Anne, of course not. He just wants you to be safe, that's all.'

Isabel stroked her arm, seeking to offer comfort but Anne wrenched it away.

'No,' she cried. 'You are wrong, Isabel, or you're deluded, or lying. Why would I not be safe with Richard? George would not even let him across the threshold. I saw the fear upon his face, Isabel; it was just that, naked fear. I know I'm right; I am George's prisoner, and he means to use me for his own ends.'

'Don't be ridiculous.'

Anne followed Isabel as she crossed the room.

'Oh, he has only ever thought of himself. What is he up to now Isabel? Is it more treason?'

Isabel watched her usually placid younger sister, her braided hair bobbing on her shoulders as she paced the room and wracked her brains for a solution. Isabel was uncannily reminded of her father, the great Lord of Warwick, who had always paced back and forth whenever he lost his temper.

Anne suddenly stopped.

'I have to go, Isabel. I have to leave here, and you must help me.'

Isabel's jaw fell.

'But George and Richard will make up soon and then everything will be well again. You know what they are like, Anne; they have always fallen out over one thing or another. It always comes right in the end.'

Anne snorted, unable to believe such gullibility.

'It only comes right, Isabel, because Richard gives in. He loves George and so he lets him have his way, but you must understand that Richard will never give in over this. Richard believes George's treatment of me to be worse than treason. No, I must escape George's clutches. Once I am out of his power, the situation will be defused and there will be no cause for enmity between them. Help me, Isabel, I beg you.'

Subterfuge did not come easily to Isabel; she betrayed herself in a thousand ways as she aided Anne's escape. She was prone to hysterical laughter and her colour came and went from her face at the most innocuous of questions.

Jayne, party to the plan, stashed away a few of Anne's clothes and some bread and wafers in sacks in the small room off one of the kitchens. Anne was far more skilled at duplicity than her sister. She spent her afternoons sewing calmly in the solar and answered George politely, and with apparent interest whenever he addressed her. Anne knew he was leaving for court first thing in the morning and her plan was to leave the house as soon after his departure as it was safe to do so.

She would go to her mother at Beaulieu, or if that failed, to Richard's mother at Crosby Place. Lady Cecily had always been her friend and was as aware as anyone of George's vagaries. She loved all her sons very much but would not hesitate to shield Anne. When she retired to bed that night, Anne was confident her troubles would soon be over. All she need do was escape George.

Isabel stared at the reflection in her polished pier glass while her woman brushed and braided her hair. The chamber was dimly lit, and a fire burned in the grate, injecting a warm glow into the room. When the door opened and George entered, Isabel welcomed him warmly, as she always did. He dismissed her woman, who curtsied to her mistress before quietly closing the door.

Isabel finished plaiting her own hair, looking at George's reflection in the mirror. For all his faults, she couldn't help but love him. From the first night of their acquaintance, when she was eight years old, she had marvelled at his handsome looks and fine manners.

His manners were not quite so polished these days, and she had to admit that he drank far more than was seemly but, although she regretted his former treason, it had not altered her love. And it also seemed that he loved her in return, for she had never had the least suspicion that he kept paramours, unlike the king, who had more than he could count.

Isabel felt sorry for the Queen who, despite her celebrated beauty, could not manage to keep the faith of her husband. It was as if Edward couldn't help himself, he had even made rude overtures to her on occasion. But Isabel had eyes for no one but George. He was in his prime, tall, golden and beautiful. He stood behind her as she surveyed them both in the glass.

They made an impressive couple.

George's doublet was unfastened, the dim light in the chamber, concealing the wine stains on his linen. He leant forward and kissed his wife's ear, and she leaned back against him as he began to undo the tightly knotted braids again.

He arranged her hair softly around her shoulders, and she watched in the glass as he slid his hands beneath the neck of her shift and cupped each small breast. His were the rough hands of a soldier and horseman, and his skin rasped over her nipples, making them stand out, proud and rosy. He pulled her chair around, so he was standing in front of her. When he knelt and began to draw hot wet circles on her skin she ran her fingers through his hair. Involuntarily, her thighs opened, and she gasped with anticipation when he lifted her and carried her to the bed.

Once beneath the safe canopy of their marriage bed, Isabel gave herself up to the pleasurable demands of her husband. Skilfully and inexorably, he brought her steadily closer to the brink of pleasure, until she was breathing fast and hard. He reared above her, his golden-haired chest solid and strong beneath her hands. Isabel strained toward him, craving his mouth on hers. She closed her eyes and opened her lips, relaxing as his face lowered to hers, his breath hot in her ear.

'What is your sister up to, my dear?' he whispered.

Isabel's eyes flew open, her passion replaced by fear.

'What, George? What do you mean? Don't be silly, come on, don't stop now.'

'Oh, I don't mean to stop,' he said, nibbling her ear and sending armies of goose pimples marching across her bare skin. 'You can tell me what she is up to while I take you, and each time you falter or lie to me, I will spank you like the naughty child you are.'

In the cold light of day Isabel was deeply shamed of her behaviour the night before but things had always been so between her and George. Until her wedding night she'd had no idea of the pleasure that awaited her in the marriage bed. George had been delighted to discover the wife he'd chosen solely for her wealth, possessed an appetite to match his own. Her delight in bizarre bed sport kept the relationship fresh and, if she ever raised objection, he had never yet failed to persuade her to relent.

Maybe that was why he never strayed.

Isabel's libido was a weapon with which George could rule her by night and by day. The guilt she suffered after a night of sin prompted her to undertake hours of penance for, although the church blessed the sexual union of marriage partners, it still regarded the act itself as sin. A woman, not a decent one anyway, wasn't supposed to enjoy it.

Sometimes George waited for Isabel to emerge from chapel where she'd been seeking consolation and immediately persuaded her to err again. There was nothing gave him more pleasure than watching her piety degenerate into debauchery.

George grinned as he reflected that, unlike other men, the rod he used to control his wife was considerably thicker than his thumb.

If Isabel seemed nervous the next morning, Anne put it down to fear of discovery; she shared her sister's anxiety. Not long after George made a noisy leave-taking, Anne, Jayne and a groom, set off on their own journey. Since Richard's mother lived much closer, Anne had decided to ask for her help first.

As they made their way through the green countryside that surrounded the city of London, for once Anne was optimistic about the future. A leafy canopy shaded her from the sun, but the road was so dusty they had to stop frequently to refresh themselves. Blackbirds sang in the trees and tiny flies danced mad circles over the sun-warmed road and, on entering a green wood, Anne saw a rabbit dart into the undergrowth and a red squirrel darting up the limb of a tree.

'I am as free as they,' she thought, with a glimmer of her old self. Unaccustomed as she was to travel without the protection of a cavalcade of armed men, she felt light-headed with freedom. She urged her horse into a canter, laughing gaily as they careered along the path with her skirts billowing about her knees, her high headdress like the sails of a ship. She ducked beneath low branches and set her horse to leap over a fallen bough.

The sun flickered through the canopy and the drumming of the horse's hooves pounded in her ears. She was hot and breathless as she sped onward, happy at last. She rode her horse toward another fallen bough, and they cleared it easily, laughing out loud as they emerged from the darkness of the wood into the sunshine.

Dazzled, she reined in her horse and blinked in the sudden light. As her vision cleared she heard the chink of harness, and low male laughter. She almost fell from the saddle when she found herself surrounded by armed men. She tugged at her skirts to cover her limbs and twisted in the saddle in search of Jayne and the groom.

As the circle of men closed about her, her mount, excited by the gallop, sidled and skipped, forcing Anne to concentrate on calming and controlling it. She patted its neck with an unsteady hand and, when she felt able, raised her head to face the soldiers.

The man at the fore urged his horse close and took hold of her bridle.

'My Lady Anne, you must come with us.'

'No, I am travelling to visit my aunt. She is expecting me.'

She looked around at her captors and noticed with a plummeting heart, that his sleeve bore the arms of the House of Clarence.

Anne paid little attention during the dreary ride. George hadn't yet shown his face, but his henchman had a firm grip on the reins, and she was unable to see a way to escape. Her captor made no attempt at conversation, and Anne was too proud to tell him she needed to stop to relieve herself. Miserably, she wilted in the saddle, uncomfortable, hungry and hot, keeping her eye on the ground as she contemplated how just a short time ago she had been celebrating her freedom. What will George say when he comes? She was confident he wouldn't resort to violence for fear of the king hearing of it, but he may well ensure she remained in a locked chamber, forbidden the few pleasures left to a woman in her position. He might keep her away from Isabel.

When the horses came to a halt, Anne looked up, startled to discover they had not returned to Erber House at all but were dismounting outside some tumbled disused manor house.

'Why have you bought me here? What is this place?'

The man, without looking her in the eye, removed her foot from the stirrup and proceeded to lift her from the saddle. She tugged her arm free.

'Tell me where we are, and why!'

As the horses were led away, he grasped her arm, led her protesting up the steps to the house.

Thrust rudely over the threshold, Anne rubbed her upper arm and looked around. The chamber was grubby, dry leaves on the floor, spiderwebs draping the windows, ashes and stray sticks spilling from the hearth.

They are going to kill me.

A sound from the far corner made Anne spin on her heel, she peered into the gloom, fist clenched as she prepared for attack.

'Relax, I am not going to lay hands on you.'

George strolled from the darkness, rested an elbow on the mantle and shook his head at her. 'Why must you be such trouble? Did you really think to outwit me? Did you really believe I would let you ride away, seek out our dear Richard and beg his protection?'

'I – I was going to visit your mother.'

'Of course, you were and then no doubt you'd have whispered poison into her ear and tried to drive a wedge between us.'

He kicked at the piled leaves, jerking in surprise when a mouse ran out and disappeared into a crack in the wainscot. George was a bully, and a liar. Anne knew he'd be behaving very differently if either of his brothers were here.

'Youi have to let me go, George. People will begin to wonder where I am. Isabel will send word to the king, or to Richard that I might be in danger.'

He scoffed, swung his head to and fro.

'No, she won't. My wife does as I say. It was your sister who informed me of your intention to flee.'

Isabel, how could she?

'I wonder how hard you had to beat her, George. You will not get away with this. I swear, whatever you do to me, I will get word out and you will be punished. The king may very well strip you of honours or throw you in the Tower.'

'He wouldn't do that; I am his little brother.'

Silence fell as they surveyed one another; George was not as relaxed as he pretended. She could see the sheen on his forehead, the way he chewed his lip and kept peering from the door. Perhaps he was summoning the courage to kill her, his hand had not left his sword hilt. Her eyes fixed on it, her body preparing for his pounce. She had no hope of fighting him off. Persuasion was her only chance. She had to make him see sense. She moistened her lips.

'I am thirsty, George, and hungry. Can you not at least let me drink while you consider my fate.'

After a moment, George sauntered toward her, unhooked a leather drinking skin and handed it to her. She drank greedily, her bound wrists making it difficult to manoeuvre, water cascading down her chin, wetting her bodice. She handed it back to him. Tossed her head.

'Thank you.'

George returned to his place at the hearth, brushed his hair from his eyes and stared into the empty grate. Anne noticed the collar of white roses he wore, a token reminder not just of the king but of his father, Richard of York.

'Would your father be proud, do you think, George?'

He looked up at her through his hair. She wondered anyone thought him beautiful. To Anne, he seemed small and mean. Lily-livered to treat a lady so.

'Proud of what?'

She let her eyes roam around the room.

'Of this. Your treatment of me, your lowly, dishonourable behaviour.'

'It hardly matters what he thinks now, does it?'

'If you kill me, my blood will stain you and yours forever. It will end your tenure as duke, your marriage will be ruined, your marriage and all your off-spring cursed.'

He tossed back his hair, his laugh uncertain.

'What, are you a witch now?'

'I might be, George. If I were I wouldn't tell you. But if you kill me, I will curse you with my last breath.'

Pushing himself away from the fireplace, he came to stand close to Anne, peered deeply into her eyes, forcing her to look away. He was mad, mad as a jack rabbit.

'I'm not going to kill you,' he said at last. 'But you'll not see Isabel again, or your mother, or the king, or Richard.'

'You can't keep me here.'

'No, I can't, but I have a connection who has undertaken to care for you. Perhaps not in the way that you'd like but you will have food and shelter. You will be safe, but you will no longer be Anne of Warwick. She is dead or fled. No, you will become Nan – Nan of Nowhere and you will work as you have never worked in your life. And in the meantime, I will have your sister, and your fortune.'

September –1471

It was before dawn when Anne blearily dragged herself from the straw pallet. Her companion, Elayne, who was also stirring sat inelegantly upon her mattress and scratched her inner thigh.

'Blasted little biting buggers,' she exclaimed, surveying the red marks on her skin. ''Ow come they don't bite you, Nan? Don't they like blue blood?'

The joke was without rancour and Anne had come to look upon Elayne as her only ally in this friendless place. The girl shielded her from the master's wrath, stole scraps of food to supplement the scanty fare they were given, and when Anne grew faint from fatigue, she helped her finish her allotted tasks. When the long day was finally over, they crawled back to the haven the straw pallet had become. Since her arrival, Anne's existence had become one round of work, sleep and work.

From the day she first met Anne, Elayne had known there was something different about her. She spoke with the soft, cultured voice of a lady and, after her first full day of labour, Elayne had daubed goose grease on her red, bleeding hands. It was clear Anne had a secret and a big one at that. Whatever the mystery was, Elayne decided on her first day to adopt and protect her.

Elayne never laughed at Anne as the other kitchen hands did. Each time she dropped a tray of tankards or tripped with a hot pan of gravy, a shout of hilarity broke the sombre mood below stairs. It was Elayne who helped her collect the scattered jugs or mop up the slowly spreading mess. In the end, Nan, as they called her, proved so inadequate a kitchen wench that she was consigned to the washing tub and spent her days bent over a sink.

At first her belly had rebelled when she was shown how to rinse the thick greasy plates into a bucket which was later taken outside to feed to the pigs. Then they must be scoured with sand until they shone. The quickly cooling water soon became rank with fat and food scraps, and had to be changed regularly, carried all the way from the fire to the sink in a pot so large that Anne could barely lift it.

As a result, Anne's hands and stomach bore red, angry scald marks that she daubed each night with more goose grease. When the pile of plates grew too large to be contained on the drainer, she wiped them dry and piled them on the dresser in dull, pewter towers.

Sometimes, she caught sight of her reflection. She was dirty; her hair hung in lank greasy tangles, but it did not really matter. Nothing mattered anymore. She had a new life now and sometimes even managed to take some comfort from the strict routine of her day.

As a child, she had been trained in the duties of a noblewoman and was well-versed in managing a large household or organising a banquet, but the menial tasks she now faced were completely outside her scope of experience. She missed Middleham, she missed Isabel, she missed her mother, but she did not allow herself to wonder about Richard. She tried to be grateful that she had work, she had a roof over her head and food to eat. The only thing she needed was more sleep.

She was constantly tired and was sometimes in danger of dozing off as she leaned against the corner sink, and lulled herself into a trance as she washed dish after dish, after dish. She had lost all notion of time and could have been here weeks or months; even her monthly flux had ceased and gave no clue as to the length of her incarceration. She should ask Elayne, but perhaps it was better not to know. In this place, the important thing was to ensure things ran smoothly below stairs, and to spare themselves the wrath of the master.

Elayne broke into Anne's reverie, holding out a hand to help her to her feet.

'Thank you' she smiled and the girls linked arms, left the room and clattered down the stairs to the kitchen.

The shutters had been thrown open and a sulky sun was peeping into the gloomy room. The cook was already bustling by the ovens, fanning the flame to speed up the heat, and the centre table was heaped with joints of pork and beef and a few fowls hung from the rack above. A pot over the fire began to bubble, heralding the start of Anne's working day.

Hastening to retrieve it, she filled the sink with hot water and soap, and began to methodically work her way through the many dishes piled in wait. She barely noticed the stench of grease and putrefying flesh that had been so nauseating when she first arrived but, as she worked, Anne turned her face toward the window to catch the faint aroma of drying herbs that hung there.

She daydreamed of the banquets she had attended and never given a thought to the kitchen staff who had laboured so to provide it. While her stomach growled with hunger, she remembered the mouth-watering dainties she had always taken for granted, the half-eaten dinners she had sent back to the kitchens, and the sweet cooling wine with which she had quenched her thirst.

Now, having eaten nothing since yesterday afternoon, her fast would not be broken until mid-morning, when a hunk of bread and, maybe, some hard cheese and a swig of half beer from a crude jug, would seem like nectar. She longed for it with as much anticipation as if she faced a banquet of roast swan, the very thought of it making her stomach growl. Elbow deep in greasy, dirty water, she remembered with longing the clean, rose scented baths she had once taken for granted.

Oh, how she longed to immerse her whole body in warm, scented water and scrub herself clean.

In all the time she had been here, she had not left the precinct of the house and was forbidden to climb the stairs to street level. Having made no enquiries as to her whereabouts she could have been a hundred miles away from home. The inn was a popular one, and the serving girls were kept busy carrying vast quantities of food up and down stairs to the customers. The ever-present stench of stale ale wafted down from the upper floor, along with Male voices, and the odd squeal of female laughter. But the staircase in the corner was used only by the serving wenches and, occasionally, the master himself.

It did not seem strange to Anne that the staff should be so in awe of the inn keeper; his power over the kitchen servants was no less severe than her father's authority had been over his household. Whenever he appeared she was as servile as the others. She might be the daughter of Warwick the kingmaker, but that fact served her little good now.

Unfortunately, the innkeeper had taken a serious dislike to Anne. He resented being forced to give her shelter by George of Clarence but had no choice but to accept. But each time she dropped something or failed to move out of his way quick enough, he glared at her as though he'd like to beat her with a stick. It wasn't that she was arrogant or refused to work, she was just incompetent. She was clearly of the blood, a breed he detested, and it infuriated him that the kitchen grease and grime that was smeared over her person, failed to obliterate her obvious gentility.

She would get him trouble; he was sure of it. There was something about her that spoke of ill-omen. She stood out from the other wenches, not because she was more beautiful but because she was more refined. She worked hard, if not well, and refused to be cowed by exhaustion or fear, and whenever she was spoken to, she had a discomforting habit of looking her betters directly in the eye.

It was mid-morning and work ground to a brief but welcome halt while the centre table was laid with bread, cheese and jugs of short beer. The kitchen staff clustered around to rest their feet and feed their hungry bellies. As they broke their fast at the rough table, a crude banter was batted around, fanning mirth and laughter.

Anne listened and smiled at their humour but did not join in, for it was very different to that which she was accustomed. But, although she did not contribute to the conversation, she nevertheless felt part of the gathering and took some comfort from that unity.

Alyce, one of the serving wenches, a bold, comely looking girl with golden hair and plump, rosy cheeks, stuffed a piece of bread into her mouth, observing at the same time.

'There be a couple of nobs upstairs today.'

Her words meant little to Anne, but Elayne sat up, her curiosity piqued.

'How do you mean? Nobs? What nobs?'

'Upstairs, there be a couple of nobs. They've been hanging around all morning, supping wine and looking suspicious like. I could tell they were nobs straight away by their fine clothes and fancy manners. They were asking odd questions too?'

'What sort of questions?' whispered Anne urgently. It was so unusual for her to speak that everyone at the table turned and looked at her.

'They wanted to know if there were other girls here, or if Nell and I were the only ones. They asked if our master were at home. Of course, I told them he was at market on Tuesdays. Then, they asked me if any other Lords had been calling. No, I says, we don't get no Lords in 'ere, not usually anyways. They were nice enough though, friendly like and they gave me a tidy tip for my trouble. It's a shame we don't get more like them, I say. It beats the rough lot we usually 'ave in.'

'Maybe you can make yourself a few extra pennies later on then, Alyce. When your feet be worn out with serving, you can earn a crust on your back.'

The raucous laughter that followed masked Anne's voice as she turned and took Elayne's wrists in a painful grip.

'It must be Clarence, Elayne. You must hide me. I'm afraid it must be Clarence, come to take me away again.'

'Ouch! Who the 'ell is Clarence?'

Elayne rubbed her wrists but at Anne's bidding, followed her into the back scullery. They retreated to the large storeroom at the back of the kitchens where sides of beef hung from the ceiling and barrels of pickled herring were stacked on the stone flagged floor. When they were safely out of the hearing of the main kitchen, Anne continued with her tale.

'Clarence is the man who pays the master to hold me prisoner, Elayne. If he takes me away again there is no telling where I shall end up. At least here I have you; I don't want to be sent elsewhere so I must hide. Don't let them find me, please.'

As Elayne opened her mouth to ask further questions, loud voices sounded in the kitchen, and Anne and her friend stood frozen and wide eyed. With her hand to her mouth, Anne strained to listen. They could not see the speakers, but the cultured accents betrayed their station, and there was no doubt that the clear, carrying tone of the voice belonged to a nobleman.

'We are seeking the whereabouts of the Lady Anne Neville; we mean her no harm, and any who help us to find her will be richly rewarded.'

A murmur broke out among the servants, but they were too over-awed to speak aloud. Elayne, in the cupboard with Anne, opened her eyes wide at her raggedy companion whose name apparently was Lady Anne. She cringed to recall poking friendly fun at Anne and calling her 'Duchess.'

From their hiding place they heard Alyce retort loudly.

'Well, I ain't no Lady and neither are the rest of us, unless of course, you care for Peter here. He's a bit of a girlie on the quiet.'

A ripple of laughter spread around the room, but the noblemen did not respond to the joke. The cold silence killed the levity abruptly and when it was quiet, one of them continued to speak.

'If any of you should hear of a lady of breeding secreted hereabouts you must send word to the Duke of Gloucester. You will be well-rewarded, for it is a matter very close to his heart.'

Anne whispered to Elayne.

'It must be a trick, but George can't fool me. Richard has no idea where I am. Oh please God, don't let George find me.'

'I thought he was called Clarence?' whispered Elayne but, before Anne could explain, the storeroom door opened, and they turned in horror to find Peter gloating in the doorway.

'Well, well, My Lady,' he mocked with a sweeping bow. 'Whatever are you hiding from? The gents outside have offered a fine reward for the return of a certain Lady Anne Neville. That wouldn't be you now, would it?'

As he inched closer, Anne began to back away, but he lunged, suddenly, for her hand and Elayne screamed.

'Let her go, you bleedin' brute.'

Snatching a large pan, she began to beat him about the head and shoulders while Anne, finding herself freed from Peter's grasp, grabbed a knife from the side and stood against the shelves with the blade held defensively before her.

With one, last, echoing buffet of the pan, Peter slumped unconscious to the floor. Anne and Elayne crept forward to bend over him.

'Is he dead?' Anne asked, fearfully but, before she received an answer, the scullery filled with curious servants. At the back of the crowd, she glimpsed a rich velvet doublet and raised the knife against attack. She did not know the man who was pushing through the crowd of servants but guessed he had been sent by Clarence.

'Just leave me be,' she warned fiercely. 'I will not be moved from prison to prison at your master's whim. I am not a chattel, so just go away and tell him to leave me be. He can keep all my money; I shall not attempt to return home just so long as I am allowed to make a new life!'

All eyes were upon her, questions on every lip, the babble of voices increasing until a second man pushed through the noxious company.

'Anne?'

She lifted her chin, the hand that held the knife, trembling. When she raised her dirty, tearstained face to him, he repeated in horrified tones. 'Anne? Is it really you?'

'Richard?'

The knife fell to the floor. She placed her cold hands against her flaming cheeks and turned to Elayne. 'It's all right, Elayne. It is not George. It is Richard. Everything will be well now.'

Richard stepped forward and caught her as she fell.

PART FOUR
'Wife'

<u>April 1472</u>

It was over. The horror of the past few years was finally put to rest, and Richard and Anne were safely and happily ensconced in their childhood home of Middleham Castle. To Anne's disappointment, Edward when he learned of her ordeal, had treated George lightly. He put pressure on Clarence to reach agreement with his brother, but Richard had been so relieved that Anne was safe he settled for just Middleham Castle and Sheriff Hutton. Never again would Anne trust George and relations between the two brothers remained strained but she knew time would heal. The only positive aspect of a truce between the brothers was that Anne would once more have access to Isabel.

Isabel begged Anne's forgiveness, claiming George had placed her under duress to reveal her plan to escape, and Anne was so happy to finally be back where she belonged, forgave wholeheartedly.

Anne recalled how patient Richard had been after her rescue from the inn kitchens. He had taken her directly to the guest quarters of the nearby Sanctuary of St Martin's where she had made a slow recovery. How wonderful it had felt to bathe her grimy skin in scented water and anoint it with soothing, fragrant oils before robing herself in soft, cool fabrics.

Her hair, once it was washed and brushed and scented, quickly grew lustrous again. Good food and warmth chased away the troublesome cough that had plagued her at night and with her health restored, her spirits soon began to rally.

When Richard visited, he found a very different girl to the one he had delivered there a few weeks earlier. She was still unnaturally silent but seemed quite resigned to the quiet life at St Martins. During the weeks that followed, he visited frequently, never failing to bring her a gift, a set of ivory brushes, a hand glass and a book of hours. On warm afternoons, they walked in the gardens and dined together, sharing trencher and cup, but he never forced her to speak. The intimacy of old had not quite returned, and unspoken barriers lay between them.

Anne did not confess it, but she was afraid that Richard's interest in her was the same as George's, and they were both lured by her dowry. As for Richard, acutely aware of her widowed state, he wondered if she had loved Edward, and if she secretly mourned him. Sometimes at night he had to force from his mind the recurring image of Anne in another's bed. She never spoke of her tormented marriage, her shame and grief at her father's betrayal and subsequent death, and so Richard continued in an agony of uncertainty.

Although she longed to speak of it, she could not bring herself to confess how frightened and lonely she had been. Richard saw how she suffered but did not know how to get her to talk. Instead, when they did talk, they spoke of harmless things. But, one afternoon, looking out through sheets of falling rain, Richard announced that he had brought her a gift.

'Another one Richard? Really you shouldn't, I will become avaricious.'

'Not you, Anne, you can never be that. This present is a little out of the ordinary, and I'm not entirely sure you will approve. Just remember that I only wish to please you. If you don't like it I can take it away. Wait there while I fetch it.'

He hurried from the room leaving Anne curiously trying to guess what he might have chosen for her. When he re-entered the chamber, he had someone with him, someone whom Anne did not at first recognise.

The girl with him threw back her hook and Anne looked at her scrubbed clean face. She was about sixteen, not much younger than Anne, and her square chin and short square stature suggested that she was of simple stock. The girl was clad in plain but clean homespun and wore a white cap upon her head. She bobbed a ragged, inexpert curtsey and whispered,

'Allo, Nan.'

'Elayne,' mouthed Anne, grabbing her hands. 'I can't believe it! What are you doing here? Richard?' she demanded. 'Explain to me, please.'

'Anne don't be cross, but I know you are in need of a friend. I must travel north for a few weeks, and I didn't want you to be lonely. I thought Elayne could keep you company while I am away. It was obvious when I found you that she was a loyal friend. She guarded you like a she-wolf. I asked her if she'd like to serve you and she agreed. She wanted to come. She loves you, too, Anne.'

Anne stared at Richard, surprised that a man had even noticed her loneliness.

'Thank you, Richard,' she said, 'you are very kind.'

Then she turned and hugged Elayne again. 'You are so very welcome, but I do not want you to serve me. You were a friend when I was in dire need, and I should like you to remain so.'

'Whatever you do say, Duch…Milady,' she blushed, remembering just in time that things had changed.

'I mean it, Elayne, call me Duchess if you wish. I want us to be equals. I'll teach you to sew and play the lute, maybe we'll find you a fine husband.'

The girl blushed and giggled. 'That'll be the day, Milady.'

Later, when it was time for Richard to take his leave, he looked into Anne's eyes and groped for her fingers. When he kissed them, he thought she seemed less nervous. He drew her hand into his chest, so their faces were very close.

'Anne,' he said. 'You know I have loved you since you were five years old, don't you?'

'Have you Richard?' she blushed prettily. 'I'm very fond of you too.'

'Would, would you then consider marrying me, my *dear* Anne?'

She took a deep breath, her eyes darting to and fro, as she considered the question.

'What about George? He'll be livid.'

'Damn George, he can't hurt you anymore. I want you and I want to keep you safe. Don't you understand how hard all this has been on me, Anne? I rode into London to see Ned one afternoon in '69, never dreaming that when I came back you'd have disappeared overseas with your father. I didn't know if I'd ever see you again, and ever since, I've been wanting you back. Now I've found you, I need to wed you before you disappear again.'

She looked into his troubled eyes and recognised the sincerity of his words. The warmth of his hand was beginning to make hers perspire but she clung to it anyway. Richard was her friend; she knew that he would never intentionally hurt her. The idea of him bedding her was not wholly pleasant, not if sharing a bed was always as it had been with Edward, but she would be forced to marry someone. If she must be intimate with a man, then it may as well be Richard.

The only other option was to give herself to God, but she knew the king would do all in his power to prevent that. Anyway, a religious life was not really for her; she longed for children and a real home of her own, and she had always been safe in Richard's company.

Smiling suddenly, she made her decision.

'I promise never to leave you again, Richard' she whispered. 'And yes, I would like to marry you, very much.'

<u>Westminster - July – 1472</u>

It seemed to Anne that all the birds in England conglomerated outside her window on the morning of her wedding day. A blue sky cradled a brilliant sun, and the early air was heavy with the fragrance of lilac that lathered the Abbey walls. Jayne moved quietly around the room, laying out her bridal gown and preparing her bath. When Elayne entered with a tray, Anne sat up in bed and prepared to break her fast. Her hair hung in braids over her shoulders and her eyes were bright as she called a good morning to her friend. How different this wedding day was to her last.

She shuddered as she recalled the dim, cheerless chamber that had never seemed warm. How she had shivered in her jewelled gown and how miserable the whole day had been. Today was very different; Anne bit into a honey-filled wafer and sighed with deep contentment while she watched Elayne sprinkle rose petals into a steaming bath.

'I can't see as how you need another bath already,' she laughed as she gathered towels to warm at the hearth. The water was delicious, while Jayne lathered her hair and Elayne rinsed it with jug after jug of fresh water, Anne hugged her knees and closed her eyes. It felt so good to be pampered, she was loath to get out.

'Time's getting on, my lady."

Reluctantly, she stood up, water cascading from her body, and allowed herself to be wrapped in a soft towel. She stood by the fire while they anointed her with scented oils and her hair was combed to a perfumed soft sheen.

The wedding was to take place at St Stephen's Chapel in Westminster in the presence of the king and queen, Richard's mother and a few select members of his household and friends. George was conspicuously absent and, to Anne's disappointment, so was Isabel. But she forgot to be sad when the priest declared them man and wife and when Richard turned toward her, kissing her for the first time as man and wife. The bells rang, the sun shone through the stained-glass window, bathing them in multicoloured light.

The feast that followed was in strange contrast to the tortured celebration of her last wedding. She shivered convulsively, remembering Edward's hands beneath the table, exploring her body before the proper time. Richard, sensing her sudden fear, turned and smiled, lifting his cup, his eyes twinkling and friendly. Anne smiled back; no matter what indignities followed, she told herself, it will never be as bad as the nights with Edward. Picking up her cup she drank deeply, remembering how a surfeit of wine had helped her handle marriage before, but she had barely touched the food piled high on her plate.

'Eat up.'

Richard meticulously rinsed his fingers in the scented water bowl as the first course was removed and the next ushered in. Anne noticed that he drank sparingly, and gallantly shared with her the choicest morsels from his own plate. Her belly twisting with nerves, Anne could only nibble on a wafer.

At last, the meal was drawing to an end prompting the king to stagger to his feet. He belched loudly as he raised his cup. The room fell quiet in deference to their King and while the company waited for him to speak, he turned to his favourite brother and noted the fearful, flushed face of the bride.

Edward had never been the most intuitive of men but even he realised that Anne would not welcome a bawdy speech. He surveyed his sister-in-law, reflected on the past year or so and decided she had suffered enough. To the disappointment of those anticipating a display of lewd royal humour, he raised his cup.

'To the most gracious, the most beauteous, the most fascinating, the most loyal, and the sweetest Lady Anne, and my most fortunate brother, Richard. May your happiness be unsurpassed.'

Anne pressed her hands to her flaming cheeks, her eyes filling with tears. She hadn't expected that, not after all the trouble her father and husband had caused the king. Richard stood up, gave thanks to the king, and bowed to the company before ushering his wife through the cries of good fortune that accompanied them to their chamber.

A hot fire burnt in the grate and expensive wax candles illuminated the room just enough to spare the bride's blushes yet providing the groom enough light to see what delights were in store. Anne sat bolt upright in the bed wanting, yet not wanting Richard to come to her.

Her hair was bound as tightly as her nerves. Her fingers twisted and contorted on her lap as she eyed the flagon that stood by the bedside. Glancing at the door, Anne considered whether she had time to drink enough wine to supplement her dwindling courage. Now the time was upon her she wished she had drunk more, although Richard wouldn't want to find his wife in her cups. Quickly, she grabbed the goblet and took a long draught before drawing the back of her hand across her mouth. As she replaced the cup, the door opened and Richard entered, bearing a tray piled with vitals and dainties.

'I noticed you ate very little at supper, Anne, so I thought we could partake of something by ourselves.'

He was wearing a loose gown, embroidered at cuff and hem with roses, a white boar on the breast. It seemed strange to see him with no jewels or weapons. His hair was ruffled, and he bore little resemblance to the great lord to whom she had so recently been wed. Anne decided she liked this new Richard who seemed younger and friendlier, more like the grubby boy she had grown up with.

He climbed onto the mattress and, placing the tray upon the covers, began to rip apart a small roast capon and pass her the choicest pieces. Anne relaxed and, to her surprise, found her appetite returning. With Richard feeding her, she ate with enjoyment, rinsing her mouth and refreshing her palate with wine after every few mouthfuls. By the time Richard removed the tray and climbed back into bed, her head felt quite light. She giggled when he pulled her toward him, her head coming to rest on his shoulder. His bare chest was unfamiliar territory, the proximity reminding her of the last time a man had bedded her. But Richard's body was very different to Edward's. Richard was a seasoned soldier while Edward had been little more than a boy when he was killed. She let her fingertips roam through the dark hair. Edward's chest had been smooth and white, his breasts almost more pronounced than her own but Richard's was hard, hairy and scarred. It was the torso of a warrior, the body of a man; the problems he'd suffered as a child hardly noticeable from the front. It was only when he turned that you noticed his spine was awry, snaking up his body rather than straight as it should have been. She remembered the consternation when, as his body began to transition from man to boy, his problems had first begun. Anne's nurse had said he was cursed, the physicians said he would never be a knight but should study books rather than the art of warfare. But Richard, of course, refused to listen. He worked harder than any other trainee at Middleham and forced his body to grow strong, even as it twisted.

'Look at all your scars,' she remarked. 'Did you get them all in battle?'

'All except that one.' He pointed to a mark that had paled so much it was barely noticeable. 'Your dog did that, Troy. Do you remember? When he had a piece of stick lodged in the roof of his mouth and I was trying to get it out for him.'

Anne sat up to look closer.

'I'd forgotten,' she murmured and reached out to trace the thin white line with her forefinger. Richard stiffened imperceptibly at her touch and his pupils darkened.

'What about the others?' she said.

He laughed and looked down at his own torso.

'My chest represents a record of the wars between York and Lancaster. I got that one at Barnet, that one at Tewkesbury and that ... erm, I think it was at Middleham, practicing in the tilt yard. You can blame Francis for that one.'

They laughed in the semi darkness and peace fell upon them. The comfortable silence lasted until Anne hiccupped and put her hand quickly to her mouth. Richard took her glass.

'Are you tipsy, my Lady?'

'I think I might be, Richard. I do feel strange, almost as though I could float right out of the chamber window.'

The laughter died.

'Oh, don't do that, my love. Don't ever do that.'

He placed his lips upon hers.

Anne had no time to object, and it did not take her long to discover that kissing Richard was very different to kissing Edward. His lips were dry, soft and warm. As he tentatively explored her mouth, her tummy turned over quite unexpectedly and when he began to run his hands softly over her body, exploring the contours of her breasts through her shift, a soft moan escaped her. Richard paused; his dark, gleaming eyes penetrating hers.

She smiled shakily and licked her lips. Now he had stopped kissing her, her worry returned, making her wish it were all over so she could stop being afraid of what was to come. Richard pulled at the ribbons holding her hair in place and began to untwist her plaits, she closed her eyes.

'So beautiful,' he whispered as he bent to kiss her again.

The sensation of his mouth on her skin was having an extraordinary effect. What with the wine and the probing of his tongue, her head was spinning, making her breath come in gasps, and her breasts were tingling. As his insistence grew, she opened her mouth as though tasting her first strawberry. The kiss continued until she became dizzy. When he took his lips away she was sorry for a moment but then her eyes widened when his tongue travelled along her throat, and his hand crept inside her shift to encircle her breast.

He pulled her chemise higher; she lifted her hips to aid him, raised herself from the pillow so that he could pull it over her head. His hands, hard and horny from years in the saddle, rasped across her tender skin, raising goose pimples, her nipples as hard and as pink as unripe fruit. His mouth tugged gently at her nipple, his hand skimming across the triangle of hair further down. Anne had never dreamed she could feel like this; she rolled against him, squealing as he gripped her bottom and pushed against her, his need for her digging hard into her belly.

Forgetting the pain and disgust at the consummation of her first marriage, Edward of Lancaster was forgotten and there was only Richard. He was inside her head, inside her body, consuming her soul.

There was no sense of wrong as there had been before; it was as though she and Richard were running hand in hand up a great green hill. He helped her over the rocky places and carried her across the streams, and when they finally reached the summit, he paused and looked deep into her eyes and when he kissed her, they soared and swooped through the clear blue air like new fledged eagles. And, once air borne, Anne opened her talons and let her fears and inhibitions fall.

Middleham-1472 -73

Anne's laughter rang across the dales as she raced to the top of the hill. Quickly catching up with her, Richard grabbed her around the waist and pulled her to the ground, twining his fingers in her hair and attempting to kiss her bared throat. Their attendants, who were waiting with the horses, averted their gaze.

The duke had been a different man since he returned home with his bride. For the last few weeks, business had been kept to a minimum and most of his waking hours were spent playing with his wife. His habitual frown had gone, and his rich laughter could be heard at all hours of the day and night.

There were those who thought the behaviour unseemly, but most were glad to see the Duke so obviously happy. He was a man apt to take things to heart, and the months leading up to and following Tewkesbury, and the long traumatic time he had spent searching for Anne had robbed him of his youth. It was good to see him restored.

Richard rolled off his wife's body and sat up, encircling his knees with his arms while Anne rested her face upon his shoulder. She giggled as she poked a daisy behind his right ear, and then followed his gaze across the vast Yorkshire landscape. The undulating green of the dale melted into the cloud-tossed sky where a lone hawk circled in the blue, his cry spiralling back to earth. Since their wedding day she had been euphoric, and with the unblemished future stretching before them, the past no longer haunted her.

Jayne and Elayne remained Anne's closest companions, seeing to her needs and helping her assume her new status as Duchess of Gloucester. In due course she would invite a handful of young gently born women to enter her household but just now, she wanted peace. Not that there was much chance of that.

It was a mammoth task to oversee the running of the huge castle and ensure that enough food was stocked up for the winter. As a girl, despite her mother's teaching, she'd had little idea the work involved in running a household the size of Middleham. It was home to hundreds and every member had to be nourished throughout the harshest months of the year. Even the supplies required to keep the horses fit had to be considered, involving cartloads of hay and grain dry stored. The household linen must be kept clean and mended, the servants must be clothed, as well as the fine garments for the family, which required more skilled care.

At least once a year, the castle was vacated, leaving only enough men to carry out a thorough clean and replace the old stinking rushes on the lower floors with fresh. The yearly spring clean was unpleasant to say the least for, as the layers of rushes were lifted, the most noxious of discoveries were made. Discarded or misplaced items along with grease, dog faeces and animal bones were all heaved from the castle windows to rot at the bottom of the moat. It was a job best carried out when the Duke and his Duchess were far from home.

Once her daily duties were attended to, Anne often visited the nearby Abbey where she left alms for the parish poor. The local people, who remembered riding through the streets beside her father, loved her and called out in greeting when she rode by. Although she was a grand lady now, Anne always took the time to acknowledge them.

On wet days she sewed in the solar with her ladies or practiced her lute while listening to the gossip of her companions. The only shadow on her life was that as Lord of the North, Richard was kept so busy he was often away. Even though he told her he was safe, she knew it was his job to keep the Reivers in check. It also fell to him to dispense justice among the local people; and she worried constantly that he would be injured, or some vengeful criminal would harm him.

He was gone often and for too long and Anne spent many afternoons watching from the tower for a sign on the distant road that betokened his arrival. On sighting him she would run down the twisting stairs, her gown catching at her legs, the dogs barking at her heel, to be waiting at the door when he cantered into the bailey.

His homecomings never failed to remind her of her father returning from court. She had been thrilled as a child when he cantered through the gates, thundering over the drawbridge to be greeted by similar barking hounds and bowing servants. She counted her blessings that her new life so closely resembled the halcyon days of her girlhood.

Yes, life was wonderful, and they were well content, but today, as she waited, she hugged a secret; a secret that would increase their happiness a thousand-fold, for this morning it had been confirmed that she was carrying Richard's child.

Written this day of our Lord, February 15th, 1473.

To my dear sister Isabel,

I hope this letter finds you well and your Christmastide was joyous. I am, as you know, presently expecting the arrival of an heir for Richard. I don't know if it is because of this that I find the winter season has been uncommonly warm. We both, of course, long for a son for although Richard's base-born children, John and Katherine, bring us joy, they can never approach the rapture that this child within me will herald.

I understand the Queen gave Edward a second son in August, I am sure the court celebrations have been vast. Although I have little love for the queen, I find myself in sympathy with Elizabeth at the moment and wholly approve of the decision to name the babe Richard.

My own Richard has been from home far too frequently of late, both at the parliament and also about some private business which he does not disclose. My lying-in fast approaches and the chamber is ready prepared and the midwife already in residence. I am grateful Jayne and Elayne will be here with me although I wish with all my heart that you and mother could be here also.

I am finding the confinement a little oppressive, and long to stride upon the moors with Richard again. I have never been very good at being idle. However, I do not suppose it will be too long to wait now and soon I will ...

The dogs suddenly began barking and Anne leapt in her seat, hurrying to the window as soon as she realised a company of horse were riding into the bailey. She craned her neck to discover the cause of such a hubbub, her hand idly stroking the velvet bump of her belly.

At the first blast of the horns, the castle burst into activity. Grooms and horses were milling around as the bailey filed with banners showing the white boar, the white rose of York. Riders dismounted, stretching their legs as they exchanged a few words. A cluster of people, all well-wrapped against the chill, moved up the steps directly below Anne's window. She sighed, frustrated at not discovering their identities.

Elayne was folding baby garments by the fire.

'Run down and see who it is please, Elayne.'

Another sigh escaped her. She hated the incapacity of childbearing. It seemed such a short time ago that she had been able to run errands for herself, and she grinned wryly at her matronly ways.

'Not much longer though,' she assured herself as she leaned her forehead against the thick window glass and tried to imagine the face of her son. She didn't turn around when Elayne slipped back into the chamber.

'You have a visitor, my Lady.'

Anne turned in surprise to find Richard, accompanied by a heavily veiled woman.

'Richard, you are home, how lovely.'

She moved forward and placed her hand in his, squeezing his fingers, watching with curiosity as the woman unwound a vast array of scarves. As the last folds were drawn aside, Anne flew into her arms.

'Mother, oh, Mother. Oh, I am so glad to see you.'

Open displays of affection had not been encouraged while Anne was growing up but this time it was gratefully received. Life had been hard for the Dowager Duchess since her husband's inglorious death two years ago at Barnet. When the king had removed the duchess' wealth and properties and she found herself friendless, she had sought sanctuary at Beaulieu Abbey, living quietly ever since. She missed her former grand lifestyle, she missed her daughters, she missed the gossip and intrigue of court.

Anne Beauchamp had married Richard Neville when she was just nine years old, three years senior to her husband. Her dowry had given him control of the vast Beauchamp estates, including the immense wealth that she inherited from her mother who had been a Despenser. Together with the title and castles already possessed by Warwick himself, their marriage had resulted in unsurpassed power and prestige. Once they were of an age to live as man and wife, despite their union being the product of diplomacy rather than love, she had fallen quite swiftly beneath Warwick's charismatic spell. She had been shattered by his loss.

He had spent much of their married life on one campaign or another, but she had never seriously doubted he would come home. His defection to the Lancastrian camp had both puzzled and wounded her but she remained loyal, doing nothing to dissuade him because it wasn't her place to do so. Since his death she had come to regret that, and it had taken many tears and prayers for her to come to terms with the fact that he was gone forever. Consequently, the woman Anne received that afternoon was not the mother she remembered;

she was aged, her grandeur ravaged by grief. Now, she greeted her daughter with tears and contrition.

The dowager duchess had come to realise she could have been a much better mother. She had given Warwick not just her love but her idolatry too, and her daughters had always served to remind her of her failure to provide him with the son she had promised him. Now, reunited with Anne who was replete with child, she hoped it was not too late to make amends. But Anne was unaware of any to be made.

'Take off your cloak and come and sit beside the fire, Mother, you must be frozen. Have you been in the saddle all day?'

'No, no, we have been on the road for a week or more, stopping to rest at Abbey guesthouses on the way. There were only a few remaining miles to cover today. It is Richard to whom I owe thanks, for he spoke to the king in my favour and has undertaken to care for me. It would have been wiser to wait and travel in fairer weather, but I was impatient. I wanted to be here for your confinement.' She turned to Richard who was waiting quietly by the door. 'I shall never be able to thank you sufficiently, my Lord.'

Richard crossed the room and slid his arm around Anne's shoulders.

'You must address me as Richard, as you always did.' he said. 'I require no thanks. I well recall my childhood when you welcomed me to Middleham and offered me a home. I am glad to do the same.'

The dowager looked around the room, remembering when she had been mistress here. This very room, the table, the hangings and the chairs were all familiar. Suddenly she wondered if she would be forever expecting Warwick to stride through the door.

Glancing at Richard now, she pondered what manner of man he really was. There had been rumours, after Barnet, that Warwick had died at Richard's hand, but it was clear her daughter didn't believe it. They must just be wicked rumours. Nobody, least of all loyal little Anne, would willingly bed her father's murderer. With a deep breath she settled more easily on the heavily cushioned seat, close to the fire. 'No,' she thought, 'the past has passed, and I must look forward once again.'

February – 1473

The lying-in chamber was ready with new hangings, the usual vibrant hunting scenes replaced with gentler scenes of gardens and flowers which were far more suitable for a birthing. All windows were covered, leaving just one to allow in a little light. The cruel winter draughts managed to creep beneath the door, but a massive fire was kept burning in the hearth. Sweetly scented thyme and rosemary were scattered, and the bed was piled high with richly embroidered testers, pillows and blankets. The bed itself was luxuriously draped to provide relief from harsh light and cold, and wax candles cast a soft glow upon the scene.

Fustian wraps, linen swaddling bands and several lengths of flax twine for tying the umbilical cord were placed beside a large copper bowl in readiness for the birth and, close to the bed, a small table was stocked with wine and herbal concoctions to relieve any pain and stress the mother might suffer. Confinements could last for days, and the strength and well-being of the mother vital to ensure the safe delivery of the infant.

Anne inspected the chamber with her mother, ensuring nothing had been overlooked. Anne was wearing a loose velvet gown with fur trim; her face was plump and rosy with good health. It was good to see her so obviously flourishing; the unhealthy pallor and troublesome cough she had picked up during her incarceration in the kitchen was now gone. Anne had still not grown accustomed to her generous bosom and rounded belly.

'I look like a female partridge,' she joked, 'plump and succulent, ready for the pot.'

'I'd eat you,' Richard's eyes gleamed wickedly.

It was only at night when she lay in Richard's arms, listening to him breathing that she allowed any fears to creep in. She never spoke of it but the memory of Isabel's labours onboard the foundering ship were never far away. Anne had been young then and ignorant of female matters; her education that night into the realities of motherhood had been abrupt and harrowing. She recalled so plainly the pinched blue features of Isabel's dead son and shivered as she thought of the tiny body slipping into the cold, unfriendly sea. As much as she tried not to think of it, the images would creep up on her when she was least expecting it. The midwife said unhealthy thoughts could result in a difficult birth.

Anne shook away the memory and stroked her velvet belly, silently praying that all the careful preparations keep her child from harm.

'Not long now,' she said for the hundredth time, as if she couldn't wait. Her mother placed a hand on her elbow, and they left the room. As the chamber door closed behind them and they entered the draughty corridor, Anne felt a nonspecific pop and her thighs were suddenly drenched in fluid. Instinctively, she put her hand at the base of her belly.

'Mother, the waters have breached. Quick send somebody to Richard with the news.' She gripped her mother's arm in a mix of fear and excitement. Her child would soon be here.

Hours later, as the day dawned brittle blue and cold, freezing the waters of the moat and petrifying the trees in the fields, Anne was delivered of a son. While Elayne cleaned her tender parts with a soft cloth and warm water, she lay like a plucked lily upon her pillows, her fine chemise ruined but dispensable, and her hair damp upon her brow. But she smiled and gazed toward the hearth where her son was undergoing similar treatment at the hands of the midwife.

'He has all his fingers and toes,' the woman said as she gently washed away the detritus of birth. While she anointed him with scented oil he screamed, red faced and furious until she wrapped him up and carried him, still squawking, across the room to his mother. Exhausted as she was, Anne did not feel the need for sleep. She reached out and held her baby close to her face, inhaling the incomparable fragrance of newborn hair. She was examining his red wrinkled features for a likeness to his father when Richard entered the chamber. Ignoring the child, he touched her face.

'Are you sure you are quite well, Anne? I have been in such anxiety, I thought he would never come.'

'I'm fine Richard; I can honestly say that I have never been better. I'm merely tired. Look to your son, my Lord.'

As she placed her son in his father's arms, Richard looked at his heir for the first time. The baby opened his eyes and Richard saw he was small and fragile but perfectly formed. A soft brown down covered his head, and his blue eyes winked up at Richard.

'It is as if he is laughing at some secret joke,' Richard said. 'He reminds of my brother. Maybe we should name him Edward after the king, if that is acceptable to you, Anne.'

Anne laughed. 'I'm so happy, I'd let you name him George, if you wanted to, my Lord.'

They were still giggling when the new grandmother was ushered into the room but, as Richard laid Warwick's grandson into his grandmother's arms, they sobered. With her tears anointing the baby's head, the Dowager Duchess whispered, 'Oh, well done, Anne, well done. Your father would have been so proud.'

Anne broke the rules and insisted upon feeding Edward herself. She had so much milk that she could not bear to allow someone else to nourish him. When her mother protested, Anne was adamant.

'It's important to me, Mother, for just a few weeks I wish to nurture him myself. It makes me feel useful to him, and I have nothing else to do. I have engaged a wet nurse for a few weeks' time; I shall wean stop then.'

The lengthy lying-in was proving to be a source of frustration to Anne who was bursting with good health and desperate to leave her bed. On this point though both Richard and the dowager stood firm; she must stay in bed for the good of her health. Anne would not be allowed to resume normal life or relations with her husband until after she was churched, and this peeved her. She felt so well and had already been confined for so long that she wanted to live fully again.

When she wasn't playing with Edward, she passed the time embellishing his robes and embroidering his blankets. The continuing harsh weather kept visitors away, making her all the gladder of her mother's company. Despite sharing the same roof for so many years, the two women had never spent so much time in one another's company and their mother/daughter relationship flourished into friendship.

As the months passed, Richard and Anne's son grew and thrived under the watchful eye of his parents. Although Anne ceased to feed him herself as she had promised, she continued to spend most of her day with him. As soon as she had dispensed with her daily duties, she would hurry to the nursery and, much to the astonishment of the wet-nurse, romp with him upon the floor.

When the weather grew more clement, she and Richard carried him up onto the dale so that he could feel the wind in his face and the good Yorkshire sun upon his head. They sat him on the grass and laughed when he tried to pluck handfuls of it and put it in his mouth. He was not a large baby, but he was a happy one and doted upon by both parents.

They introduced him to the horses in the stable, allowed him to pet the castle dogs and taste morsels of food from their own plates, a thing much frowned upon by Anne's mother. Edward, or Ned as he was more often called, had inherited his mother's sunny nature but Anne was pleased to see he was developing his father's dark good looks. On the day she noticed his eyes were changing from a milky blue to a deep, rich brown she took him with her to the stable where Richard was busy with the steward.

Richard, took him from her, turned him into the light and agreed they were going to be brown. He even went so far as to ask the opinion of the steward.

'Yes, I think you're right, my lord. He is certainly a bonny child.'

Anne beamed with delight as she took him back into her arms again.

'I shall go and tell his siblings,' she said, with a smile at her husband.

Ned was not the only child resident at Middleham, the nursery already housed Richard's two bastards, Katherine and John. Katherine was just four and John was six and both were grateful to their new mother and delighted when she presented them with a new brother. Anne harboured no ill-feeling toward children born long before she and Richard were married. But, although she cared for them, they in no way matched her adoration for little Ned.

Completely fulfilled, Anne continued to blossom and, the more she blossomed, the more she indulged her husband and child and the more those around her fell victim to her charms. At the end of the summer, news came that Isabel had given birth to a daughter at Farley Castle. They named her Margaret, and Anne dreamed of summer visits, the children playing under the watchful eye of the Warwick sisters. Isabel wrote that the child was healthy and although the birth had been arduous, she was making a steady, if slow, recovery. George, Isable joked, was already planning the next child and assuring everyone, it would definitely be a son.

Anne let the letter drop into her lap, Isabel's words injecting a pang of longing. It had been so long since they were together but ... she was still wary of George, and the relationship between him and Richard not yet properly healed. But soon, she hoped, soon the breach would be mended, and the two families reconciled.

After a wonderful summer, Middleham castle prepared to receive a visit from her mother-in-law, Cecily Neville – proud Cis, as she was known. Anne scurried around Middleham, issuing orders and ensuring that everything was ready. Richard was annoyingly calm.

'Don't be so anxious. My mother will be happy just to admire her grandson and spar with your mother. Everything will be fine.'

That was all very well but Anne feared she would fail to live up to the exacting standards of the devout Cecily. In her youth, Cecily had been celebrated as a great beauty, and known as the Rose of Raby. During the tumultuous days of the last reign, she had faced danger with calm fortitude, never once allowing darkness to drive her, as it had her rival, Marguerite. During his quest for the crown, she had supported her husband unwaveringly, sacrificing both him and her son, Edmund to the cause.

Since their deaths and her son, Edward's accession to the throne, she had gradually retired from court life, appearing in public less and less until she was practically a recluse. She was a generous patron of many Cistercian abbeys and people said her piety was so great that she listened to devotional works, even while dining. Anne had heard it said that even in age her beauty remained unchanged.

Anne still felt sure she would find fault in her; her looks, her housekeeping and maternal skills. She might well decide Anne was an unsuitable wife for her youngest son. Still seething with doubt, late one afternoon, Anne stood at Richard's side and watched Cecily's cavalcade arrive. Despite her reclusive lifestyle she apparently still liked to travel in style. She arrived to a blast of trumpets, her insignia emblazoned on every pennant and the surcoats of her retainers. The white rose of York was painted prominently on the door of her litter, the fluttering curtains embroidered with fleur de lis. Anne's stomach churned with trepidation as the slim, upright figure ascended the steps and threw back her hood.

What rumour said was true and, although Cecily was beginning to show signs of age, she still retained the beauty she was famed for. Her eyes shone with vigour.

'Anne, dear,' she cried, kissing her on the cheek before turning to embrace her son. Anne noticed how she held on to him for a few seconds longer than necessary. As they moved into the depths of the hall, Cecily chatted about the journey while she removed her travelling cloak and let it drop. A servant scurried to retrieve it while Cecily paused, noticing Anne's mother for the first time.

'Anne,' she said, the two women bowed their heads guardedly.

They had been close in their youth, but much had happened since but Anne's mother, taking the initiative eased the awkwardness by launching into virtues of their grandson. Anne could have kissed her.

'He is such a forward boy,' her mother said. 'He recognises me already, and loves the dogs, trying to grab at them from our laps.'

After a quarter of an hour listening to his wondrous feats Cecily grew impatient.

'Well, let's not sit talking. Take me to the nursery so I can make the acquaintance of this paragon.'

Ned had just finished his evening feed and on the nurse's lap. He grinned a milky greeting as the women swept into the room closely followed by his father. Ned had already learned the presence of the women equated to attention and spoiling. As Cecily took him onto her lap and looked him over from head to toe, he raised a chubby hand and pinched her cheek.

His grandmother laughed and kissed his fist.

'Well,' she said, 'aren't you just the most exquisite baby in the world?'

Over the next few weeks, while Richard was busy, Anne was left to entertain her mother-in-law; a task made much easier by their mutual adoration of baby Edward. It also afforded Anne the opportunity to understand her father, Warwick, better because while they sewed, the women reminisced about his childhood. To Anne, her father had always been something of a stranger, so it was illuminating to hear stories of his youth.

Her memory of him softened as she learned of a boy who had been thrown from his first horse into the moat, and of a young husband who had often proved too drunk to climb the stairs to his marriage bed. The tales humanised him and enabled Anne to almost forgive his many errors of judgement, although she could not quite acquit him of the crime of marrying her to the enemy. She watched her mother, prematurely aged and shrouded in sorrow, and Richard's mother, equally bereft but her grief armoured with pride. They had both lost husbands but dealt with their loss differently but, of course, Richard of York had died a hero whereas Warwick had died a traitor to his king.

Anne wondered how she would cope with widowhood herself. She had been widowed before of course, but Edward's death had been a release. She felt no guilt for that but, at the mere thought of losing Richard, her heart quailed. Hastily she forced herself to concentrate on other things.

Middleham -1474

Ned was standing by the settle, with Anne hovering just behind. Experimentally, he let go and took three faltering steps into the middle of the room. Anne followed, stooped and ready to catch him should he fall. Cecily's brow creased as Anne put dangerous objects out of the baby's reach and spread cushions upon the floor to soften his many tumbles. When Richard made his excuses and quit the room, she put down her embroidery.

'Anne, may I speak to you about something?'
'Of course.'
Anne sat beside her, keeping one eye on her son.
'I am not criticising you, my dear. I merely wish to warn you … about loving your son too much.'

Startled, Anne turned to the older woman and frowned.

'Too much? Is that possible?'
'If you love them too much, sons can break your heart, Anne. They go away and forget you or marry unsuitable women and break your heart that way. You cannot protect them forever and if you cushion their every fall they do not learn to fend for themselves. When life is cruel to them, the final injury can wound you so deeply that recovery is impossible. Remember Marguerite …?'

Anne gasped as Cecily's point found its mark. She remembered too well Marguerite's incessant fussing of

Edward. She had been jealous, her affection for him embarrassing. Marguerite had hated Anne not because she was Warwick's daughter but because she was Edward's wife. Anne recalled her secret scorn whenever Marguerite stroked her son's face as she bid him goodnight. She had sneered at Marguerite's refusal to allow him to leave France until she was certain it was safe enough. Her reluctance to let him engage in combat, even after he attained manhood.

Edward had longed to take part in battle, but his mother had always forbidden it. Marguerite's insatiable mothering had robbed him of his manhood just as surely as a Yorkist sword robbed him of life. At Tewkesbury, when she had listened to his mother rage at the news of his death, Anne had not really understood, but she could now.

The thought of her Ned butchered by an enemy sword made her blood run cold. She must protect him but how could she when protection might lead to his destruction. She turned to Cecily, speaking through tight, white, lips.

'I watched as she went mad, Cecily. How can I prevent that from happening to me? How can I protect Edward from the world without smothering him?'

Cecily stared through the oriel window into the distance.

'Women must learn to love their sons with a loose hand. We must learn to let them run, let them fall, and be there for them afterwards. It is you who must wear the armour, and guard against excessive love so that you have the resources to cope with whatever fate brings. It's a hard lesson, Anne, and I'm probably trying to put an old head on young shoulders, but my sons have hurt me more than you can ever understand. Of all my sons, only Richard has been steadfast, only Richard.'

Middleham Castle -September 1475

The late September rain lashed the castle windows, painting the rooftops with a glistening sheen. The wind howled, piling mounds of wet leaves into doorways and the foot of the hall steps. The castle dogs skulked, head down against the rain, seeking the protection of the outer walls.

Inside, Anne was warmed by the roaring fire in the great chamber. She looked from the triple arched windows across the rain-lashed valley of Swaledale. The letter she had been re-reading lay discarded in her lap. It was a lively account from Isabel detailing the circumstances of another lying-in and the perfection of her baby son. The child had been born in February and she and George had named him Edward. Isabel reported he was golden haired like his father and so placid that he had quickly become the delight of all who beheld him. Apparently, he rarely cried, even when due a feed, but waited with beguilingly contentment for his food. On reading this, Anne reflected that he was clearly nothing at all like his father. She couldn't imagine George had ever been content, even in the cradle.

She wished for the thousandth time that Richard would return. He hadn't yet heard the news for he had already been gone for some weeks and was not expected to return until Christmastide at the earliest. Edward had levied taxes to raise money for war and was calling for men at arms to accompany him on his challenge for the French crown. The magnates were expected to respond, and as royal dukes, Richard and George were at the head of the list.

The landowners paid up, some grudgingly, grumbling about royal extortion but Richard and Clarence were both eager to teach King Louis a lesson. They had summoned one hundred and twenty men at arms each, plus a further two thousand archers. In fact, Richard's ever-increasing popularity in the north had resulted in three hundred extra men answering his call to arms. While the warriors of the north checked their weapons, Richard ordered the making of cognisance's and banners displaying the *Blanc Sanglier*, the White Boar of Gloucester.

It was May when Richard bid Anne farewell and mustered with his army at Barham Downs near Canterbury. She did not once complain as he prepared to go for she understood it was his duty, but she missed him acutely, thinking of him constantly and counting the days until his return. He wrote regularly, his letters full of amusing anecdotes on the lighter side of a soldier's life. But once he had accompanied the king across the channel, news became less frequent.

His last letter detailed a visit to his sister Margaret, Duchess of Burgundy in St. Omer. Anne had read it so many times, the missive was becoming dog-eared and when Isabel's news arrived, Anne anticipated fresh news of the French campaign. She skimmed her sister's salutation and the praised heaped upon her newborn but found little news of import. It seemed she was so happily engaged with her new baby that Isabel was not missing George as she usually did. She told Anne she felt very tired and sometimes retired to bed for the entire afternoon and slept until vespers. Anne frowned. Isabel's son was seven months old, and she should really have fully recovered by now. Perhaps it was just as well George was absent, affording her some much-needed recuperation. She folded the letter, tucked it away, and peered miserably out at the darkening afternoon.

Elayne and Jayne mended clothes while keeping Anne company.

'Ned is doing better now, my lady,' Jayne said, nodding toward her son who had been suffering with a summer cold. Anne turned to look. It seemed he was going to be one of those children who were prone to sniffles. She had ordered him brought to the chamber so that she could keep an eye on him. He was propped up on a day bed playing with some wooden animals, his cheeks were flushed and his eyes heavy.

Every so often, one of the women, usually Anne, left her work to encourage him to take another drink. It was important to keep him warm and they were constantly tucking the bedclothes tighter about his body but, with a strength of will only to be found in a two-year-old, he immediately kicked off them off and complained of being too hot.

'Don't be silly, Ned, you must keep warm,' reprimanded Elayne. 'Look, why don't you call Troy over to sit beside you.'

She slapped her thigh and called to the dog who roused wearily from his slumbers. It was not the Troy of Anne's youth, but his namesake and Ned adored the little dog. He allowed his ears to be pulled and the pads of his feet to be examined but his patience was not universal, and he had been known to snap. It was only Ned whom he allowed such liberties and Troy was the self-elected bodyguard of the castle's most precious inhabitant. He sat up, ears alert, trembling in anticipation as Elayne balanced a sweetmeat upon his nose. Ned laughed when the dog began to drool, crossed his eyes trying to see the treat but making no move to eat it until Elayne gave him leave. Then, at her command, he tossed it in the air, caught and swallowed it all in one movement much to the delight of the sickly boy.

'Again, again!' Ned clapped his hands.

Anne, glad to see her son so entertained, rose from her seat, and as she did so, a lone rider cantered over the drawbridge. She craned from the window, frowning at the muddy stallion, trying to determine whose badge he wore. She did not recognise Richard until he threw back his saturated hood, then with a cry that made the dog bark, she sped from the room and down the stairs.

Before Richard had even crossed the threshold, she was in his arms. Disregarding his dripping cloak and chilled hands, she clung to him for a long moment. She could feel the tension of his journey draining from his body. Then she pulled away.

'Come,' she said. 'There is a fire in the solar.'

Back in her chamber, while retainers heaped victuals onto a side table and, Elayne and Jayne made themselves scarce, Richard peeled off his sodden garments.

He stood before the fire, towelling his hair dry and attempting to answer the questions Anne fired at him. Every so often, her examination was interspersed with the high-pitched excitement of their son as, his chill forgotten, he sought to gain his father's attention. At length, when the last of the servants quietly closed the door leaving the family alone together, Richard was able to freely discuss the events of the past few months.

As he spoke Anne could almost envisage the triumphant entry of the most impressive army England had ever led into the French capital, numbering in excess of one thousand five hundred men at arms and eleven thousand archers and a huge train of artillery. She saw the pennants and pikes, the glint of armour the tramp of many feet. But the picture was blighted when Richard began to describe the ignominy of Charles of Burgundy. The disappointment of those who had expected to fight.

'Burgundy reneged on his deal with the king, and never sent the promised support. Instead, he pursued his own war upon the insignificant city of Neuss! From then on the whole campaign was a farce.'

Richard's jaw clenched angrily as he thought on it.

'Edward refused to listen to me. He placed financial and diplomatic consideration above honour and valour. Instead of a second Agincourt, the affair degenerated into an ignoble pay-off.'

'What do you mean?'

Richard scowled and thumped the table.

'I mean that that Louis wriggled his way out of the battle by persuading Edward to accept seventy-five thousand golden crowns immediately, with the promise of a further fifty thousand crowns a year for the remainder of his reign. Oh, and he also pledged to wed the dauphin to Elizabeth.'

'But …she is …'

'A child, yes.'

Anne listened with a mixture of relief that her husband was home and not to face battle after all, and dismay that Edward had sunk to such dishonour. Richard spat out the words as he described the meeting of the two kings on Picquigny Bridge.

'Oh, Edward made a magnificent display in his velvet and jewels and cloth of gold, but Louis was not so splendid.

A barrier was erected in the centre of the bridge and the two kings embraced through the bars, signed the treaty and swore on a piece of the true cross. Louis then tried to ingratiate himself with as many English courtiers as he could by offering huge pensions.'

Anne gasped, waiting for Richard to continue.

'He promised them money and plate, and most of them were easily bought, and agreed.'

Richard took a long draft of ale, the despair in the action betraying his sense of personal dishonour. Anne knelt at his side, offering comfort in the only way she knew how. She patted his arm inadequately as his voice broke.

'Edward's actions were not like those of my brother, Anne. He was shady and calculating. He listened only to the opinion of his Woodville sycophants and ignored my plea to reconsider. He is my king and I have never argued with him before but this … this latest act emits a foul stink, Anne. Even without Burgundy we could have won the victory or died in the attempt. Our father would never have considered such a discreditable truce. I was shamed to be his brother and I felt for our men who had left their homes and families, abandoned their crops for sake of their King, only to be sent home untested.

And afterwards, I was shamed afresh to witness our English soldiers drunk in the streets on Louis' hospitality and, by God, the French king is sly, Anne. He invited me to dine with him and I couldn't, in courtesy, decline but I did refuse his gifts. I could not hide my disdain, and I fear I have made a very powerful enemy.

The whole affair has left a bad taste in my mouth so I came home as soon I could. Edward kept trying to bring me round, he is eager to make amends. Of course, I am still his man in my heart but, by God, Anne, I have no faith in his foreign policy. He is there, at court, surrounded by Woodville's and there's not a man or woman among them that is not out for what he can gain. Why can't he see what is before his very eyes? How can he believe they have the good of the country at heart? They've made us a laughingstock. Do you know what I heard being bandied about in a tavern on my way home? '

Anne shook her head, aghast at this outpouring of vitriol.

'Evidently, Louis is so pleased with the outcome he joked publicly about it. *'I have chased the English out of France more easily than my father ever did; for my father drove them out by force of arms, whereas I have driven them out with venison pies and good wine.'* The whole of Europe are laughing at us. God's teeth it makes me mad t' think on it.'

Anne leaned forward, refilled Richard's cup and handed it to him. He took a long draught before smiling up at her and drawing her onto his knee.

'Oh, Anne, you are such a good listener. I can't tell you how good it feels to be home. I won't be leaving the north again for a long time to come. Wild horses couldn't drag me from you.'

Middleham - Christmas 1476

The Christmastide celebration was underway. The torches in the hall leaping and dancing. Trestle tables, draped in snow-white linen groaned beneath the weight of gold and silver plate and crystal stemware. The cloths were sprinkled with fragrant dried rose petals and heaped with half-consumed festive dishes. An enormous fire burned so fiercely that the people closest were over-warm and those farther away were not quite warm enough. Richard and Anne sat in their customary places at the top table in the company of Anne's mother, and their guests, Francis and Anna Lovell. Ned was on Richard's knee, sharing his parent's trencher and applauding the festivities by banging his plump fist upon the snowy board.

The company had plenty to celebrate. Richard had finally quelled the trouble on the northern border and Francis and Anna Lovell were enjoying an extended celebration of their recent marriage. Added to this was the news from

Warwick castle that, after a problematic pregnancy, Isabel had been delivered of a son whom, rather surprisingly, they had named Richard. Both mother and child had come through the ordeal although the child was said to be very frail. It was now two months since the birth and the danger period past. Cups were raised to the mother and child and the hall of Middleham rang out with a heady, happy laughter.

The first course consisted of porpoise and peas, baked herring with sugar, roast swan, venison, roast woodcock and of course the traditional stuffed boar's head eating an orange. A clarion of trumpets announced the arrival of the boar and, while the diners rinsed and dried their fingers in the tiny bowls provided for the purpose, a minstrel stepped forward into the torchlight to sing.

> *'The boris hed in hondes I brynge,*
> *With garlondes gay and byrdes syngynge;*
> *I pray you all, helpe me to synge,*
> *Qui estis in convivio.*

The revellers took up the well-known refrain and young Ned beat with his spoon upon his roundel in accompaniment.

> *The borys hede that we brynge here*
> *Betokeneth a Prince withowte pere*
> *Ys born this day to bye us dere;*
> *Nowell, nowelle!*
> *This borys hede we brynge with song*
> *In worchyp of hym that thus sprang*
> *Of a virgine to redresse all wrong;*
> *Nowelle, nowelle!'*

Their faces were flushed and happy and Christmas tidings were called repeatedly as the wine flowed ever more freely. Beneath the table, the fun continued with dogs of various sizes fighting over scraps and bones. But Troy, who was no match for the large castle dogs, curled on Anne's lap where he was sure of only the choicest dainties.

Deprived of fine food during advent, now it was over the diners fell upon the feast. The initial course took the edge off their appetites while the subsequent courses were consumed at a more leisurely pace. The leftovers would be sent back to the kitchens to be distributed to the poor who lingered at the castle gates.

Music issued from the minstrel's gallery throughout the meal and the volume of the conversation rose to challenge it, mingling with the din of growling dogs and the clink of fine plate.

Another fanfare heralded the arrival of a minstrel who, clad in red and green in the old manner, strode to the centre of the hall. A hush fell as the company waited for him to begin. He struck a pose, enjoying the drama of the moment before launching into *The Legend of St George*.

> *'O yee folk that heer present be,*
> *Wheeche of this story shal have inspeccion,*
> *Of Saint George yee may beholde and see*
> *His martirdome and his passyon.'*

The heroic tale of the man whom every young boy strove to emulate was greeted with such thunderous applause a stranger might have imagined it had never been heard before. In most popular literary tales, a great feast always heralded the climax of the drama. At King Arthur's court, the Green Knight interrupted a Christmas repast to issue a challenge that was taken up by Gawain. The revellers at Middleham were so deeply embroiled in the tale that when a great hammering fell upon the castle door, they mistook it as part of the entertainment. Nobody was expecting a half-frozen messenger to stagger into the hall. Their hilarity suspended while the company watched the travel-stained page fight his way to the high table. He bowed before the Duke and Duchess.

When she saw the badge he wore, Anne groped for Richard's hand.

'My Lord of Gloucester,' he gasped. 'I bring news from your brother, the Duke of Clarence.'

Richard passed Ned to Anna Lovell and took the letter. Anne rose unsteadily to her feet, spilling her indignant greyhound to the floor and peered over her husband's shoulder.

In the silence that followed, the Dowager Duchess pressed a kerchief to her mouth and tried to swallow the bile gathered in her throat. Every face in the hall was turned toward the high table, knowing intuitively that disaster loomed. Richard broke the seal and frowned at his brother's untidily scrawled note.

Brother,
This is to inform you that my wife Isabel died on the twenty-second day of this month.
George.

Richard turned to his wife and, without speaking, confirmed her fears.

Tewkesbury Abbey – January 1477

Tewkesbury, the abbey where Anne's first husband had met his death was now her sister's burial place. As Richard accompanied her and her mother south, the frigid northern frost gave way to warmer southern climes and the crack and drip of thaw sounded all around. They were wet through by the time they arrived at the abbey and Anne's limbs and fingers were stiff with cold when Richard helped her dismount.

Anne, lodged in the same chamber that once witnessed the lonely confusion of her widowhood, looked sadly at the hated walls she had hoped never to see again. Now her grief was for Isabel and her baby son, who had lived just a few weeks. Each time she thought of it, Anne's heart broke afresh. Mother and son were tucked together in a shared coffin, and would remain in the Abbey, lying in state for thirty-five days.

When Anne's limbs thawed and she had taken food and drink, she refused Richard's offer to accompany her, and made a sad journey across the churchyard. Pausing outside the great doors of the abbey, dwarfed by the vast pillars Anne prayed for courage.

As soon as she entered she saw her sisters coffin, the candles flickering, and thin beams of light from the high glass windows piercing the impenetrable dark. Anne took a few tentative steps toward the bier, her feet loud on the marbled floor. The velvet cloth, emblazoned with the arms of Clarence and sprinkled with silver stars was draped across the casket, leaving just Isabel's head and shoulders on view.

Anne sent up a swift prayer and peeked over the edge. Isabel could be sleeping. Her alabaster face was smooth, depersonalised by death. The once rosy lips devoid of colour, her hair tidied away beneath a headdress. Heartbreakingly, in the crook of her arm, lay the tiny body of her son.

Apart from the unnatural stillness, her sister appearance was not much altered. As Anne looked at her, images of their shared life, danced across the theatre of her mind. Isabel teaching her to curtsey; Isabel dressing her hair, Isabel running with their dogs across the dale. Isabel, spinning triumphant circles in her first grown-up gown and then, an older Isabel, defying the king to marry George.

Anne also remembered Isabel stinking of vomit on that cursed boat as she fought to expel her firstborn. She recalled how Isabel had forced herself free from post-coital madness to offer comfort to a sister in need. Unable to recall or imagine life without her presence, grief tore at Anne's heart like a knife.

Reaching into the coffin and lifting a strand of the hair she had brushed so many times, she snipped off a glossy brown tress. Soon, Isabel's body would corrupt and decay, her skin would shrink, her flesh would shrivel until even her bones would moulder into dust. But the face of her dead sister and the child who had barely lived, would remain in Anne's consciousness for the rest of her days.

For a long time, Anne prayed. When her knees grew too painful on the unrelenting marble floor, she wiped her tears, turned and walked away. As she stepped into the cold January air, Richard emerged suddenly from the shelter of a doorway and took her in his arms.

'I've been waiting for so long. I didn't wish to intrude.'

Anne pushed him slightly away, keeping hold of his elbows.

'Why are you wet?' she asked, and then noticed steady rain was falling.

'How touching.'

George wove an uncertain path across the precinct and, although it was only a little after midday, it was plain to see he was far gone in drink. His unfastened doublet revealed the soiled and crumpled linen beneath, and his eyes were red from grief or lack of sleep. He halted a short distance away, and swayed, unheeding of his sodden hair dripping rain down his shoulders.

'And what comfort can you offer me, Dick? It will take more than a brotherly embrace to heal my hurt.'

Richard flinched as he imagined how he'd feel were it Anne in Isabel's place. His guts twisted to think of her silenced and stilled by death. He reached out in brotherly welcome.

'George, come back with us and take some sustenance. Isabel's mother is inside and will wish to see you. You look as though you've neither eaten nor slept. Come, good fellow, come with me.'

George pulled away.

'No. I'll not leave her alone. I only withdrew when I saw Anne approach. I won't leave her.'

He rubbed his nose, a childish gesture that revealed the extent of his wretchedness. His gaze flitted around the churchyard as though in search of something or someone and, as pity vanquished her dislike, Anne swallowed her fear and stepped forward, placing her hand upon his arm and blinking raindrops from her eyes.

'Go with Richard, George and I will wait with Isabel until you have refreshed yourself. I swear I will not leave her; go with Richard.'

After a long moment, George nodded, as close to despair as Anne had ever seen. She watched the brothers walk slowly across the precinct and as they turned a corner, Richard slid a comforting arm around George's shoulder.

For the next few hours Anne kept Isabel company, praying in the cold, dark church until the silent piety of God's house began to offer her just a little comfort. But the peace of the deserted abbey was abruptly shattered when rapid footsteps sounded in the nave. She raised her head to find George running toward the coffin. Catching sight of Anne, he yelled,

'Go on, get out of here. Go back to your pious fool of a husband.'

With her heart banging, Anne hurried toward him.

'Whatever is the matter, George? What has happened now?'

It was obvious that something had enraged him; she didn't think she had ever seen anyone so angry, not even her father. Spittle clung to his lips and his eyes were wild as he repeated through clenched teeth.

'I asked you to leave. I don't even want you near her, do you hear?'

Richard, appearing as if from nowhere, took Anne's arm and tried to pull her away but she turned back to George.

'George,' she said, holding a hand toward him, but Richard dragged her back. As she skipped and hopped to keep up with his rapid step, she said.

'I have never seen such grief, Richard. I fear for him, really I do.'

Richard shook his head as George's sarcasm followed them up the aisle.

'Farewell, Lord and Lady Righteous.'

'What happened, Richard. What did you say to him?'

By the time they had reached the comfort of their chamber they were both soaked by the relentless rain. Anne shook the drops from her hair.

'Has he gone mad, Richard? I've never seen anybody behave like that. Do you think his mind has become unhinged?'

'I fear so, and you did not hear the half of it, Anne. He seems to be channelling his grief into his hatred for the Woodville's. I have no love for them myself, as well you know, but George is accusing them of murdering her!'

'What?' breathed Anne in disbelief.

'He swears she died as a result of some Woodville plot and fears he is next on their list. He said the king hates him because of his knowledge, I repeat *knowledge*, of Edward's bastardy. He started to bandy about the old rumour about Ned being the son of a Flemish archer. When I warned him he was speaking treason, he said he didn't care. When I pointed out that the rumour slanders our Mother he couldn't see that he was at fault. We argued horribly. I can't see us ever reconciling after this, Anne. I think he really believes his own lies, maybe that's why he has continually challenged Edward's right to the crown. He thinks if the king is a bastard then he must be the rightful monarch. He must have harboured this resentment for years, and Isabel's death has triggered something in his head. It's a very dangerous situation.'

Anne stepped out of her gown, accepted the robe that Richard handed to her and moved closer to the roaring fire.

'Surely he must have some love for Edward though, Richard. The king has always been a good brother …to both of you. He has forgiven George for many terrible things and heaped him with power and riches, regardless of his behaviour.'

Richard lifted her hand to his lips.

'If it were only as simple as that, my love. I did try to remind George that there is more to brotherhood than mere blood, but I could not make him see sense.'

He sighed and reflected that the only thing about George that had ever been sincere was his love for Isabel. She had somehow steadied his more unstable tendencies. Without her, George was likely to prove ever more difficult.

Isabel's death was over-shadowed just two weeks later by the more politically threatening death of Charles of Burgundy. His widow, Richard's sister, Margaret and his heir, Mary, were now vulnerable and unprotected, a fact King Louis of France was not blind to. He immediately claimed the lands as French territory and it became imperative for Mary to find a powerful suitor. Burgundy was of immense import to English trade, and Edward was now caught in the middle. If he sided with Burgundy and his sister he ran the risk of jeopardising his treaty with Louis and losing a considerable annual income.

Margaret herself favoured her favourite brother, George, as a suitor for her stepdaughter. He was conveniently widowed and, in Margaret's eyes, would provide a powerful alliance for her adopted country. Although still smarting from his recent loss, George hastily agreed to it, but Edward had different ideas and to George's fury, promptly scotched the plans.

George's indignation was further fuelled by the king's proposal of his brother-in-law, Anthony, Earl Rivers, as a more suitable consort for Mary. The proposal was refused but the knowledge that Edward considered Anthony to be the better choice confirmed George's belief that Edward was against him. George tipped completely over the edge of reason.

May - September 1477

The pleasant spring weather, together with the almost constant company of her husband and son, helped Anne come to terms with the loss of Isabel. Although she missed the regular communication from Isabel, and rued the void left in the world, her mother's company ensured that her memory at least was not lost.

But, if Anne's spirits recovered, the same could not be said of her health and the chill she contracted at Tewkesbury continued to plague her. She returned from the miserable journey suffering from fever, probably the result of travelling through inclement weather, and kneeling for too long in the freezing church.

'I reckon it were the ghost of that first husband o' yours,' declared the superstitious Elayne. 'When you took them flowers to his grave, I bet he leered up out of the earth and laid a curse on you.'

The girl's eyes were wide with terror of her own devising, making Anne laugh.

'Elayne, you are frightening yourself,' she cried, bending her head over some embroidery she was unpicking. Elayne pulled a wry face and rubbed her nose.

'I just don't understand why you went out in the rain just to give flowers to a man you never loved.'

Anne looked up, her face showing signs of strain.

'No, I never loved him but, he was still just a boy; a silly, frightened boy in a grown man's shoes.'

Just as Anne began to recover and normality returned to Middleham, the king sent an urgent summons for Richard to attend court. Anne's smile died. Her dismay was so great, she lacked the strength of will to hide it but she agreed to Richard's request that she remain at home until she was well enough to join him.

'I've no idea what the king wants this time,' Richard said as he ran his eyes over the message again, 'but perhaps he won't keep me long. I might be back before you've even missed me.'

'I already miss you,' she murmured miserably.

Promising to write as soon as he knew the likely length of his stay, he kissed her tears away and bid her goodbye with a heavy heart. Anne watched from a tower window until the small troop of horse dwindled into distant dust, then she returned to her chamber, too miserable to resist the pressure from her mother and Jayne to take to her bed for a few days.

Written this day of our Lord, June the tenth 1477

Well-beloved wife,

I trust that you and my son are in good health and spirits and that the saints watch upon you both in my absence. It seems that my stay here may well be an extended one, but I earnestly beseech you not to follow me until you are fully recovered in health.

It seems that George has been misbehaving, his actions forcing the king to send him to the Tower to simmer down. I was allowed to visit him briefly yesterday and found a very sorry fellow; he continues to drink to excess and, within the hearing of his guards, continually smeared the Queen's reputation. As you can imagine, my mother is very distressed by the ill-feeling between her sons, and I am lodging with her at Crosby Place until the situation is diffused.

For a while, Sweeting, my pen must needs take the place of my lips in communicating to you the depth of my regard.

Richard

The summer was cheerless without Richard, and Anne's recovery was hindered by lack of joy. Although the fever abated and she regained some appetite, the cough lingered for so long it became as familiar a sound at the castle as her laughter had once been.

Little Ned provided her only sunshine and, at almost four years old, he mischievously filled each hour with new discoveries and adventures. The highlight of Anne's day was the hour after supper she spent helping Jayne and Elayne ready him for bed.

The warm room clamoured with his chatter as he sang her songs, and related stories that featured himself and Troy.

His half-brother, John, was too old to be a playmate but Catherine, loved to include him in her games in which he figured as her child. But it was John whom Ned admired. He watched him practice in the tilt yard, learning the skills of the battlefield, and honing his horsemanship. Ned longed to be like him. One afternoon, John allowed Ned to hold his sword. It was only a half-sized weapon, made to accommodate a boy's stature, but Ned had been unable to wield it. Later on, in the evening, as his mother was overseeing his night-time rituals, a messenger arrived with a missive from Richard.

Wiping her hands on her skirts, she excused herself to read it in the privacy of her chamber. Anne swept so swiftly into the room that she made the torches and candles gutter. It was late September, and she had not heard from Richard for a full month. Impatiently, she tore open the seal, moved into the light and began to read.

Dearest wife,

I was much relieved to learn from your last letter of your recovered health. Believe me, the distance between us has not lessened my desire to be with you or the amount of time that I spend dwelling upon your beauty. Indeed, I miss you more than I can say for I am in great need of comfort and, therefore, I write to you in hopes of some relief.

It is with heavy heart that I send you this ill-news, but I confess to being in need of your ever-gentle wisdom. There is no easy way to begin so I shall be brief.

The king has indicted George, and he is awaiting trial for conduct derogatory to the laws of the realm and most dangerous to judges and juries throughout the kingdom.

I wonder if you recall the conversation that we had at Tewkesbury concerning the state of George's mind? It seems that we were correct in our conclusions, and he is indeed suffering from delusion or some manner of sorcery.

You already know of his outrageous behaviour after Edward refused his marriage to the Burgundian heir but since then, he has become increasingly paranoid. He truly believes the king and the Woodvilles are intending to do him harm. He is obsessed with poison and refuses to eat a morsel until his food had been tested; he all but accuses the king of wanting rid of him.

His behaviour seems to have grown worse subsequent to Edward's refusal to allow his marriage to the sister of the king of Scots and I must confess that the second refusal makes George's belief that Edward is against any profitable match seems possible. Maybe it would be beneficial for George to marry somebody; perhaps a wife is just what he needs. Isabel usually managed to curb his lack of reason.

It seems that George has conspired with two fellows, Thomas Blake and Thomas Burdet, to use astronomy and metaphysics to imagine the king's death by sorcery. Edward was very lenient at this juncture and, although Burdet and a man called Stacey were hung, he pardoned Clarence and Blake. But my brother, instead of appearing grateful, then proceeded to speak out against the conviction.

Why can he not let things rest? Surely he can see the dangers of casting doubt on the justice and validity of the king's court.

It would not be like George to apply half measures though and he was not content to leave it there. I pray that the following news will not distress you too much, I fear that your present lack of health affects your usual stalwart courage but take heart my love.

It is with great dismay that I must confirm George is indeed beyond the help of physicians. He will not heed my council. I had hoped his accusation against the queen's family's involvement in Isabel's death would be forgotten but that is not so.

In May, he ordered the arrest and trial of one Ankaret Twynyho, and one John Thursby and suffered them to be taken to Warwick castle. He then rushed through a trial, all stages of the proceedings taking place in a single day and executed them both without recourse to a legal court of law. Edward, of course, is livid at George's highhanded manner and has him fast in the tower.

I did manage to obtain a brief interview with him although he is allowed no visitors, but he remains unrepentant and swears that the Queen paid Mistress Twynyho to poison Isabel while employed to nurse her through her confinement and that Thursby did murder his son in much the same manner. It is a crazed idea. Isabel died weeks after the woman had left her employ and it is common knowledge that the child was weak from the time of his birth.

George believes Edward will execute him or have him poisoned. He says he will receive no justice because the king intends to silence him. He swears Edward is a bastard with no right to rule and also swears he has further knowledge even more detrimental, both to the king and his heirs.

It is hard to watch as madness takes one's brother, even if that brother has always been trouble.

I must stay here, Anne, and urge Edward to show some leniency. After all, how harmful can a lunatic really be? He should feed Clarence physic and, when he is calmer, let him go peaceably home to Warwick. I will return as soon as I can, my sweet, fare you well and care for our son.

Keep in your heart the knowledge of my great love.

Richard.

Once she had read the letter, Anne could no longer rest. Richard needed her, she was of no use to him here. After a few weeks' preparation, she set out with her son, mother and household to travel the long, weary miles to Crosby Place where Richard was in residence.

A messenger was sent on ahead to warn of her arrival, but she knew they would be warmly received. Although she had recovered from the chill, apart from lingering bouts of fatigue and she had not yet regained the weight she had lost. To conserve her strength, she travelled mostly in a litter with Ned.

Her son divided his time between riding in the litter with Anne and riding on the pommel of Elayne's horse. They amused him with songs and stories and there was plenty to see at the roadside to keep him entertained. Rabbits, foxes, deer and once, a family of wild pigs added to the tally of animals that they spotted.

Ned stored away the new sights and sounds to relate to his father when they arrived and after nine long, weary days, he had plenty to say. As they passed through the city gate, and they were assailed but the stench of London, the failing light hid the worst of the grime. Edward peeped from the litter curtains in wonder at the unaccustomed noise and bustle of the city. Crosby Place stood close to the river at Bishop's Gate and candles burned in every window in welcome. Almost immediately, Anne spotted Richard peering anxiously into the gloom and when the horses slowed, she slid from the litter and ran into his arms.

He held her tight, his hands reacquainting with her body. The promise of the coming night drove goose pimples across Anne's flesh, and she gasped at the force of her own need.

'My Lord,' she smiled, glancing around to ensure nobody had seen. 'You are like a great drooling hound.'

'Grrrrr,' roared Richard, astonishing Cecily as she appeared on the threshold. Anne straightened her clothes and hurried to greet her mother-in-law. Even in the dim light, it was easy to see the effect the breach between her sons was having. Her once glorious beauty was obscured by lines, anguish marring her once bright yes, but she was still Cecily and greeted them with a smile.

December 1477

Christmas in London was very different to Christmas in Yorkshire. There were more feasts and entertainments than she could count but they managed to avoid many of them. The garish display of wealth and ostentation seemed heartless when George was locked in the Tower. Neither Richard or Anne felt like celebrating, and Cecily spent most of her time in prayer.

Richard, after visiting George twice more, confirmed he remained unrepentant. He arranged for a daily supply of good food to be taken in, and ensured George's appetite for malmsey wine was catered for. There was little else Richard could do to make him comfortable.

The chamber in which he was confined was luxurious, with a hearty fire in the grate and warm furs for his bed. For people of George's status, and others with the money to pay for it, the Tower of London could be a gilded cage. As the king's brother, he was treated deferentially, even if he didn't deserve it. Richard said, it was the boredom that plagued him most.

George had always been an active man and the hours of ennui ate away at his good looks. His torso grew flabby, and his face paled from lack of sunlight. No longer part of the wider world, he failed to change his linen or keep his beard trimmed, and the gaunter he grew the more his red eyes dominated his face.

But, despite all the comforts of his brother's prison, Richard could not bring himself to feast in the ivy draped halls of the king's court where jesters tumbled, and minstrels sang. After making a dutiful visit to the king on Christmas Eve, Richard and Anne shunned the entertainments and crept home to the more sombre celebrations at Crosby Place.

Had it not been for Ned, they would have kept things even more simple but for his son's sake Richard shook off his depression and attempted to be joyous. Anne, who did a rather better job, even managed to clap her hands when the Yule log was lit, and excitedly tear the wrapping from the small gifts.

Excusing herself, Cecily remained in her chapel with memories of happier Christmases, trying not to weep for the days when her sons were boys, and their father was still alive. Throughout the festivities, while England made merry, George was left in limbo, untried and captive, because the king refused to either release or try him until after the holy season.

On January the fifteenth a celebration was held they were glad to attend. The king arranged a huge Royal pageant to celebrate the marriage of his younger son, Richard, aged four, to Anne Mowbray who was his senior by two years. She was the heiress of the House of Norfolk, a match both beneficial and enriching to everyone involved. The king made it clear that Richard and Anne were expected to attend, and Richard was given the honour of escorting the child bride from St. Stephen's Chapel to the king's great chamber for the marriage banquet.

As they passed through the city, the Duke of Buckingham and Richard showered handfuls of coins to the crowd. But all the while he smiled and waved at the onlookers, he was aware of George's absence. He kept forgetting to appear joyful and stood in sharp contrast to the flushed pleasure of his strapping cousin, Harry of Buckingham. It didn't help that the Duke bore such strong Plantagenet features. Each time he caught a glimpse of the brash smiling face, he was struck by the strong resemblance to George, and the king.

At the wedding feast, Richard watched the king revel with his Woodville in-laws. He frowned at the frequent use Edward made of his wine cup and trencher. He hated the way he quickly became bellicose and flushed. Richard wondered what had become of his warrior brother. His velveteen belly shook each time he let loose a bellow of easy laughter. It was hard to reconcile this gross figure of excess with the hard, firm victor of Towton field.

At his side, his long-time friend, Lord Hastings, flirted with a golden-haired girl who laughed at everything he said. Richard knew of Jane Shore, one of Edward's mistresses but hadn't met her before. For the first time, he gave credence to the rumour that she shared her favours with both the king and the Lord Chamberlain. That was friendship indeed, Richard thought as he mourned the ideals that Edward had once promised to bring to the throne. *What had changed him so?* ... and then the Queen laughed at something Edward had said and Richard remembered.

Elizabeth.

He had never warmed to Elizabeth Woodville; her harsh beauty had never touched him. He saw her for what she was, and knew she was not driven by love of Edward but love of power. As he watched her lift her cup and drink the king's health for the twentieth time, Richard was certain she was to blame for George's continuing imprisonment. Usually by now, Edward would have grown bored and freed his brother, had the queen not wanted him to remain.

Anne, aware of the train of Richard's thought, reached out and covered his hand with hers. He turned and smiled, grateful for her presence, grateful for her lack of brittle artifice. How easily, he reflected thankfully, could he have been saddled with a shrew, and how glad he was to possess the triple blessing of Anne who was his friend, helpmeet and lover.

Not knowing his thoughts but sharing them, Anne leant across to whisper in his ear.

'If you wish to leave, my Lord, you can tell the king that I am overly fatigued; he knows I have been ailing.'

Richard read the invitation in her eyes and his face lit up. He kissed her wrist and rose from his seat to approach the king.

Edward was sprawled upon his chair of state with his wineglass resting on his stomach. The Queen was bending over him, a tress of her long hair escaping from her veil to drape across her husband's chest as she related some bawdy story. Edward let out a sudden burst of laughter, his amusement continuing to bubble inside him as Richard approached.

'Little Brother,' he roared in delight when he noticed him. 'You are welcome indeed. Here, Bess, get up and let Richard sit beside me for a spell. How goes it, brother? Where is your pretty wife?'

As Elizabeth moved sulkily away, Richard bowed briefly but did not avail himself of the proffered seat. When he spoke, his voice was as cold as his expression.

'I am afraid, Ned, that she is fatigued, and I must escort her home, she is not yet fully recovered from her ailment, and I don't wish to tire her. I will wait upon you in the morning if I may; there are things we must discuss.'

Edward became drunkenly guarded.

'Do we?' he said, 'what things might they be?'

'George,' replied Richard and the name sobered Edward for a moment while he considered the implication behind his brother's request.

'Oh yes. George. We will see to that tomorrow.'

February 1478

George's predicament caused those at Crosby Place much anxiety during the next few months. After he received his sentence, Richard and his mother visited him. It was hours later when Anne heard the sound of their return and ran out to greet them. Anne watched Richard assist the old lady from her litter. Cecily did not pause to greet Anne but crept on painful feet to the comfort of her chamber. Once she was there she refused food or drink and instead, spent the night kneeling at her *prieu dieu* begging for her errant son's reprieve.

After repeatedly trying to offer Cecily comfort, Anne retired to their chamber where she found Richard alone, staring across the dark gardens. Although his back was turned, she knew from the dejection that hung about his shoulders, the visit had not been an easy one. When she placed a gentle hand upon his fur collar, he turned and buried his head in her thin shoulder.

She stroked his head and crooned to him as she would Ned and, after a while, he straightened up, composed and in control once more, and moved to the ewer to wash. He spent over-long with his face hidden in the towel.

'Can you speak of it, my Lord?' she asked as they moved toward a seat. He looked vaguely around the room, fighting to contain his raw emotion, his voice, when it came, was hoarse with grief.

'The worst thing is my mother's grief. I don't understand how Edward can do this. There is no comfort I can offer; the whole thing is in the king's hands, but he refuses clemency. I could have understood if he'd done this when George defected with your father all those years ago, for that was not just treason but also a personal affront, but this time ... this is something else. Something lies behind it; something I cannot see.'

Richard examined his wife's face as though he had never seen it before, absorbing her thin cheeks and encircled eyes, and then stroked back a stray strand of hair, tucking it behind her ear. 'I never thought the day would come when I'd see my mother beg, Anne, but that is what she did. She went down upon her rheumy old knees and clung to Edward's coat, pleading for George's life but still ... he would not relent. Proud Cicely Neville, stripped of dignity by her own son.

When Edward turned away from her and said it was out of his hands, I wanted to kill him. She was unable to rise, and he even refused to help her to her feet. He ignored her tears, her pain. This has made an old woman of her, and I warrant my father is turning in his grave. What would they have done, Anne, in such a situation? I tell you what my father would have done, he'd have mustered his men, stormed the Tower, freed Clarence and said, *To Hell with the king!* Am I less a man because I cannot do that? I have the power, the resources and the motive, so why do I lack the will?'

Anne thought for a moment before replying.

'It is loyalty that prevents you from defying the king, Richard; and it's the best thing about you. It's why I married you. *Loyalte me Lie* is your motto and you live by it. And besides, the king's treatment of Clarence does not change the fact that he is your brother too, and since he is both brother and king, as such you owe him loyalty two-fold. I for one would not want you any different.'

Anne stood in the centre of the room, her face pink with passion. She reminded Richard of her father whom he had often seen similarly impassioned. She was right, of course, he could never fight against an anointed King, it was against his nature. It didn't matter how many men waited in the north to ride to his summons, he would never use them against Edward.

He reached for Anne and pulled her close, tearing off her wimple and burying his face in her hair, searching for oblivion.

'I am nothing without you,' he mumbled.

The king dallied for a further ten days before signing the order of execution and, during that time, Richard was more often at court haranguing for a pardon than at his own home. Any real hope of reprieve had faded long ago but he was driven by love. He craved to free his brother, spare his mother further grief and prevent Edward from committing the sin of fratricide.

Each evening as Anne waited for his return, she readied herself to offer whatever comfort she could, in whatever form he required it. She knew how many different strategies Richard had taken; some days he tried flattery, sometimes he applied guilt, sometimes he yelled, coming fearfully close to treason himself. Anne marvelled at his tenacity and his capacity for forgiveness. There had been little love between George and Richard for years now, but all animosity was forgotten in the face of their former childhood bond.

But, at last, on the seventeenth of February, they received word that the deed was done. George had been executed in the Tower of London. Word spread that he had drowned in a butt of malmsey wine but Richard and Anne, knowing George so well, believed he had been poisoned. But the malmsey rumour stuck, becoming a metaphor for the sin of drunkenness that led to his downfall.

George's body was laid with Isabel and her child, behind the high altar at Tewkesbury Abbey. Once Richard and Anne had safely settled Cecily at Baynard Castle, they journeyed home to Middleham.

Before they bid her farewell, Cicely and Anne exchanged a few words on the subject. Cecily's voice quavered, her face working with emotion.

'When you are safe home, I'd like you to tell Richard how proud I am. I know how hard he worked to save George and I am grateful. It doesn't matter that he failed; that sin is Edward's, not his. Richard has never shamed me. Of the four sons I safely raised, two are dead, one is lost and now only Richard remains ...my ever-constant boy, ever-constant.'

The old lady's eyes misted with emotion as Anne covered her hand with her own.

News filtered slowly to the north, and it was some time before Richard and Anne learned Edward had reversed the attainder placed on Clarence and his heirs, so his son, Edward, would now retain the title of Earl of Warwick. It was a small comfort to Anne to know Isabel's son would carry their father's title and maybe one-day restore honour to the name of Warwick.

But for Richard it offered none.

From the day of Clarence's death, smarting with grief and a sense of failure, Richard remained in Yorkshire attending to his duties as Lord of the North. He still regarded himself as the king's man but his faith in Edward was severely damaged, and his animosity for the queen's family barely containable.

One of his first acts on his return was to found two colleges, one at Barnard Castle and one at Middleham, where he housed priests and choristers to pray for the king and Queen, for himself and Anne and little Edward and for the souls of the king's dead brothers and sisters.

The following June, on his return from a visit to York, a young squire informed Richard that Anne was sick abed, and a physician had been sent for. He handed him the reins of his horse and sped up the stairs, bursting into the bedchamber to find Anne, her face as white as the sheets, lying limply on her bed.

He almost collided with Elayne who was hurrying across the room bearing a slopping bowl of bloodied water and gore spattered towels. Jayne was at Anne's side, mopping her mistress' brow. Obviously the physician had not made it in time.

Richard almost knocking Jayne to the floor, pushed her aside. Anne looked tiny and fragile, and very alone in the huge bed.

'What's the matter, Anne? What is it? Why was I not summoned?'

Hot tears rolled down her cheeks. At first, she could not find her voice and merely clung wordlessly to his proffered hand while she further tears fell. But, after swallowing painfully a few times, she wailed,

'Oh, Richard. I lost our baby. I've failed you again! I am so sorry, so very sorry.'

Regret twisted his innards. She had not yet even told him of the expected child. It was too soon for her to have been sure. How acutely she mourned it. He thought of the ease with which Edward's queen produced infants. It was not fair. Gently, he touched Anne's sweat-darkened hair.

'Don't be sorry, my love. I already have all I could wish for. I have a fine son and heir, and a loving wife. I'd never want another son at the risk of losing you. As long as you are well then I am blessed, nothing else matters.'

1478 - September 1482

Richard's self-imposed exile ended when Edward summoned him to London to assist him in dealing with the combined nuisance of Louis of France and James III of Scotland. Louis was determined to keep Edward occupied while he continued his quest to rule Burgundy and had enlisted the aid of the Scottish King. In the winter of 1479, James had violated his truce with England by making large scale attacks on the northern border and there had been trouble ever since.

It was a council of war and when he left London Richard not only had the king's instructions on how to proceed with the campaign but was also appointed Lieutenant General in the North. It was high favour, but he could not help wondering if the king was attempting to purchase loyalty which was already his.

Richard would be working closely with the Duke of Northumberland, an uneasy ally who had never forgiven Richard for replacing his family as chief Lord of the North. But, in early September, after mustering the men of the Marches, Richard led an army across the Scottish border.

The campaign was brief, but enough to subdue the Scots for a while and buying King Edward valuable time in which to raise the funds to finance a full-scale attack. Meanwhile, in Burgundy, Maximillian appealed to his English ally for aid but Edward, careful of his treaty with Louis and loath to relinquish the 50,000 crowns a year, failed to respond. He was determined to prioritise the Scottish problem.

During this time Richard and Anne saw little of each other. She amused herself by planting a new herb garden and making winter preparations for the castle. In August, she and her household visited Sheriff Hutton castle while Middleham underwent its thorough annual clean. It was no coincidence that logistically, it was far easier for Richard to pay fleeting visits to Sherriff Hutton as he made preparation for the approaching battle.

Anne hated the very word *battle* for it summoned memories of the many loved ones she had lost in conflict. When Richard was away, each time a messenger galloped into the bailey her heart beat hard and fast until she was satisfied of his safety.

Rumour had it the king was not well enough to take part in the campaign, but he assured Richard that he'd be recovered enough to join him for the main assault. Edward's ever-increasing bulk made him unwieldy in the saddle, but he did manage to make a slow progress as far north as Fotheringhay where he consulted with Richard and introduced him to his new ally, the Scottish Duke of Albany.

It was typical of Edward to have singled out Albany and recruited James' weakest link, promising to place him on the Scottish throne in James' stead. Albany was James' embittered brother, and nobody knew better than Edward how a younger brother could prove a thorn in the flesh. Albany was an unprincipled and rash man, very much in the mould of George, a fact that had not gone unnoticed among the English who immediately labelled him 'Clarence in a Kilt.'

And, if it went hard with Edward to wait at home while the men went out to fight, then the winning-over of Albany went some way to appease it. Richard, however, from the first moment they met, distrusted and disliked Albany and, as they rode out to war, he kept a wary eye on him.

The army progressed north, collecting further troops on the way, and when they reached the city of York they were unprepared for the welcome the people gave to its favoured Lord, the Duke of Gloucester. Because of his careful diplomacy and general concern as to the well-being of the citizens, Richard was popular in the city and the obvious esteem with which he was held, did nothing to defray the resentment of the Duke of Northumberland. Sometimes, when they rode together, Richard could feel the man's dislike burning into the back of his neck.

'It is with little relish that I ride out with two such dubious companions,' he wrote to Anne. 'Albany, I am sure, will turn his coat again and Northumberland has too much power to make a comfortable enemy.'

In July 1482, Richard reached the gates of Berwick at the head of an army twenty thousand strong. Faced with such numbers, the town quickly yielded, leaving only the castle holding its own. The Scottish king, angry at the burning of the town, gathered a large army of his own and marched south to launch a counterattack.

But things were not going well for King James who due to his favouring of lowborn artisans over the nobility, had never been popular. As he reached Lauder, the discontented Lords seized the king and his followers and, after locking James up in Edinburgh castle, they hung his favourites from Lauder Bridge.

Knowing nothing of this, Richard left Lord Stanley in charge with instructions to lay siege to Berwick. Then he and his men rode north to intercept James on his journey. Disappointed to find that the Scots had no stomach for a pitched battle, the army progressed north, burning and pillaging on its way, trying to goad them into taking the field. At the end of July, Richard marched unmolested into Edinburgh and, quickly and without bloodshed, took control of the city. He then immediately dispatched an army to attack the retreating Scots at Haddington, some eighteen miles east of the capital.

It was some hours before he found the leisure to write to Anne.

Well-Beloved,

I trust that God continues to keep you safe, and you are not pining too much in my absence. Here in the land of the Scots business passes surprisingly easily and I think I may well be returning home to you soon. It ill-behoves a military campaigner to yearn for his wife and the familiar things of home but, I must confess, I do.

I have little affection for the company I keep here and, unlike my comrades, find no comfort in this alien land. We subdued the Scots with ease. Indeed, it was harder to convince Albany to give up his ideas of the crown and accept instead the return of his forfeited lands and castles. But, I had the wit to ensure that he signed a treaty promising to keep faith with the English crown and, in the end, he was restored to his estates.

The Scots have returned all of the monies paid by Edward for the dowry of the Princess Cecily and she is now freed of the obligation to marry either James' son or Albany.

I will return as soon as I can, but my first duty is to continue with the siege, but I've been assured, the town will be returned to English hands forthwith.

I believe that I have done Edward, and England, proud and that any debt that I owe to my brother in the way of disloyalty has now been paid.

The remainder of the letter dealt with the more private side of marital life and bore words that went a long way to salving a lonely wife. Anne took heart from the love he sent and was reassured by his promise of a prompt return. On the same day, however, she received a second letter from Cicely who, although she did not visit her son's court, somehow managed to obtain gossip almost as soon as it was aired.

Dearest Anne

My prayers are with Richard, still in peril in the land of the Scots and my thoughts are also with you. I well remember the lonely sojourn of waiting for a husband's return. War is hard on us. Do remember, my dear, that more often than not, they do return.

I trust that you continue to recover your health after your last miscarriage and hope you will listen to the advice of the physicians. It will be wiser not to make further attempts for children. It may seem easy advice for one as well-blessed as I to proffer but it may be best to be thankful for the son that you do have.

The real purpose of this missive is to inform you of the latest news to reach me from the court. Apparently, Edward has received word that Maximillian and Louis have made a treaty at Arras which includes the promise that Margaret, the baby daughter of Marie and Maximillian, will be betrothed to Louis' heir. I have not seen Edward, of course, but I can imagine his enormous rage and keen sense of betrayal. As you know Burgundy has been in turmoil for some time and Edward refused all their pleas for help simply because his treaty with Louis was of such import to him.

I also have heartfelt sympathy for my granddaughter, Elizabeth, who for so long has been trained for the Queenship of France. For seven years now she has been addressed as, Madame la Dauphine, only to have it snatched away by a babe in arms.

I do wonder if the worst of Edward's anger is for the loss of his fifty thousand crowns or the loss of his daughter's suitor. I only hope that the affair does not lead to further war. I can only estimate the extent of my son's rage, but it will not be he who rides out to war, will it? The excesses of food and drink have made sure that he must remain safely in England while he sends his little brother out to face the wrath of France.

Mind you, I am reliably informed that the French King is close to death. He has recently suffered two major seizures so mayhap will not live to fight a war, and his thirteen-year-old heir may, God willing, prove a much easier fish to fry.

Other news has reached me that may also touch you, Anne. I learned of the death of Marguerite last August, at her château of Dampierre in Anjou. I understand that she had been ailing for some time and I hope she now finds some measure of peace. Evidently Louis has demanded all her dogs be sent to him for he claims she named him as her heir and the dogs are the most valuable things she possessed. Poor Louis, quite lacking in all the virtues one admires in a man.

Well, the summer season draws too soon to its end, and Michaelmas will soon be upon us. I regret my tardiness in not visiting with you while the weather was more clement but perhaps I may be able to journey to Middleham with the onset of spring.

May God keep you and yours, dear Anne,

Cecily of York

PART FIVE
'Queen'

Middleham – April 1483

Sheltered from the April wind, Anne risked a freckle and turned up her face to enjoy the gentle kiss of the sun. She had escaped the company of her women and accompanied Elayne to gather early herbs. A half-filled basket lay at her feet, but Elayne continued to snip sprigs of newly emerging rosemary and mint to her hoard. Anne lay back against a sun-warmed stone and closed her eyes.

She was often weary in the afternoon but had learned that, if she dozed for a few minutes, she would wake revitalised. Richard teased that she was like the castle cats, whose real task was to control the infestations of rats and mice but were more usually found dozing in a sheltered spot or curled up before a cosy hearth.

Anne smiled as she considered what sort of cat she resembled. Not a fat tabby cat that was for certain, for she was still far too thin, and Richard was able to circle her waist with his hands. She despaired at the unfashionable saltcellars above her collarbone. The current fashion was for women to be plump, and she fell far short of that ideal. Her face was pretty enough but the structure of her bones was clearly visible beneath her skin, and a delicate lacing of pale blue veins decorated her temples.

If she was appearing in public, she supplemented her sparse bosom with extra padding, and was grateful that her voluminous skirts disguised her narrow hips. Unfortunately, there was little artifice to assist at nighttime when she went naked to her husband's bed.

Although Richard never seemed to think so, she always felt somehow lacking. Despite Cecily's advice, she hadn't given up hope of conceiving another son and had not told Richard of the physician's advice to avoid intercourse. She could imagine nothing worse than foregoing Richard's bed, and since she had so far failed to conceive, it was quite likely sacrifice would have been an empty one anyway.

As she sat lazily dreaming, she could hear Richard and John sparring in the tiltyard while nine-year-old Edward shouted encouragement from the grassy ruin of the ancient motte. She could hear the clash of steel and an occasional high-pitched cry of enthusiasm followed by the deeper tone of Richard's reply, but she could not determine their words. She basked happily in the certainty of summer's approach, her love of her family and the fact that Richard had been home for almost the entire spring.

As yet he had no plans of leaving. The promise of a lasting truce on the border meant peace not just for England but for Middleham too. If it lasted, and Richard was at home more often, it may even result in the longed-for pregnancy. Anne knew she could conquer anything as long as Richard was by her side. As she drifted off to sleep, the happy voices of her family played in her ears, but when they made their noisy way into the garden in search of her, she woke and stretched her arms.

'Mother; Father says I can have a sword of my own now that I can almost lift John's. Not a wooden one but a real one, especially fashioned to fit me.'

Anne exclaimed enthusiastically as he continued urgently. 'How long will it take for the smith to fashion one, Father? A week? Two weeks? Oh, I plan to train so hard to be a Knight. I want to be as brave as you are, and ride into battle with John and smite down our enemies. My sword arm will be so strong by then my opponent will tumble from his horse, and then I will run him through.'

John laughed, and Richard ruffled Ned's hair as Anne exclaimed in mock disgust.

'How blood-thirsty you are, my son. I am sore afraid.'

She shifted along the seat to allow her husband space and Richard took Edward onto his knee while John perched beside her on the edge of the turf. Catherine and Elayne's heads were just visible above the shrubbery.

Anne barely noticed the sound of a single horse hurtling into the inner bailey. The first indication that anything was amiss was when the man ran uninvited into the privacy of the garden.

'My Lord of Gloucester. I must speak with my Lord of Gloucester. Where is he?'

Richard stood up, concerned at the urgency of the man's voice. The messenger halted by the fountain, bowed from the waist, panting, his words tumbling over one another in his haste to convey his message.

'My Lord of Gloucester, I come from Lord Hastings with grave news from court.'

Richard hesitated, shuddered before taking the letter and, it seemed to Anne as she watched him that the sun sank behind the clouds. The birds ceased their song.

'Elayne, take the children into the house.'

'But Father, I am old enough …'

'Leave us …'

While the children were led sulkily away, Anne took the letter.

With regret, my lord, I must inform you of the king's passing. It was sudden, a chill taken the day before while out fishing. His death was quick and merciful. Trouble is brewing though. On his death bed, the king – the late king – left instruction that you should be named Lord Protector until his son is old enough to rule wisely. But, I have since learned that the queen's son, Dorset, has taken control of the treasury while her brother, Edward Woodville, has control of the channel ports. Anthony Woodville is bringing the heir from Ludlow for the coronation. They are making no mention of your role, but the king has left all under your protection – goods, heir, realm. Secure the person of our sovereign Lord Edward the fifth and get you to London.

Anne looked up. Richard thrust aside his grief and focussed on the action he must take. Without further consultation, he turned to the messenger.

'Tell Hastings, the Duke of Gloucester is on his way.'

The Woodville's were in a prime position to assume power. The dowager queen's son, Dorset, as Constable of the Tower, held the reigns of the treasury and armaments of the realm, and the appointment of her brother, Sir Edward Woodville as commander of the fleet, bolstered their strengths further. Neither Richard nor Anne were surprised by the snake-like duplicity with which the queen's family moved.

It was no secret that Richard had no love for the Queen and her Woodville kin, he had borne with them for the sake of the king and had no intention of standing by while they assumed control of the realm. In an anxiety of indecision, Anne hovered in the bailey as hasty arrangements were made to travel south.

'We can meet with Prince Edward and his escort at Northampton. I will confer with Anthony Woodville there.'

It could only mean trouble. Anne had to force herself not to hold him back, not to beg him to have no part in it. It matters little who ruled the king, they were happy and safe here at Middleham. But she knew Richard would not heed her. His sense of duty would demand he act in the best interests of the country – his duty was to Edward's son now. King Edward V.

Polished harness was thrown onto the backs of horses while servants darted back and forth with weapons and supplies for the journey. Word was sent out and new arrivals constantly thundered over the drawbridge into the inner bailey. The castle dogs and children, not comprehending the crisis, ran about laughing and barking in excitement and added to the chaos.

Richard, refusing to heed Hastings' advice to travel with a heavy escort and only ordered three hundred men to make ready for the journey. He was unwilling to ride into London enforce and had already refused an offer from the Duke of Buckingham, of an additional force of one thousand men. However, he was glad of his support.

'I am merely accompanying the king on his entry into London,' Richard explained. 'To turn up with an army will make it look like a military coup.'

Before they left, a state of mourning was issued and requiem masses for the soul of the late King Edward were ordered at the castle chapel. Richard also ensured that the men who were to ride with him swore an oath of fealty to King Edward the fifth.

At last, the preparations were over, and they were ready to leave. The white boar banner unfurled, and after ordering his man to swear fealty to King Edward V, Richard leaned from his stallion to kiss his wife. Trumpets sounded, the dogs barked, and armour glinted in the sunshine as the cavalcade moved off. Watching them go, Anne acknowledged that England was a demanding mistress, and if Richard was to become Protector it would be a long while until they could resume their idyll.

Try as she might, Anne could not concentrate on the domestic demands of Middleham; her heart was with Richard. She understood his grief. Edward had always been so more than a brother, and so much more than a King. Hero-worship had blinded him to Edward's faults and he'd made excuses for his worst failings. Perhaps it was easier for him to blame the queen than acknowledge the king's mistakes.

If Edward had withstood Elizabeth's demands, things might have been very different. But, to conserve peace in his marriage, Edward had allowed her to manoeuvre her family into positions that now enabled them to seize control.

It was Richard's task to clear up the mess and put the queen and her kin back in their place. It was time to acquaint himself with his nephew and attempt to turn him into a wise and clement king. To Anne and her family, it would mean the upheaval of leaving Middleham and spending the majority of the year at court.

In the meantime, she drifted from task to task, plucking a few weeds from the garden one moment before wandering off to oversee the cleaning of the tapestries in the great hall. In a fit of pique, she stormed from the chamber, leaving her servants open-mouthed, and climbed the twisting steps to the battlement that skirted the outer limits of the castle. The view from there always calmed her, she leant over the parapet and saw, far below, the blacksmith working at his anvil, the clang of his hammer reaching her ears a few moments after it fell. How much easier life would be had she married a blacksmith. Looking along the road threading across the purpling moor she saw dust betokening a rider travelling at haste toward the castle. She straightened up, shielding her eyes from the sun, and peered into the distance, trying to determine his mark. It was not until he was almost at the drawbridge she was able to confirm that he bore the badge of the *Blanc Sanglier*. Swirling around, she hurried back down the stairs, arriving breathless and dishevelled in the inner bailey just as the rider passed into the keep.

He bowed low, the letter held aloft, and she snatched it from him, waving him toward the kitchen for refreshment. Then, seeking the privacy of her garden arbour she tore open the seal.

Written on this day of our Lord the fourth day of May 1483

Dearest wife,

I have much to relate to you but first must apologise for being so tardy in my communication. I have been sore busy almost every waking moment since I left Middleham and, although I have determined to write to you every evening, I find myself much in demand, both with my own business and the king's. Do not doubt though that it is your face that I see each night as I fall asleep.

We met with Buckingham on route to Northampton and rode into the town just before dusk on the 26th of April to be told by a courier of Lord Rivers that the king had travelled onward to put up at Stony Stratford to allow for the lack of accommodation in the town of Northampton. Both Buckingham's suspicions and mine were raised at this juncture, as Northampton is a sprawling town with plenty of room for both the king's escort and my own. Rivers visited us in the evening, and we dined together in feigned conviviality. He is a self-important, foppish sort and not my chosen style of companion. I find his ostentatious religion offensive; true piety, in my opinion, has no need of display. I wonder at the stories that circulate as to his habit of wearing a hair shirt beneath the stylish garments that he so favours. All in all, the man is a strange combination of earthly avariciousness and heavenly humbleness. I do not trust him and neither does my cousin, Harry of Buckingham.

Harry, however, I find a welcome ally. He reminds me of both Edward and George, having a fair share of Edward's good humour and more than a little of George's recklessness. He is, I think, a good fellow on the whole, and one whom I regret not knowing sooner. As you know, he was married as a boy to a sister of the queen, and such is his distaste for her that he keeps as far from her as possible.

I was, at first, startled by his good looks that are so reminiscent of my brothers' but now I think I may find some comfort for my losses there. Anyway, back to my tale, after Rivers left us late after supper that night, Harry and I fell to talking and found ourselves in agreement that Rivers was not to be trusted. The Woodvilles are determined to prevent me from fulfilling my role as Protector, a fact borne out by the testimony of Hastings. If the boy is crowned before I assume the appointment then I will be legally unable to do so.

It is critical that I undertake the role appointed to me and oversee the early reign of Edward's son. So, after much deliberation, it was decided that we should seize Rivers and lay hold of the body of the king to protect him from further Woodville taint. At the dawning of the next day Buckingham and I rode with force to arrest Rivers, Grey and Sir Thomas Vaughn and then faced the considerable task of befriending my nephew.

He is not at all what I expected, for the last time I saw him he was a rosy-cheeked infant and full of smiles but now, he is a sullen, puny, undersized boy, balanced on the brink of manhood. I know not what they have told him of me but he both hates and fears me. I am afraid his years at Ludlow have not only educated on kingship, but also included demonising me.

I'd give anything to know the nature of the poison whispered by his uncles. In appearance, he does not favour the Plantagenets at all but seems to be a male image of his mother. Since we met, I have tried hard to gain his friendship and have explained that his father put him in my care, but he fails to listen. He is presently ensconced in the safety of the Tower royal apartments where he awaits his coronation, and I have requested that the queen allow his brother, Richard, to join him soon.

I believe I forgot to mention that the queen has taken herself, the princesses and young Richard into the sanctuary at Westminster. I will never understand the workings of that woman's mind, but she was in such a fever to escape my dreaded clutches that she caused a large breach to be made in the walls of the sanctuary to allow for the passage of coffers of gold and plate, along with much of the palace furniture. I may dislike her, Anne, but I am sure I have never given her reason to fear me and, I suspect, she judges me by her own failings.

I am presently residing at Crosby Place and would ask you to join me as soon as you may. I know that Ned had been ailing but if you deem him fit enough to be left in the care of your mother and Jayne then please join me where I remain,

Your ever-loving, Richard

London –Crosby Place - June 1483

On the fifth day of June 1483, Anne's travelling party clattered through the gates of Crosby Place. It had been a long and weary journey, the lumbering coach hampered by roads that had been baked to a crust by the unseasonably hot weather. On two separate occasions progress was slowed when the horses fell victim to the potholes that peppered the dusty roads. In the end, Anne abandoned the lurching coach and took to the saddle instead.

At her journey's end, she dismounted stiffly and was escorted into the house by the steward who informed her that her husband was from home but expected to return at any time. Her heart sank. She had spent the last part of the journey dreaming of Richard's arms. But at least his absence gave her time to refresh herself, and it was a rested and fragrant wife that greeted Richard when he finally arrived.

'Anne' He pulled off his gauntlet, slapped dust from his robes.

'Richard! Oh, I have missed you!' Anne flew into his arms.

So was so engrossed in the greeting that at first she failed to notice he was not alone. A subtle cough made her let go her husband and spin around toward the figure at the window.

'Oh, oh, forgive me. I hadn't realised …'

Richard smothered a smile.

'My love, you remember my cousin Buckingham, do you not?'

'Of course,' she replied, holding her hand out to be kissed. 'I hope you are well, my Lord.'

Buckingham, a huge man, dressed like a jewelled butterfly, bowed.

'Unfortunately, not as blessed as my cousin of Gloucester, here.'

Blood flooded her cheeks at his teasing, but her discomfiture soon gave way to laughter when Richard punched his cousin playfully on the shoulder.

'Damn you, Buckingham, must you make a jest of everything? My poor Anne is quite disconcerted. Come, love, don't mind him, the man's a jade. As you come to know him better you will realise that he thinks every woman he encounters is fair game.'

Feigning shock, Buckingham winked at Anne again.

'My Lord, that is unfair. I have never been one to poach in another man's pond.'

Richard laughed and pulled her onto the settle.

'And what about that wench at the Red Lion, the one as wide as a carthorse; was she not married to the innkeeper?'

'That cannot be counted, it was an honest mistake and, besides, he was not known to me.'

Richard's roar of laughter was welcome to Anne's ears, and she began to warm to Buckingham, appreciating for the first time, the deepening friendship between them. Maybe he was just what Richard needed.

Richard fiddled with the ends of her hair.

'So, if a man does not have the acquaintance of the husband then it makes the wife fair game, does it? A useful philosophy indeed, in this land of unmet spouses.'

Taking pity on Buckingham, Anne rose.

'Will you be joining us for supper?' she enquired. It took some persuading but, in the end, he agreed to stay, promising to be gone long before dark.

As they shared a simple meal, Buckingham watched Richard and Anne together and noted how often their hands touched, and how Richard's eye scanned Anne's face as she spoke to her, as if he was drinking in every detail. When she rose from the table, Richard followed her about the room with his eyes, and it soon became apparent to Harry that he was in danger of outstaying his welcome.

With a stab of envy, he took his leave, regretting his shrewish Woodville wife whose very name was hell. When he bent over Anne's hand, he noticed how every finger bone was visible beneath her skin, skin that was chilly against his warm lips. Then, after nodding a bright farewell to Richard, he left them alone.

As he pulled on his gloves he pondered the unlikely pairing, wishing his own match had been so fortunate but, as he trotted jauntily down the stairs, Will Catesby fell into step beside him.

'Have you time to share a cup of ale?' Catesby asked. 'I have some news to relate.'

Buckingham, who always had time to share a cup of ale with a friend, clapped his arm about Will's shoulders.

'Point the way to the nearest tavern, my friend,' he said, and the two disappeared into the night.

Made languourous by love, Anne rose late the next morning and didn't emerge from her chamber until sometime after ten. Richard was already in conversation with Harry of Buckingham and, after intercepting the warmth of their good morning, Harry restrained from bawdy innuendo and kissed her hand in a seemly greeting.

'Good morrow, Cousin. I trust you are well-rested.'

'Very, my lord, I thank you.'

Anne sat on the window seat and looked out over the garden while the men continued their conversation.

'You were saying, cousin?' Richard prompted, but Harry hesitated, glancing doubtfully in Anne's direction who, until a slight hostility crept into Richard tone, had not been listening. 'My wife can hear our counsel,' he said and, curiosity piqued, Anne pricked up her ears.

'According to Catesby, Hastings can no longer be trusted. He has been seen in secret meetings with Morton, Stanley and Rotherham. There can be little doubt they are plotting against our government.'

Richard began anxiously twisting his rings on his fingers.

'But Catesby is Hastings' man. Why would he betray him? And why would Hastings betray us anyway? He is a good man; he has ever been my friend, and a good friend to Edward, and my father before that. I don't like this, Harry, it smacks of deceit but not on the part of Will Hastings. I would rather suspect the Woodvilles of slandering him and using it as a wedge between the Chamberlain and our council.'

Buckingham ran a hand through his hair and shook his head.

'I don't know, Richard, all I know is what Catesby told me, and I also know he is unhappy about his Lord's dealings. He told me Hastings lost no time in making up with the king's mistress, Jane Shore, and spends every night in her company. It is common knowledge that, although she hated

Jane Shore when Edward was alive, the Queen is now her friend and receives visits from her daily. Shore even takes her gifts and dainties.'

He paused, organising his thoughts before continuing.

'Richard, it occurred to me and Catesby that the Woodvilles are plotting with Shore to wean Hastings from his allegiance to you. With the aid of the old king's government, namely Morton, Stanley and Rotherham, they intend to seize the Protectorship.'

Richard's frown grew deeper. He picked up a goblet of wine and finding it empty, slammed it down again. Anne moved soundlessly to the table, and reached out to touch his sleeve, looking suspiciously at Buckingham and wondering how so fair a face could conceal so sordid an imagination.

'Richard. Hastings has always been an ally of York. He followed Edward and you into exile in Burgundy and fought at Barnet against Marguerite and my father. He cursed Clarence for his treachery. Surely he would never stoop so low.'

Richard hoped she was right. He stroked her hand before turning again to Buckingham.

'I pray my wife is right, Harry, but I suppose we cannot take that risk. I shall speak to Hastings; he will not be able to hide the truth from me. I know him, his eyes will give his mouth the lie. We shall call forth a meeting of the council in the White Tower on Friday, but I pray God you are misinformed.'

In the days that followed, a mist of deceit and mistrust pervaded Westminster, and each morning Richard dreaded discovering the truth. Anne, tried to offer what comfort she could, and their bedtime conversations were monopolised by Hastings and his suspected divided loyalty. Richard alternated between white-faced defence of his life-long friend, and rage that such duplicity was possible.

The intervening days dwindled and Richard's last night of torture was upon him. Tomorrow would reveal all he needed to know. He had spent long hours with Harry, discussing the strategy of the meeting but no hard and fast decision had been reached. Richard remained certain that Hastings' face would either reprieve or condemn him but, at Buckingham's insistence, he sent to York for two hundred men at arms.

When Richard took his leave he assured Anne it must be a misunderstanding. She watched him ride away, thinking how sorrow made him seem smaller, and then she turned into the house to resume the waiting game. By the time dusk was falling, Anne had fallen asleep on the settle, her head lolled uncomfortably to one side, resting on the hard wooden edge. When the three men slammed into the room, she woke with a cry, clasping a hand to her stiff and aching neck.

'Ha! I told you we were right, Dickon.' Buckingham exclaimed, 'Well done, Catesby. You did a great thing warning us of this plot and you will be well-rewarded, Sir.'

Anne looked at Richard, dismayed at what she found there. His face was grey and his eyes red-rimmed with unshed tears.

'Richard?' she enquired gently but when he made no response, she hastened to the table and ignoring her duties as hostess to see first to the requirements of her guests, slopped wine into a cup and handed it to him.

Buckingham, with one hand resting on the mantle, continued to heap praise on William Catesby, who, judging from the looks he cast in Richard's direction, was more alert to his discomfiture. Richard drank deeply but said nothing. Anne hovered, desperate to learn what had happened but appreciating Richard's need to tell it in his own time but Buckingham made certain her wait was short.

'We've got them, Anne. Rotherham is locked up. Morton is locked up. Stanley is locked up. And Hastings! Well, he won't be making any more trouble; not from where he is.'

Laughing, Buckingham slapped Catesby on the back, spilling wine on his doublet. Catesby, still overawed by the great company in which he found himself, mopped at the stain ineffectually until Harry roared.

'Leave it man; I'll get you a new and better one. I'm telling you; you've earned your place on our council now. He saved your husband's life, Anne. They were plotting to kill him.'

'Richard?' breathed Anne. 'Is this true? Will Hastings plotting to kill you? Oh, God please, tell me this is not true.'

Richard nodded mutely before adding huskily.

'It is true, Anne. I saw it written on his face, just as I knew I would. He was never one to dissemble, and he couldn't look at me. Bluff, brave Will Hastings unable to meet my eye. Worse than that though, Anne, is that I have probably committed the worst crime of my life. I only hope God will understand and forgive me, and you, too.'

Images of Catherine and John flashed briefly through her mind before she dismissed them; there were, after all, worse sins Richard could commit than take another woman. But it was certainly guilt she was seeing on his face. It was the nature of his guilt that eluded her. Watching him fight for self-control, Anne turned to Catesby who seemed a gentler man than Harry.

'Mr Catesby, could you please tell me what happened, from the beginning?'

Catesby, startled by the attention from the legendary Warwick's daughter, cleared his throat.

'Well, I've served Hastings since I was a lad, and I've followed him through thick and thin, good times and bad. I've seen him do things that I've not liked before now, but never anything like this. Before, it was things with the late King, immoral behaviour with women of loose morals and that sort of thing, if you pardon my saying so, ma'am.

Well, soon after the king passed away, he began to see Mistress Shore openly. They'd been secretly meeting for months before the king died, but now they were open about it, and he more or less lived with her. I don't like her at all, Ma'am. She has not a virtuous bone in her body, or a moral thought in her head. After a while, I saw them more and more in the company of Dorset; another worthless scoundrel in my eyes, and then, what with her visiting the queen in sanctuary so often, I began to suspect that Lord Hastings mind was being poisoned against his real friends. He was drinking more than ever, and when he was in his cups he began to criticise the Protector, saving your presence my Lord, and declare he would make a better guardian of the young king. He began to question why King Edward did not make him protector.

It became regular practice for Hastings to meet with Morton, Stanley and Rotherham, all of whom, I knew, were no friends to my Lord of Gloucester. I began to suspect that they were hatching a plot. We all know that King Edward left Gloucester in charge because of his loyalty and integrity, and I don't believe the Woodvilles be right for the job. So, I informed my Lord of Buckingham of my suspicions.'

Catesby paused and fiddled with the tassel on his gauntlets.

'Go on, Will, tell me what happened today,' pressured Anne. As he began to speak further, Richard rose and looked from the window. Will cleared his throat.

'Well, my lady, today we attended the council meeting as ordered by my Lord of Gloucester in the White Tower, as is usual, and all summoned were present. My Lord of Hastings sat at the table with Morton and Stanley while we awaited the arrival of your husband. When he first entered he was so pleasant to everyone, I thought he must have decided against his plans to confront them. He attended to some trivial business and asked Morton about the strawberries that grow in his garden, and the bishop promised to bring him some. Then, after some further business was dealt with, my Lord of Gloucester left the chamber for about an hour. It was on his return that things took a turn for the worse. He sat down and looked around at those present, dwelling for some time on the face of Hastings, as he related the tale of a dastardly plot hatched by the family of the queen. To which news those assembled pretended great surprise and disgust. I saw my Lord of Gloucester fix his eyes upon Lord Hastings, and then all of a sudden, he jumped up and banged his fist loudly on the board. Everyone in the room took fright, the loud strike shattering their wits. I was afraid myself, although I knew that

I had committed no offence. My Lord Duke then accused Morton, Stanley and Rotherham of treason and had them borne off to prison. But he grabbed Hastings by the collar and spoke to him through clenched teeth. 'I will not go to dinner until I see thy head from thy shoulders.' Then he ordered them to take Hastings below and strike off his head. Which they did, my Lady … which they did.'

His words trickled away and through sheer strength of will, Anne managed not to faint. Slowly she turned her head toward Richard who remained by the window, his head bowed, and his shoulders slumped.

'Could you give us leave a while, my lords?' Anne's voice was quietly authoritative, and obediently the men quit the chamber, leaving them alone. Neither one of them knew quite what to say but, at length, sick of stomach, Anne cleared her throat.

'Is this true, Richard, did you really have him slaughtered without shrift or trial?'

His reply was cold and clipped.

'I did, Anne, and had there been no one else to do it, I would have done the deed myself. However, I am informed that a priest was summoned; he did not die unshriven.'

Despite the warm June sunshine, Anne felt cold. She looked on Richard's familiar face and thought she hardly knew him at all. Suddenly, she grasped his arm, forcing him to look at her.

'Why Richard, why could it not have waited for a trial?'

She laid her head in his lap and felt him stroke her hair. Richard closed his eyes and grit his teeth.

'He was my father's trusted henchman. He was my brother's trusted companion. He was my mentor and my friend. When he took up with traitors against me, he betrayed all of us - my father, my brother and the entire faction of York. He deserved to die, Anne, his actions condemned him to lawful death but, had I waited, I would have lost the strength to do it. If he had gone to a cell to await trial, he would have escaped death because I would not have been able to bring myself in cold blood to destroy a man I had once called friend. If nothing else, Anne, it has helped me understand what Edward suffered when dealing with George.'

Anne stared at the man she loved and knew this day had changed him. Richard was now aware of his own capabilities.

The Tower, London- June 1483

Preparation for the coronation was underway and the new king, and his brother, Richard, were lodged in the Tower royal apartments. On the morning Anne decided to pay them a visit, the sun shone brightly, and she found them shooting arrows on the green at the foot of the white tower. At first they were so intent on their shooting match that they didn't notice her. But when they became aware, they put down their bows; the elder boy remained where he was while his brother hurried forward.

'I am pleased to meet you, my lady. I am Richard, and that is my brother, Edward. He is going to be king soon.'

While Richard waved him over, the elder boy held back, acknowledging her with a cold nod. The younger boy seemed not to notice his brother's reserve. 'You have a boy called Edward too, don't you? Is he in London? Will you bring him to see us; we are short of company here?'

'I am afraid my son is in Yorkshire. He has been ailing but, once he is fully recovered, I am sure he will love to get to know you. You must also visit us at Middleham. There are several children in our household.'

Informally, Anne sat with him on the close clipped grass and listened to him chatter about his sisters and his favourite dogs. Every so often, she glanced toward Edward, but the boy did not look at her. She guessed he disliked her as much as he resented her husband.

The young Richard was very much in the mould of his father. He was plump, blond and, as a result of the hot June weather, somewhat sweaty, and red-faced. He had taken off his doublet and discarded it on the grass some way off, and his white shirt was unlaced at the throat. Beads of moisture adorned his top lip and his hair stuck to his forehead. He smelled and acted exactly like a puppy, and Anne had the urge to take him in her arms and appease some of her longing for her son.

Richard didn't seem at all shy or display any lack of confidence as he plucked daises and piled them into Anne's lap so she could fashion them into chains while he plied her with questions. Edward sat down a short distance away and watched them, his chin resting on his raised knees, pretending not to listen.

'My father had a lot of dogs,' Richard continued, 'and I mean to get more too. Edward has a nice pup but mine was lost. It really isn't fair because Edward prefers books to dogs.'

Anne glanced at Edward again who was diligently poking the dusty soil with the toe of his shoe, he scowled when Anne spoke to him directly.

'I wanted to bring gifts for you today, Edward, but I couldn't think what you might like. I thought I would get to know you better first. Tell me, is there anything you need?'

On receiving no answer, she turned her question to Richard and the boy thought for a while.

'I do miss my lurcher, Smoke. He got left behind when my mother dragged us all into sanctuary. You should have seen it. They were smashing down walls, and my mother was raging at the servants and when her maid dropped a whole bundle of gowns into the mud, I thought she was going to box the girl's ears. I don't expect I shall ever see Smoke again though, and my playthings were left behind when I came here to join Edward. I like presents very much though, Aunt; I will be pleased with anything you care to bring.'

He sprang up and held out a hand to assist Anne to her feet. 'We must look at the menagerie before you leave. Come along, Ned.'

Swept along in the tide of his enthusiasm, Anne and Edward followed but Edward offered no conversation until Anne asked him a direct question.

'Are you sure there's nothing I can bring next time I come, Edward?'

'No.'

'Oh, surely there must be something. What about some more books, or a lute, maybe? Your brother says you play very well.'

Edward stopped and glared at her, his fair head thrust forward, his eyes full of hostility.

'There is one thing I would like. I would like my Uncle, Earl Rivers, and my half-brother, Richard Grey and my tutor released from Pontefract and returned to my service.'

Surprise robbed Anne of speech. She fumbled for the correct response. She had huge sympathy for the boy and understood the depth of his pain. After all, she knew better than most the misery of a child at the mercy of adults. She wished she had the answer but, as she looked into his steely grey eyes, she knew he would never heed her advice. She swallowed her impatience before making a careful reply.

'You know I have no power over state matters, Edward. I realise that you must miss your uncle and brother sorely, but I also know that the Lord Protector has your welfare at heart, and the good of the country. He believes that your uncle was not acting in a way that was beneficial to England and it is his duty to rectify that. I know that he will not fail you; he takes his duties very seriously. When you come to know him, you will realise this, Edward. Richard is a good man, and he is determined to raise you as your father wished, to be a good King.'

Wrenching his sleeve from Anne's grasp, he yelled,

'Gloucester has never been a friend to my family, and he will never be trusted by me. As soon as I am crowned and his role as Protector ceases, I shall reinstate my uncle and banish Gloucester and you from my court …from England!'

Anne stared at him, grieving that one so young should harbour such bitterness. Gaining his trust was going to be an impossible task. As was customary for princes, Edward had been raised at Ludlow under the sole tutelage of his mother's family. He was perfectly schooled in Woodville ethics and

Woodville prejudices, and when he ascended the throne of England, it would be as a Woodville. His coronation day would be the crowning glory of the dreams and aspirations of his maternal family. York had fought too long and hard for the throne to allow it to fall into the hands of the Woodville's who were essentially, Lancastrian.

At a loss for words, Anne shook her head and turned away, hastening her step to catch up with Richard who was pulling heroically ugly faces at an ancient lion through the bars of the cage. For the remainder of the afternoon, although she laughed and pretended to be gay, Edward's unhappiness cast a deep shadow over her spirits.

In the evening, as she pondered all possible solutions, her sighs dominated the solar and brought concerned glances from her ladies. Had young Richard only been born first, the future would be so much brighter. He was York through and through; courageous, endearing and, already very chivalrous. She smiled as she recalled the gallantry with which he had bowed over her hand, very much as his father would have done. But Edward left a nasty taste in the mouth, and despite his tender years, Anne didn't trust him.

'I visited the princes today,' she said when Richard arrived later on that evening.

'The devil you did. You didn't tell me you were going to. What did you think of them?'

Anne put down her embroidery and took a sip of wine, letting the liquid refresh her palate before responding.

'Richard, I found enchanting. He is affectionate and open, and I could happily spend every day in his company but Edward, well, he is quite a different matter.'

Richard's hair gleamed in the firelight as he played with the rings on his fingers.

'I know, Anne. I have tried more than once but I just can't reach him. He hates me, although I cannot fathom why. I've never done anything to hurt him.'

'Well, you did arrest his uncle and stepbrother. Of course, he resents that; it is only to be expected. What I fail to understand is why they turned him against you in the first place? It is almost as if they knew you would one day be named Protector.'

'Maybe they did. They certainly seemed to be in a rush to have the boy crowned, knowing the post ends at the coronation. We have been discussing it at council today, and it has been decided to extend the Protectorship until Edward reaches his majority; that way I have longer to teach him how think and act like a king. I need time if I am to distance him from the queen's family, and I cannot let him loose upon England until he is fit to rule. Apart from anything else, it would be suicide, for he would lose no time in wreaking vengeance on me.'

'He admitted as much today. He said that he intends to reinstate Rivers and Grey and banish us from his realm.'

Richard sighed and shook his head.

'That, I can well believe. And, as welcome as the idea of Middleham is, I have no intention of allowing either of those things to happen. The prisons are filling up. I have sent Morton off to Brecknock under the care of Buckingham; Jane Shore is imprisoned along with Rotherham and the former secretary, Oliver King. I see no reason to keep Shore locked up though. She will do penance as a harlot and then, I may let her go free.' He ruffled his hair and stretched out his legs. 'I must be seen to act decisively, and the queen's continuing intrigue gives me no option but to take a stand. This morning, I issued the execution of Rivers, Vaughn and Grey. Northumberland is to supervise at Pontefract, so it seems, my love, the young prince will soon despise the name of Gloucester even more.'

Crosby Place – June 1483

The beautiful June weather mocked the darkness in Anne's heart. She longed to escape the oppressive city and breathe the fresh air of Middleham. She missed her son, her home, her routine. Richard was out so often and, even when he returned after darkness fell, it was only the shadow of her husband that came home. He was distracted, exhausted and she was sure still suffering prolonged grief at his brother's death.

The noise and grime of London depressed them both, and they longed for the freshness of the Dales but, as Richard's responsibilities increased, so did their hopes of returning home dwindle. Anne was also concerned about Buckingham's influence for, although Richard was his own man, he was also a lonely one, and seemed to be relying more and more on Harry to replace his brothers. But, as the initial charms wore off, Buckingham began to strike her as greedy. Not only was he profiting from Richard's position but had benefited greatly from the late Lord Hastings' estates.

Sometimes, when she overheard their council, Anne was uncomfortably reminded how her father had manipulated King Edward. It was Richard's role to govern in Edward's stead until he became of age yet more and more Richard took Buckingham's ideas on board. She wondered what further reward he could hope for because, after Richard, he was already the most powerful magnate in the country; his estates and riches were unsurpassed.

Nobody but Anne seemed to notice the deepening lines of strain on Richard's face. Although matters had settled down since the removal of the most prominent traitors, Anne was still concerned for Richard's health. She wished they could escape to some quiet place where she could pamper and love him back to health. It was to this end that Anne insisted he return early for an intimate supper. She ordered a table laid in their chamber and told the cook to prepare all his favourite foods.

While Richard washed away the megrims of the day, Anne watched the warm water trickle like silver snakes across his chest. It seemed so long since they had lain properly together, and recently their lovemaking had become brief and perfunctory. She missed him and planned the leisurely evening would extend into a lazy morning.

Richard, clad in a velvet robe, his hair still wet on his neck, lounged with her close to the hearth. Anne could barely wait for the meal to finish. She had left her hair to hang loose, knowing that he liked the way the firelight burnished it. Very soon, the meal over, he would run it through his fingers, his lips would ...

Her anticipation was interrupted by someone pounding on the outer door.

'Ignore it,' Anne said, as her contentment evaporated but a few moments later, Elayne peeped around the door.

'I'm sorry, my lady but the Duke of Buckingham and another gentleman are here and wish for an audience with the Lord Protector.'

Richard swore, straightened his clothing and, while Anne disappeared from the room, stood ready to receive the uninvited guests. His annoyance melted into surprise when he saw the Duke was accompanied by a rather dusty Robert Stillington, the Bishop of Bath and Wells.

Buckingham unfurled his cloak and tossed it onto a nearby chair before helping himself to some wine and stealing one of Anne's wafers. Offering no apology for the disturbance, he took a bite and waving his goblet summoned the clergyman to come closer.

'Wait 'til you hear this man's story, Richard. This'll put the cat among the pigeons and no mistake. Come on, man, come over here and tell the Duke of Gloucester what you told me.'

As Anne re-entered the chamber, the bishop moved forward and bowed. His hair was dishevelled, and he seemed to be struggling with some restriction in his throat.

'My Lord of Gloucester,' he croaked, full of nerves. 'I do have a tale to tell, and such that has caused me many hardships. I must choose to incur further punishment if I do tell, or risk punishment in the hereafter if I keep quiet. So, I beg you to deal gently with me, Sir. I am an old man.'

Richard raised the bishop from his knees and seated him before the fire where he offered wine before asking him to begin his tale. Anne, remembering a similar visit from Catesby not so long since pressed a hand to her sinking heart, and wondered what fresh trouble was brewing.

Stillington cleared his throat. 'My Lord. The late King, at the time of his marriage to the Queen Elizabeth, was already trothplight to another. His alliance with the Queen was unlawful and therefore all his children are illegitimate.'

Anne gasped. She hadn't expected that. She watched in a daze as Richard leaned forward in his chair and snarled at the old man.

'You lie, Stillington. How dare you speak such slander? And you, Buckingham, how can you give credence to such vile lies? Get out, the pair of you, and do not disturb us again this night.'

Richard leapt up and began to pace but Harry, undismayed by his cousin's anger, spread his arms wide, palms up.

'Just listen to the man and think about what he is saying. It explains a great deal. Why else are the Woodvilles in such haste to have the boy crowned? If this is true it explains the dowager Queen's insecurities and her fear of you and … it also explains your brother George's death, and why Edward had Stillington, here, imprisoned for so long.'

Richard's hesitation was long enough to encourage Buckingham to continue.

'Did Edward not accuse Clarence of speaking words injurious to the king and his heirs? Why did he insist on George dying for such a small offence, when his former crimes were so much more worthy of death? Why did he so outrageously offend and ignore the pleas of your good mother?'

Buckingham gripped Richard's shoulders, but the protector wrenched himself away and, in three strides, reached the window. He looked angrily across the moonlit rooftops to where the river flowed on its silent journey to the sea. The Thames, slow like time, waiting for no man as it wound on its inexorable way, taking anyone caught in its current to their fate. He wished he could swim against the tide.

He recalled George's wild accusations when he visited him in the Tower, and Edward's stubborn refusal to show clemency. A glance at Anne's shocked features told him she was as shaken by the news as he. He wished they were alone so they could talk it over.

She had never had any illusions about the old King and had often teased him about making an icon out of a sheep's ear. Maybe she was right, perhaps he never had really known his brother and the chivalrous knight he remembered had always been just an illusion. Some deity he had conjured up as a boy, after losing his father.

Richard turned slowly back to face the room where Stillington still cowered in his seat and, realising his innocence in all this, Richard reached out to him.

'Come, man, do not fear my wrath, it is not aimed at you. Tell me, is this truly the reason that George died? Did Edward really murder our brother for the sake of his queen?'

'Not for the queen, Richard,' Anne interrupted as she moved toward him. 'Not for Elizabeth, but for his boys; for Edward and Richard. It was a conflict between love for his brother and for his sons. Surely you can understand that now and perhaps forgive him a little? Would you not do the same for our Edward? Would you not do *anything* for him?'

Anne's obvious distress, and the ruin of their planned evening, tipped Richard over the edge and he roared at the world at large.

'And now the knowledge is mine, what am I expected to do with it? Do I imprison Stillington again and continue with the coronation, or do I plunge the country once more into civil strife? And whom do you suggest that I place on the throne? Young Warwick who can barely string three words together? Or shall I summon Henry Tudor from overseas?'

Anne bit her bottom lip, hurt by the sarcasm that was so rarely aimed at her. Looking down at her blue slippers that peeped from beneath her gown, she pressed her lips together and remained silent, ill-equipped to deal with his present mood.

Buckingham, however, was not so restrained and matched his cousin's anger with his own. 'Young Warwick is attainted by his father's treason, and besides, he is verging on idiocy. So, go ahead and summon Tudor; I'm sure we shall all thrive under his rule. It will do us all good to have a Lancastrian ruling over us again. Sometimes, Richard, I doubt your intellect.' He pointed a finger and wagged it beneath Richard's nose. 'Wake up, man. You must take the throne for yourself. You have the right. In the absence of heirs, and as Edward's brother, you are next in line.'

'Don't be ridiculous, Harry. Edward has scores of children,' cried Anne, momentarily jerked from her determined silence.

'All illegitimate, thanks to Bishop Stillington's testimony. And don't forget, it says in the bible - *bastard slips shall take no root.* Your husband, my dear, is clearly the only man for the job and the best possible choice for England. The country needs a soldier at the helm, not a half-fledged boy, and everyone will be glad of it. Show me a minority rule that ever prospered. This is our chance, Richard, and we have to take it. You have no choice.'

With a frustrated groan Richard ruffled a hand through his hair that had dried un-combed in the warmth of the night.

'There's always a choice, Harry, just never an easy one.'

Baynard's Castle – June 1483

As soon as they could, Anne and Richard rode over to Baynard's Castle where they found Cecily collecting herbs in her garden, later to be distilled into salves and medicines for her household. Although George's death had extinguished the last of her beauty, she remained a striking woman. When she saw them approaching, she put down her basket.

'How lovely to see you both. I'm surprised you could spare the time for calling, Richard, as busy as you must be.'

Richard bowed over her hand before embracing her and planting a kiss on her cheek.

'I'm afraid it isn't really a social call, Mother. We have news which may cause you distress, and I wanted you to hear it from us. I need your blessing before I take action. I've had a visit from the Bishop of Bath and Wells …'

Before Richard could finish his sentence Cecily's face paled, and she swayed on her feet. Seeing she was about to fall Richard grabbed her arm and assisted her to an arbour where she sat down. When she was sufficiently composed, she raised her eyes.

'So, you know at last, Richard, at last, you know the truth.'

'Mother, you knew of this!' exclaimed Richard. 'How could you know and never tell me? How could you let George die without me knowing the reason for it?'

'I believe George tried to tell you himself, my dear, but you would not listen. You would never allow any of us to say anything to Edward's detriment. Even now, I expect you to cast around, looking for a way to excuse him. The fact that you must face, Richard, is that Edward owned all the human failings a man can. He was a slave to his own libido, and many women have been damaged by it. Eleanor Butler was a gently bred girl and a virtuous widow who believed Edward's promise to wed her. It broke her father, Old Talbot's, heart when she was taken down. When the king married Elizabeth, Eleanor retired broken-hearted into a nunnery. His horrid lust ruined two people's lives, and now, it seems the repercussions are to continue.'

Richard kept her hand fast in his.

'You knew didn't you, even when Edward married Elizabeth you kept silent. Why did you never tell me, especially once George was taken?'

'Edward swore me to secrecy, my dear. He was always afraid of discovery, that's why they wed in secret. Elizabeth refused to yield to Edward before wedlock, not because she was careful of her virtue but because she coveted the crown. Woe betide anyone who tried to tarnish her claim to it. When George discovered the truth, she badgered Edward into destroying him and then into shutting poor Stillington away. He was in prison for months before Edward bribed him into silence with the position of the Chancellorship.'

Anne coughed gently before speaking.

'The coronation has been postponed, Cecily, and Buckingham is urging Richard to take the throne. What do you think he should do? Should he accept it, or let things lie? Do you think the secret could be kept so that life can go on as planned?'

Cecily looked at her niece and laughed mirthlessly.

'Is this truly Warwick's daughter speaking? Should Richard take the throne? Why, of course he should; for the sake of all England. Even if young Edward were not illegitimate he would make an abysmal king. Consider the last insipid man that we had on the throne and the lengths my husband had to go to remove him. Henry VI was far better off and happier praying than ruling, and Edward will be better off studying and keeping his meddling mother out of mischief. No, Richard, the throne is yours and I know your father would have urged you to take it. Just make sure you rule England honestly…as your brother never did.'

Richard knelt in the dust at his mother's feet and kissed her hand, but emotion robbed him of speech. Without further words, he left Anne and Cecily seated together in the arbour.

Anne rose to follow but Cecily grabbed her wrist.

'Are you all right, Anne? Can you cope with this? I know you are sickly.'

There was naked anguish in Anne's voice as she replied. 'Oh, Cecily, I would far rather go home to Ned at Middleham. All I have ever wanted is to be home.'

Crosby Place - 4 July 1483

Although the windows stood open to allow as much air as possible into the chamber, the curtains hung limp and Anne was sleepless. The blankets had slid onto the floor, leaving her coughing and feverish while Richard, seemingly unaffected by the heat, snored oblivious, beside her. His hair made a dark halo on his pillow and his head was thrown back, his throat bared, his breath coming in regular heavy gusts. Trying not to wake him, Anne stifled her cough.

The night candles illuminated the contours of his chest as it rose and fell steadily, and she quashed the urge to trace her forefinger along the battle scars. In the old days, she wouldn't have hesitated to wake him and urge him to make love to her but, the man beside her now, was unlike the Richard of old.

Matters of state monopolised his time, his thoughts, leaving little opportunity for intimacy with his wife and, although Anne tried to be supportive and understanding, she longed for a return of their former lives. It was an emotionally exhausted man who returned from Westminster every evening and although she tried to ease the mantle of fatigue that weighed him down, it was no longer easy; he was remote, unreachable, distracted. This was not the first night she had lain awake, miserable and afraid.

Richard, already exhausted by matters of state, reluctantly agreed to accept the crown … on condition that all was done legally and above board. Robert Stillington's address to the council informing them of Edward's pre-contract had caused an uproar, dividing long held friendships and alliances but ultimately, the majority favoured Richard as candidate for the next king.

On June the twenty-second a stunned crowd listened as a sermon was read from the pulpit of St Paul's Cross, revealing Edward's pre-contract to Eleanor Butler and denying the legal right of Edward V to the throne. To reinforce his point the biblical text, 'Bastard slips shall take no root,' was quoted, and when the sermon ended, the country swirled into a seething mess of mixed opinion.

Some raged and, denying the credibility of the plight-troth story, began to openly predict the young prince's early demise in the wake of, what they regarded, as usurpation. Others were comforted by the prospect of a strong man on the throne and wholeheartedly supported Richard's claim. The inns of London became a hotbed of conflicting loyalty, and fights and arguments broke out regularly. But, ultimately, the desire for social stability proved stronger than any lingering regret for the boy king. In the capital, preparations for the coronation of Edward V switched to that of his uncle, Richard III.

Anne, however, grew resentful, separated and unable for the first time to communicate properly with her husband. Never before had Richard failed to consult with her on a matter which affected their life together, but he was swept along on the tide of Buckingham's enthusiasm and remained unaware of her reservations.

She had no ambition to be Queen. She was desperately homesick for Yorkshire and craved the company of her son. The pressures placed on Richard and the resulting lack of intimacy considerably decreased her chances of pregnancy and every morning she woke depressed and every evening, she retired distressed. She was isolated and constantly fatigued.

Under normal circumstances she would have confided in Richard, but he was so weighed down with cares of state she was reluctant to add to his trouble. Unnoticed, the breach between them widened. By the twenty-sixth of June, when a delegation of nobles and clergy arrived at Crosby Place to formally offer Richard the crown, Anne, felt she hardly knew him.

She stood apart, excluded as Richard accepted the crown and rule of England.

London thronged with nobles and commoners eager to see the new King and Queen. Word of the events since King Edward's death had spread far beyond the confines of the city. Such was the turmoil created by the incomers that Richard issued a proclamation forbidding, *'any person under penalty of death, on account of any old or new quarrel, to make any challenge or affray whereby the peace might be broken, or any sedition or disturbance of the peace within the City of London.'* He further ordered that everyone was to be in his lodging by ten o'clock at night, and the carrying of glaives, bills, swords and bucklers was prohibited.

But London carried on regardless.

It was not until the fourth of July that Richard and Anne proceeded in state along the Thames from Westminster to the Tower, where monarchs customarily spent the night before their coronation. Anne looked askance the crowd who were rowdier, dirtier and far larger than those she was accustomed to in Yorkshire. She was a stranger to them, and they were like foreigners to her. She wondered at their strange southern accents, as they roared their approval but, for all their roughness, she was unable to detect any hostility toward either Richard or herself.

She squinted against the glare of the sun and winced at a sudden pain just her above her brows. If only she could pull off the heavy wimple and slip off her slippers to lie down and rest. It was the only thing that would ease her constant headache. But it was not yet time to sleep, so she waved to the crowd and smiled like a queen.

The Church of St Peter Westminster - 5th July 1483

There was little respite the following day and, clad once more in an uncomfortably hot gown, she accompanied Richard on a procession made up of magnates, prelates, knights and household attendants. For this occasion, however, she resorted to a horse litter, attended by seven of her ladies, all mounted on splendid palfreys.

The crowd was as raucous as the day before, and the couple waved and smiled with no visible sign, on Anne's part, that she wished herself far, far away. They were supposed to be together, but Richard was so surrounded by henchmen, all clad in crimson satin doublets and short gowns of white cloth of gold, that she could barely see him. Every so often she would catch his eye and he'd flash her an encouraging smile. *How can he be so blind to my discomfort?* Anne wondered. *How can he not see my unhappiness?*

Last evening had afforded them little privacy and when the lengthy feasting eventually ended, with no energy for anything else, they had fallen gladly into bed. Now, Anne watched as Richard responded to the enthusiasm of his new subjects.

He was dressed in a fine doublet of blue cloth of gold, decorated all over with nets and pineapples, and his sleek, dark hair gleamed. Over-warm in the velvet and ermine trimmed gown his face glistened as, with one hand, he controlled the side-stepping of his huge white horse. He looked every inch a Plantagenet King, as grand and commanding as Edward ever had, and Anne's heart warmed as she recognised his fitness to rule.

Perhaps she had been selfish; perhaps she should support his new role more wholeheartedly. Maybe, between them, they could correct the many defects in the present system and offer the English people a better future. But, just as she was beginning to think all would be well, the figure of Buckingham passed through her line of vision as he took his place at Richard's side.

Harry Buckingham's gown was cut from splendid blue velvet and emblazoned with golden cartwheels. He raised his hand and gave the crowd the benefit of his perfect smile, acknowledging the cheers as though they were for him alone. From behind the curtains of her litter, Anne watched him play to the crowd and, although there was nothing to justify it, she felt a squirm of distrust.

It all came so naturally to Harry. He carried himself like a king and rode through the teeming streets as if he had the right to be there, whereas Richard, she knew, was wishing himself elsewhere.

Westminster - 6 July 1483

The face reflected in Anne's looking glass the next morning was ghostlike. Important occasions always seemed to bring out the worse in her, she never looked her best when she most needed to. She sighed, turned from the mirror, and put herself into the hands of her women.

Her Coronation gown was exquisite, a vision of purple cloth of gold on damask but Anne knew she hadn't a hope of showing it off to its best advantage. She fingered the rich cloth between finger and thumb, remembering the tales Richard had told of Elizabeth Woodville's coronation long ago. He'd said Elizabeth was a great beauty, surpassed in his eyes only by Anne herself. She smiled at the memory, and regretted that now she was grown, she could not hope to match the last queen.

It had rained on Elizabeth's coronation day but for Anne, the sun shone. It crept mercilessly into the chamber to reveal every line on her exhausted face. As Elayne brushed her hair, surreptitiously hiding the strands of hair left behind after each stroke, Anne wished she were anywhere else but here.

She allowed Elayne to anoint her body with scented oils, pinch colour into her cheeks, and then finally, it was time to put on the gown. Anne shivered in her shift while she waited for her women to ease it over her head but, when it was properly laced and tied, her shoulders sagged beneath its weight. While her ladies clapped their hands and gasped in wonder, Anne didn't see a queen looking back from her mirror but just plain little Anne Neville, dressed in someone else's gown.

Before all this nonsense had started, Richard, determined to make Edward's crowning memorable, had ordered no cost be spared. When the boy was deposed, the original coronation plans had simply been adapted to fit Richard and Anne.

Only it didn't quite fit.

As they walked barefoot along the specially laid carpet Anne was dwarfed by the array of dignitaries who preceded them to the abbey. Priests, abbots and bishops held aloft a sea of mitres and crosiers that waved above the mass of faces surrounding the procession. The old Cardinal Archbishop of Canterbury shuffled along the carpet behind the Bishop of Rochester who was carrying a cross and following them, came the greatest nobles of England, each bearing the symbol of their office or royal insignia.

Lord Stanley bore the mace of Constable, and Surrey the sword of state, and close behind came Kent and Lovell with the naked swords of justice. Northumberland bore the pointless sword of mercy, but the Duke of Norfolk, as Earl Marshall of England, had the greatest honour of all and carried the coronation crown.

The Duke of Suffolk and the Earl of Lincoln, followed behind with the orb and sceptre and, in the midst of it all was Richard. Anne hardly recognised him. He was wearing a coat and surcoat of crimson satin, and a purple velvet robe trimmed and lined with ermine. A great canopy billowed above his head while a disgruntled looking Duke of Buckingham, carried his train.

While she waited to take her place in the procession, Anne's uneasiness increased. She tweaked the nap of her gown between her fingers as she cast about for a friendly face. And, just as her nerve was threatening to break, she realised the kindly Earl of Huntingdon was bowing before her.

He was the only affable face nearby, for her trainbearer was the immensely proud Margaret Beaufort. She was a diminutive woman who never failed to intimidate Anne. You couldn't tell from her demeanour but the mother of Lancaster's only remaining hope, Henry Tudor, Margaret found little favour with the kings of York. Henry Tudor was an exile in the court of Brittany where he had been for many years, and everyone knew Margaret coveted the crown for him. Right now, if it was in Anne's power, she would give it to him.

Assisting Anne to her feet, Huntingdon stepped into place with the crown held out before him and led her into the abbey. Behind, the Earl of Wiltshire followed, bearing her orb.

All she had to do was follow them while Lady Beaufort came behind, but all eyes were upon her, watching, criticising, she hesitated until Margaret poked her in the back. Anne took a few steps, so strung up by now that she held her breath all the way from the West door to the chairs of state which stood close to the shrine of Edward the Confessor.

Her heart hammered. When she reached Richard's side, he glanced at her with an encouraging smile. The voices of the choir soared and Anne, grateful for the chair, wished it could continue forever but, far too soon, the song ceased, and it was time for them to take their place before the high altar. Here, they were stripped to the waist to receive the holy oil on their backs, breasts, shoulder, palms and hair. Anne shivered as the old Archbishop anointed her.

Is this right? Is this God's will, or Richard's?

The anointing seemed to take forever but, at last, they were clothed again. This time when they took their seats on the royal thrones they were dressed in fresh robes of cloth of gold. Anne held her head high and steady, and the congregation held its breath as Archbishop Bourchier placed first Richard's and then Anne's crown on their heads.

They were now King and Queen of England.

While a *Te Deum* was sung in glorification of the new King and his Queen, Anne knew the ceremony was almost over; she breathed a little more easily and reflected that maybe now she was Queen, nobody would have the power to prevent her from returning home.

With the bells ringing out and the sun blazing, Richard and Anne emerged onto the steps of Westminster. As the crowd let out wild cries of joy, Anne wondered if her father was watching. He would have been proud this day, to see his daughter becoming Queen of England. It would have fulfilled his greatest wish.

Richard, sensing Anne's exhaustion, insisted in a short private interlude before the feast and while the court revelled, they retired to their chamber and cast off the ceremonial robes.

'Oh, Richard, It took so long. I thought I was going to collapse.'

Anne fell onto the great bed while Richard drew the drapes against the brightness of the day. It was so long since they had been together during daylight hours that, at first, his conversation was stilted.

'You are tired my love. I fear you have not been taking care of yourself as well as you should.'

Anne smiled, making little of her fatigue.

'I shall do well enough after a short rest, Richard. I did not sleep well, and the events of the day have tired me further. Did you notice Harry's wife did not attend?'

Richard gave a short involuntary laugh.

'I did, although I was not in the least surprised. You know that Harry has no liking for her. I'll swear he forbade her to come. No doubt she is closeted with her sister, cursing both my eyes and those of Harry.' He climbed onto the bed, relaxing into their old camaraderie. 'Old Bouchier bore up well, I thought; at one point I feared he would drop the crown.' Richard lifted a strand of Anne's hair. 'You looked lovely, my Queen.'

Anne coloured, shaking her head.

'No. I didn't, Richard, but thank you for saying so. I hated every minute. I was so out of place and felt so friendless. Only Huntingdon thought to smile at me all day, and Lady Beaufort dislikes me greatly, although I don't know why. And, as for the anointing, standing half-naked before all those people. I never want to go through that again.'

'I thought it was the best moment.' His laughter stilled abruptly. 'Do you know, it has just occurred to me that I've never bedded a Queen before.'

The next few weeks did much to restore Anne's faith in the future. Now that the pressing Coronation arrangements were over, Richard was much more in her company. Plans were being made for a royal progression into the north of England, a prospect that delighted them both for it meant seeing Edward. And now that Buckingham was not around so much, Anne's spirits began to recover and so did her health.

The progress was intended to be both a holiday and an opportunity to show themselves to the people. There were those who were uneasy at his new role, but he had many plans, changes to the system that would benefit ordinary folk. He wanted to show them his intention to reform the justice system, and base his rule on loyalty, rather than fear.

The first part of the progress would be taken by Richard alone. Anne was to enjoy a two-week rest period in London before travelling to Warwick, where Richard would join her. From there they would travel north together. Although this meant Richard must leave sooner than she, Anne had to admit she welcomed the respite from duty.

Richard set off from Windsor at the head of a great royal cavalcade. The intended route was to pass through the Cotswolds and rest at Woodstock, where the king planned to restore a tract of land to the town that Edward IV had annexed as part of his personal hunting grounds. While he was in the area, he took the opportunity to visit his friend, Francis Lovell's home near Oxford.

Minster Lovell was situated on the tranquil banks of the River Windrush. The king's party lingered for a few days both to recuperate and to enjoy the hospitality of his closest friend. Francis would prosper under Richard's rule and had already been made a Viscount; he was also promoted to the role of Chamberlain of the Household, and Chief Butler of England.

From the comfort of Lovell's best chamber, Richard wrote to Anne, telling her of Francis' joy in his house and land. It was a house to be proud of. Built by his grandfather in the early part of the century, Francis had been making improvements and showed the king the new oriel window he'd recently had installed. The window flooded the chamber with light and offered views of the garden and beyond.

'I must do something like this for Anne,' Richard said. 'It doesn't suit her to be so much indoors. Here, you get the feeling of being outside without the inconvenience of the chill.'

'I will give you the name of my builder.' Francis grinned. 'Come and look at this, Sire.'

Much to Richard's surprise, Francis led him along a dark passage and opened a concealed door in the panelling, after leading the king down some dark, rather steep stairs, they entered a chamber.

'What is this?' Richard spun around, taking in the sparse furniture, the supply of candles.

'We are now beneath the south-west Tower. I have no idea why or when it was built, I used to play here as a boy, although my mother always boxed my ears when I was discovered.'

On the floor, old toys and treasures were scattered, left there since Francis' boyhood. The king was impressed.

'It is perfectly secret,' he exclaimed. 'I had no idea it was here from the outside – although, of course, I wasn't looking. A room like this could stand a man in good stead in times of strife. It is intriguing, Francis. I wonder why it was built and by whom?'

'I have no idea. I used to frighten the life out of my cousins by bringing them here to tell them ghost stories.'

'I can imagine it. You were lucky. My own childhood memories are not so happy.'

'Oh, we had some good times at Middleham, didn't we, as Warwick's retainers?'

'We did,' Richard admitted. 'I was thinking of the time before when my mother sent George and me off to Burgundy on our own while Edward fought for his crown.'

'That must have been …hard.'

'It was. We didn't know what was happening. We used to worry that if the Lancastrians won, no one would care about us, and we'd be forgotten in a foreign land. I had nightmares for years, and I know George did too.'

Richard and Francis walked beside the river, where Francis pointed out huge fish lurking in the depths. Minster Lovell was a place of peace, very different from the vast, wildness of Richard's home where the world was made up of dale and sky. Here, sleepy cattle stood in tall meadow grasses, and small children splashed in the dappled shallows of the river.

'How lucky you …' The comment halted on Richard's tongue as he caught sight of Anna Lovell near the dovecot. Perhaps Francis didn't have all he longed for.

Richard and Anne had discussed Anna before. She had attended their wedding where she'd been bright and friendly, but the intervening years had wrought great changes in her. Although she played her part of hostess with ease and competence, she seemed troubled, old past her years. Sad. Richard mentioned it in his letter.

'I think you should request her presence at court,' Richard wrote. 'It might cheer her and bring her out of herself. I fear that there is little love between them, and I wish, with all my heart, that Francis might find joy in his marriage, as I have in mine.'

There were as yet no children and Richard wondered if Francis blamed her for it, or if he considered setting her aside. He wouldn't be the first man to seek a more fertile bride. During supper the couple hardly exchanged a word. Whatever the problem, childlessness was always a source of strain in a marriage; Richard knew Anne would feel for her.

It was some days later that Anne received a second letter. It too was written from Minster Lovell but this time, reading between the lines, Anne sensed he was deeply concerned about something he was reluctant to set to paper. After the usual tender greeting, he went on to say,

'I have arranged for a trusted emissary to call on you, his name is Edward Brampton, and he carries verbal instruction from me which you must follow carefully. I repeat that I *trust* this fellow and wish you to rely on him in all things. He will answer any questions you may have and return any verbal message you may wish him to carry. I have sent cryptically to one in London who will assist Brampton in his task.'

Anne curious, and worried by the tone of the note, wondered what matter could not wait until she joined him at Warwick. For a few days, her preparations for the journey were unsettled as she waited for the mysterious visitor but by the time Sir Edward Brampton was announced, her thoughts had already strayed to other matters.

Anne put down her tapestry and, forgetting she was no longer obliged to stand for any man, save the king, she rose as he entered. It was a stocky, deep-chested man with a dark beard that knelt before her.

'Your Majesty,' he said, making Anne blush to the roots of her hair.

'Sir Edward, I am pleased to make your acquaintance. I understand that you have some communication from my …from the king.'

Brampton licked his lips, his tongue appearing very red against the darkness of his beard. He glanced uneasily at the ladies who were clustered around the great fireplace and when he spoke, his voice was thick with a Portuguese accent.

'Madam, may we speak in private? It is a matter of great secrecy I have to impart.'

Anne looked into his eyes, and what she saw there convinced her that he could be trusted. She clapped her hands, and the ladies swept from the room. Most of them smiled at her as they departed but Lady Beaufort closed the door with frosty dignity.

Anne turned once more to her visitor.

'I am afraid Lady Beaufort approves of nothing I do, so do not be alarmed at her manner. Now then, Sir Edward, what do you wish to tell me?'

As if to make certain they were alone, Brampton glanced around the room and smoothed his beard with his left hand.

'Your Grace, the king commends me to you and begs you not to fear. He has received secret communication that warns of an intrigue against him; intrigue in which the Duke of Buckingham may be involved.'

Anne groped for her chair and sat down heavily, waving Brampton to continue.

'Buckingham,' she breathed.

'We do not believe the king to be in imminent danger, Your Grace, but he is concerned about the well-being of the

Lords Bastard in their present lodging. He bids me to ask your permission for them to be conveyed to Middleham with all speed, to join the household of the Prince of Wales.'

'But of course. It goes without saying that Edward and Richard should make their home with us. Clarence's boy is also there with his sister, Margaret, and I should never honour the children of my sister above those of Richard's brother. Oh God, does Richard really believe that Buckingham would harm them? What motive could he have?'

Anne gestured to Brampton to pour some wine and accepted the cup that he handed to her.

'Your Grace, we have known for some time of communications between the duke and the Earl of Richmond, Henry Tudor. We now believe that Buckingham means to eliminate the Lords Bastard and try to take the throne, either for Tudor or for himself. It is my business to watch those about the king, and I have witnessed Buckingham's ambition. If he can harm the boys and place the blame on Richard, men will not hesitate to take up arms against a Herod king. After all, his claim to the throne is almost equal to that of your husband. They are sprigs of the same branch, your Grace, and his lineage is far better than Tudor's who is, even now, clamouring for a chance.'

'But Sir Edward, has Buckingham not proved his loyalty to my husband? He would not be king were it not for him. He went to his aid at Stony Stratford and has supported his claim from the outset. In fact, if it were not for Buckingham, the story of Edward's pre-contract with Eleanor Butler would never have been discovered. And yet … for all that, I never have quite trusted him. There is something predatory, and I always believed he would lead Richard astray, but this? *This* plot is outrageous, it's unthinkable.'

'That is why the king is eager to remove the boys without delay. He is not yet ready to accuse Buckingham, but he intends to watch him and, therefore, the boys must be taken to safety. He has asked me to travel with them to Middleham as soon as can be arranged. I will need you to supply me with a trustworthy woman to care for them on the journey, but you must be certain of her discretion and swear her to absolute silence ... on pain of death.'

Placing the empty cup on the table, Anne stared distractedly from the window.

'I do have such a woman in my employ. She can be ready for a journey without delay. It is seven days to Middleham, Sir Edward; can you keep them safe and secret on the road for that long?'

Brampton bowed low over her hand.

'The manner in which I intend to travel, your Grace, we will be there in four. I shall return shortly, in secret and meet with your woman behind the kitchens ... at all speed. Perhaps some ...disguise is in order.'

As the door closed behind him, Anne called urgently for Elayne. She waved away all her other women.

'I am sorry, ladies, but I have a headache and would lie down alone for a while. Elayne, I know you have a marvellous recipe and I require you to attend me.'

Once the ladies had departed, Anne dragged Elayne into her bedchamber.

'Elayne. There is great danger and I need your help, as I have never needed it before.'

She related the tale, making clear the urgency of the situation and the peril she would be placed in. Elayne, as always, rose to the occasion with alacrity.

'I'll pack right away, my lady, I mean, your Grace. It'll be nice to see our Edward again, have you any messages for him?'

As she spoke, she moved about the room hastily stuffing garments into a bag, and her calm manner helped to steady Anne's nerves. She grabbed Elayne's hand and spoke quietly and earnestly.

'I cannot stress the danger that you may encounter, Elayne. You are to dress plainly, like a common woman and I have arranged some ragged clothing for the boys. You can trust Sir Edward Brampton with your life, and you may very well have to. You must look to those boys as if they were your own and, remember, they are bewildered by recent events and do not trust the king. On the journey perhaps you can comfort them with tales of Middleham and reassure them of their importance to us. Tell them how we care for them ... the elder boy, Edward, is quite difficult to love. He does not trust us, so watch him. You must guard them both with your life and never speak of this matter, to anyone, no matter what happens. You must take it with you to the grave.'

'I will, your Grace. You know you can rely on me.'

Elayne hitched her bag onto her shoulder and took her leave of Anne before sneaking down the backstairs to the kitchens where Brampton was waiting.

Warwick Castle - 8 August 1483

With a joyful heart Anne saw the dust on the road, indicating the arrival of the king's entourage. She longed to fly to meet him at the door as she had always used to but, now she was queen etiquette demanded otherwise. Quelling her impatience, she waited in the great hall, forcing herself to be calm but Richard, defied convention and swept her into his arms.

As he swigged down a flagon of ale, he pulled her onto his knee and demanded to hear all her news. From inside her bodice, she withdrew a much-crumpled parchment and read to Richard the contents of their son's latest letter. Edward's large round handwriting told them of his scholarly progress and, more lengthily, detailed the arrival of a litter of pups. He also revealed he'd been much troubled with a cold but was recovering well under the care of Elayne, whose sudden arrival had been a wonderful surprise.

Edward also wrote at length about a new playmate Dick who far surpassed him in the tiltyard. Anne and Richard smiled at this last, for although Brampton had reported in person the safe arrival of the Lords Bastard to Middleham, it was comforting to have confirmation from their son. Under the noses of Richard's enemies, the boys had been smuggled from the Tower and conveyed to the safety of Yorkshire.

It was a job well done, and Brampton would be well-rewarded.

Now Richard had arrived, Anne could hardly contain her impatience to continue the journey. She knew and approved of his plan to hold Edward's investiture as the Prince of Wales at York, and had begged that, instead of waiting for them to reach Middleham, the boy should travel to meet them at Pontefract. And so, on the nineteenth of August, Edward said goodbye to his cousins and, in the company of John and Catherine, left Middleham castle.

Although she fretted that he was very thin and seemed to tire easily, Richard and Anne were overjoyed to see their son. Kissing him in a manner quite unbefitting a queen, Anne could feel his bones through his doublet and resolved to feed him up. She was sure that now he was back with his mother, he would soon rekindle his strength. As ever, when she was away, his vigour dwindled, like a kitten that missed the lick of the mother cat. When they tucked him into his bed that night, Edward held onto her hand.

'I thought you might be different now you are king and queen. I thought you'd be proud and grand.'

'Silly boy,' laughed Anne, 'Why would we be different? No matter what your father or I become, we are and will always be, first and foremost, your parents.'

Anne stroked back his fine, dark hair, and he smiled with the eyes of his father before replying.

'I thought you may have been too busy to put a boy to bed at night. Edward, my cousin, is ever-so majestic and he was only nearly a king. I like Dick, though, he is looking after Troy while I'm away. Father, would you read The Tales of Arthur? You read it, while Mother sits here and holds my hand, like you did when I was little.'

Richard and Anne's eyes met over Edward's sleepy head and silently promised to spend more time with him in the future. As Richard's heir there was much for him to learn.

Middleham Castle - Late September 1483

The Prince of Wales climbed down from the litter and returned Troy's enthusiastic greeting while the small dog cavorted about his feet, his thin tail rotating like a whip. On the steps of the hall, Jayne and Elayne waited, in the company of the household. Dick laughed appreciatively at the antics of the dog, showing no sign of jealousy of Troy's obvious delight at Ned's return. He hurried down the steps and flinging an arm around his cousin's shoulders, chattered in his ear all the way to the solar.

Informality came as a relief. A welcome fire burned in the grate, and a table had been placed close to it, piled with tempting refreshments. The elder boy, Edward, was sitting on a window seat but made no move to greet his cousin. He remained where he was, staring out across the roof of the lower hall.

With Troy bounding between them, his claws skittering on the floor, the two younger boys clattered into the room with John and Catherine in tow. Richard's hunting dog awoke from his doze and warned the greyhound with a single bark. Troy wisely hurried to Ned's feet and sat on them, looking up, his tail beating a tattoo on the floor.

'Hello Edward,' called Ned cheerfully to his cousin, regardless of the elder boy's dislike. 'We have had a wonderful time in York. I've never seen such a crowd. There were mystery plays and mummery, and I ate so much, I thought I should burst. It is a shame that you couldn't be there. Catherine was with me, but she is just a girl, and my brother John was more interested in a silly lass he met there. What was her name, John? Was it Mary? Yes, I think it was Mary.'

John good-naturedly threw a cushion at his brother and when he had his attention, put a finger to his lips to silence him. Although he loved Ned dearly, he felt some empathy for the plight of the deposed Prince. He attempted to change the subject.

'What have you two been up to in our absence? I expect you are equal to me in the tilt yard by now are you not, Dick?'

Richard turned to him his smile wide.

'I practice every day, but I'm still too small to be as good as you are, John! But never fear, time will cure that problem. I mean to grow as big as my father was, so you'd better watch out.'

'And you, Edward? How have you passed your days?'

Edward shrugged a shoulder and refused to answer, his gaze fixed on something outside the window.

'He's been reading,' volunteered Dick. 'I think he's exhausted your father's library already. I hate books; give me a sword over a pen any day.'

Ned glanced from one brother to the other.

'I have heard it said,' he observed, 'that the pen is mightier than the sword, although I'm dashed if I know why. If I were to go into battle armed with only a pen I'd have little chance of victory.'

Edward got up and stalked toward his cousin.

'A fine King you'll make, then. The saying infers that intelligence is superior to brute force, you little fool. What sort of Prince of Wales is unversed in an elementary thing like that. How can a King hope to rule adequately if he is not wiser than those he governs? I think henceforth you should attend in the schoolroom with the same diligence you display in the tilt yard.'

As he absorbed his cousin's hostility, an unpleasant thought stirred in Ned's mind.

'But - but I'm not going to be King. My father is the king. I am just the Prince of Wales.'

John anticipated Edward's response and placed a hand on his shoulder, silently advising him to discontinue the argument. After all, they were hardly fairly matched, Edward's twelve years of education against Ned's seven.

'Let it drop, Edward,' he warned, but the angry boy ignored him.

'You may be right, Ned,' he cried, shrugging John's hand away. 'After all, *I* was Prince of Wales when *my* father was King, and I never became king because when *my* father died, *your* father stole my crown and now thinks to pass it on to you. If you ever *do* become King, you'd better keep a look over your shoulder because I will not allow you a minute's peace. I will kill you and take back my throne just as soon as I am able.'

Edward turned, intending to quit the room but stopped in his tracks when he saw his uncle and aunt standing in the doorway. He threw them a look of such unadulterated hate that they failed to halt his departure. Edward thrust past, leaving those in the chamber listening to his departing footsteps echo along the corridor.

Ned collapsed onto the settle, knuckling his tears while his brother and sister offered what comfort they could. He had never been spoken to like that before and Dick, feeling responsible for his brother's outburst, looked on uncomfortably.

'I'm sorry, Ned. I don't know why Edward feels so bad about it. After all, I was the Duke of York for a time, but I don't feel so angry about it now. I'd prefer it had not happened, of course. I just wish my father were still alive…'

'Don't rub your eyes, Sweeting, you will make them sore.'

Anne took her son's hand and looked up at her husband, silently begging him to help her explain. The king coughed uncomfortably and sat on the other side of Ned.

'It's more difficult for Edward. It would be hard for anyone to be brought up to perform a role, only to have that role taken away. Believe me, Richard, if I could have found a way to let Edward stay on the throne, I would have done so, but I had to follow God's laws. The laws of both God and the realm of England state that illegitimate offspring shall not ascend the throne. John here understands and accepts that as my bastard, he can never be king. It may not be an easy thing to accept but accept it we must. Your brother, Edward, feels betrayed and unhappy but, most of all, misplaced.

Dick, for all your Woodville blood, you think and act like a Plantagenet. That is why it is easier for you to accept it. You have been taught chivalry and honour, and will grow to be a fine warrior one day, just as my Ned will learn to be a fine Plantagenet King ... but what is Edward to do? Tell me that?'

The logs in the fireplace glowed red, shifting and settling as they burned, the damp lodged within whistling up the vast chimney with the smoke. The company fell silent and stared deep into the leaping flames, wondering and despairing of Edward ever finding his place in this world.

Middleham Castle - September 1483

Richard had been closeted in the privy council chamber for so long that Anne began to worry. For what seemed like a week, but was only hours, she had been constantly pressing her ear against the carved door. But all she heard was an occasional cough or the scraping of a chair leg. She was tired and strained but had several times curtly refused her ladies request that she retire to a chair nearer the hearth.

Sometimes the way her women fussed drove her mad. She had always appeared frailer than she was and was not about to start coddling a slight fever just because she was now a queen. A late summer storm stirred the heavy tapestries but, although it was not cold enough for winter, the threat of it was definitely in the air. So, when Elayne entered with a bowl of hot frumenty and insisted that Anne take some refreshment, she was very welcome.

'Sit yourself down here and take some sustenance, my – my – Your Grace or you'll be fit for nothing by the time the king does come out. I'm sure there's nothing to worry about. 'Tis the habit of Kings to shut themselves up with their ministers for hours on end.'

Much to the annoyance of her high-born ladies, Anne obeyed the commands of the serving girl and ate delicately. The bowl was not even half empty before the door opened and a group of serious looking council members bowed distractedly to their Queen before filing from the room.

Anne threw her napkin onto the tray and joined Richard in the inner chamber.

'Richard,' she said, as she closed the door. 'I know something has happened. You must tell me what it is before I am driven to distraction.'

The king, noting her strained face, was immediately contrite.

'Oh Anne, I'm sorry. I gave little thought to what you must be thinking. You were right to worry though, for there is more trouble. The rebellion is gathering strength in the south where they wish to restore Edward to the throne. Those who have cause to resent me have lost no time in joining forces with the Woodvilles in support of my brother's line. And, since the adherents of Tudor will join any faction opposed to my rule, they rise against me too. On top of all that, Francis of Brittany is threatening that if I do not help him against France, he will turn Tudor over to King Louis. We all know Louis will lose no opportunity to oust me from my throne. '

Anne began to roll up the parchments that were scattered across the table. As she worked, he stared at her thin wrists and listened to her soothing, sensible advice.

'Trouble again already? Why can't they give you a chance to prove yourself? I am sure nobody truly wants to see a child on the throne again and, as for Louis, what will he gain from this? Is he truly still holding a grudge against you for your behaviour in '75? I had hoped we could begin to enjoy our reign now. The coronation went well, and everyone seemed content to see you crowned. Even our former enemies turned out to support you on that day. What can have happened to change their allegiance so rapidly? Are people really so fickle?'

Richard sighed and, taking Anne's tiny wrist, clasped it in a palm that swamped hers.

'I haven't reached the worst bit yet, Anne. It's Harry. He's joined up with the rebels as we suspected he would. He has freed Morton whom I placed in his care for safekeeping and betrayed us. Even now, they are gathering against me. I must take action, so I fear I will be leaving soon my love. I must put down this rebellion before it grows too strong.'

Anne stood up in such haste that the blood rushed from her head and, as she fought against the shower of tiny lights behind her eyes, she stamped her foot.

'How I hate that man,' she cried. 'How I wish I'd told you of my misgivings about him. I thought I was simply jealous of the time you spent in his company. I feared he would lead you into bad womanising ways. In stemming my jealousy, I put us in peril. Oh Richard, why did we ever trust him? His army is strong; he controls many, many men. Do you think you can win against him?'

Tossing the rolled parchments into a chest and locking the lid, Richard sighed.

'I think I can defeat him, if I can get between London and Brecknok and cut him off from the rest of the rebels, we will stand a greater chance. Don't worry, my love, even if I lack the numbers, I have the experience that he lacks. The most important thing is to get Brampton to move the boys again. He must take them from the country this time. I have spoken with him this morning and it has been agreed, just between the two of us, that they should go disguised as Brampton's sons. It might even be wise to take them separately to avoid suspicion. Brampton will lodge them somewhere, in Bruges perhaps, where he has connections.'

'So, you think they are in danger here?'

He kissed the hand that was clasped in his own and grimaced before continuing.

'I know how you fret for me when I am away, Anne, and it is not easy to say this to you, but I do not think they will be safe enough here … particularly if I am defeated.'

He abruptly raised his hand, stifling Anne's horrified gasp.

'I'm not saying I will be, but the possibility must be taken into account. There is no telling what Tudor would do were he to succeed, but I think we both know what Buckingham would do, don't we?'

She nodded mutely; her constricted throat unrelieved by the tears that wet her cheeks.

'And what of our Ned, is he safe? He is your heir after all, and in your absence will surely become a target.'

Richard wrestled with his reluctance to heighten her distress but at length he broke the silence.

'No, Anne, I don't believe he will be safe but, we must face the fact, he is not strong enough to undertake a journey across the sea. We have to trust that I will defeat them all and return quickly. If I don't then you must risk all and get him, and yourself, away. I do not intend to leave you unguarded, and my most trusted knights will be with you. Remember, you are the one I trust above and beyond all others. I defy any of them to defeat the daughter of Warwick when her blood is up.'

Taking a deep breath, she swallowed a sob, steeled her strength and nodded, drawing on those hidden reserves of bravery that had stood her in such stead throughout her life. The one fact that she did not share was that previously when her life had been in danger, she had been physically strong and mentally optimistic. Now, she was simply sick and tired.

Once more, Anne stood on the battlement of Middleham Castle and watched Richard ride away. Ned was beside her, thrilled at the spectacle of knights and horses as they marched south along the winding road. His face shone with joy at the spectacle of the banner tail of his father's horse streaming in the wind as he carried the armoured King to defend his crown.

But Anne didn't see the glory.

'I may never see him again,' she thought but, for the sake of her son, she smiled bravely as she fluttered her kerchief.

When the cavalcade has shrunk into a glint on the horizon, she hurried Ned from the battlement and returned to the warmth of the hall. His hands and face were chilled to a deceptively healthy-looking pink and his eyes were bright. While Anne chaffed his fingers to bring back some warmth, Elayne flew around the chamber, packing belongings of the Lords Bastard.

Although this adventure was equally as dangerous as their escape from the Tower, the journey had to appear leisurely to avoid any undue suspicion. Ned was sorry Dick was leaving so soon but Anne promised that the boys would return as soon as it was safe to do so. Once the king had vanquished their enemies, they could begin to lead normal happy lives again.

The elder boy snorted at her optimism and Anne turned to him, annoyed at his insolence. He leant nonchalantly against the chamber wall and sneered.

Could he not sense her worry, or understand the danger he was in?

'Edward, it is your duty to cheer the younger ones who may be afraid of what lies ahead.'

But her words, instead of shaming him, merely goaded him. He leaned toward her.

'Why should I do my duty when I have been stripped of my proper rank? What defined duty does a bastard have, anyway? I hope my uncle *loses* this battle and, when I am reinstated, I shall throw Ned in gaol for stealing my title.'

He began pulling garments from the trunk and tossing them about the room, and Anne felt something snap suddenly inside her.

'I am sick of your attitude. Do you not realise that your uncle, THE KING, could have left you and your brother to rot in the tower, and that if he had then your LIVES would have been forfeit? Not from us but from those you call ALLIES! We have done EVERYTHING to make you feel better. We have welcomed you into our home, we have borne your insufferable behaviour, and we have tried to LOVE YOU! And, while we are on the subject, don't moan to me about hardship. I have suffered hardships that you can have no notion of. You are here, in my home, surrounded by those who wish to love and care for you. Can you imagine how it feels to be COMPLETELY FRIENDLESS in this world? Little more than a child, I was left alone and afraid with only enemies around me. I despaired of ever seeing a friendly face again. How would you like that? You are an ungrateful, insufferable boy and moreover, you are SPINELESS!'

The children stared at her as if she had been bewitched. And, realising all that she had said and done, tears spurted suddenly. Elayne, appearing in the doorway, immediately took stock of the situation and tried to defuse it.

'Well then, my lovelies, what's goin' on in here? I could hear the shoutin' all the way from the privy. I thought we were under attack from the Scots.'

But, straight away realising that her joke was not appreciated, she scanned the room and decided that the boys, distressed as they were, were in less need of care than her mistress. Ignoring the children, she led Anne gently from the room.

'Oh Elayne, what have I done? What have I said? Oh, I should never have spoken to him like that. What must he be thinking and poor Ned, and Dickon too. Oh no, do you think they believe everything I said?'

Elayne, drawing the slippers from Anne's feet and pulling the covers up to her chin, sniffed.

'I don't care if he does, my lady. He'll get over it. You are going to rest now, and no, you can't see them, not until I think you are recovered enough to do so.'

She came to the bed, armed with a bowl of water and began to bathe Anne's tear-streaked face.

'And another thing, my lady, if you don't mind me saying so. That boy has been asking for a good spanking since he arrived, ungrateful little monster.' Before she quit the room she sent her mistress an approving smile. 'And, tomorrow, perhaps you can tell me where you've been hiding such a filthy temper all these years.'

The chamber door closed, and Anne turned onto her side, cupping her cheek in her hand. She closed her eyes against more tears. Edward's stricken face rose in her mind's eye, and she began to chide herself afresh. How could she have spoken to the poor, misplaced child that way. She would never forgive herself, not if she lived for a thousand years.

Written this day of our Lord November 28th, 1483.

Well beloved Wife,

Greeting to all at Middleham and apologies to you, Anne, for failing to write at once. My excuse is one of constant matters which allow no respite or peace. It is over now, however, and the rebellion is quashed. My recompense to you is to bid you come, with my son and other children, at all haste to court for the Christmas celebrations. The good fortune of the last few months demand that we give thanks and praise to God for deliverance from our enemies. It seems fitting that we should celebrate the birth of Christ with as much joy as we can muster.

On a more sombre note, I expect word has reached Yorkshire by now of the executions of the rebels these past few weeks. Among those dead is of course that most untrue of creatures, my cousin Buckingham. At the last he beseeched me to meet with him, but I declined, unable to trust the germ within me that even at such a late stage craved to show him leniency. Unfortunately, he did not die well, as a Plantagenet should, but went to his death pleading and begging for mercy.

I cannot comprehend such disloyalty in men. It is a black slime that runs like poison through their souls. I dealt harshly with the leaders of the rebellion but showed leniency to their followers whom I allowed to go forth in peace. I was advised to punish more harshly but I believe that loyalty is better won by clemency than vengeance. Vengeance I will leave in the capable hands of God.

I have stripped Margaret Beaufort of all her titles and possessions and bestowed them upon her husband, Lord Stanley, and placed her under his strict care. She was deeply involved in this affair, and I will not tolerate disloyalty not even in a woman. I trust Stanley to ensure that she stays out of mischief.

'God sent weather that proved my strongest ally in all this. For the torrential rain and flooding that fell that day, swept away the crossing and kept Harry from joining his

friends across the river Severn. His associates lost no time in deserting the cause as soon as it appeared to be lost. Tudor, who had sailed from France, came close to the Dorset coast for a time but, although my men tried to lure him ashore by posing as the Duke of Buckingham's men and sending him a welcome, he was not fooled and scuttled back to Brittany where he will no doubt plot again.

I arrived in London on the 25th of this month and everything has returned speedily to normal with the majority relieved the matter was dealt with so quickly. I anticipate your arrival in London, my Queen, and convey with this letter my deep love and devotion.

Richard Rex.

December 1483

Ned was ailing again, and Anne was torn between the wish to spend Christmas with him, and the great longing to be reunited with Richard. She was loath to allow the child to spend the festive season with only his attendants for company but, at the same time, was well aware that he was not strong enough to travel the harsh roads to London in the depths of December.

The child was sick but not unto death, it was merely the return of the feverish chill that attacked him every winter and left him weak. She longed for signs of spring when his health and vigour would return but for now she supposed she must remain here and make his first Christmas as Prince of Wales one to remember.

Anne was still weak herself from a recent winter fever, but she felt well enough to travel. It was vexing that her returning health coincided with Ned's decline to frustrate their plans for the festivities. Aware that Richard would be bitterly disappointed if they could not join him, she delayed making the final decision until the last possible moment.

One morning the rain ceased, and the weather turned frosty, the scent of snow in the air but, encouraged by the blue sky, Anne ventured into the garden, well-wrapped against the wind. She surveyed her summertime idyll now petrified by the cold. Frozen waterfalls hung from the mouths of the gargoyles adorning the fountain, the water prevented from reaching the bowl of ice beneath. In the summer, the birds came here to bathe and splash but today the garden was deserted, a ghostly contrast to warmer days.

Frost rimed grass and dead flower stalks stood as tall, stiff sentinels but as she walked among them, many sweet memories lingered along the pathways. It seemed only yesterday that she had sat in this very spot with Isabel, George and Richard discussing her father's fury at Edward's marriage to Elizabeth.

In hindsight, it was easy to pinpoint that day as the beginning of all their troubles, and she realised now how right her father had been to be angry. She had been just eight years old when the king made his unwise marriage and ever since she'd been tossed hither and thither, victim of Edward's foolish choice.

How extraordinary that his actions could have such far-reaching consequences.

Anne sighed, mourning for the lost, happy days of childhood. The weak sunshine, that until now had shielded the worst of the chill, sank behind a cloud. She was just deciding to return to the hall when she heard a footstep on the gravel path. She looked up to find John had joined her. He bowed over her hand before bestowing a kiss on it. She patted the turf seat beside her, and he carefully placed his gauntlets down before joining her.

'I hope you are not sitting on the bare earth, Anne. It's very damp, and you don't want another chill. Elayne sent me to fetch you; she said you had taken quite enough air for one day.'

They laughed at the ease with which the serving girl controlled the household.

'I was just about to come in but, you needn't worry, I do have a cushion look.'

She lifted her skirt to reveal the thick padding on which she sat, and John, while nodding approval, looked about the garden.

'It's strange how the garden is so decrepit in the wet months of November or October, and yet be so elegant during the freezing months of December and January. The frost lends it a sort of dignity. It doesn't seem possible that just a few short weeks ago we were out here playing chess in the sunshine.'

'It seems an age to me,' sighed Anne. 'But I expect that is because I miss your father.'

'Anne, I have been thinking,' John turned toward her, frowning. 'You needn't stay here for Christmas. I know how much you want to be with Father, and I think you should go. Perhaps you worry unduly about Ned's health. I was never strong as a boy but, once I passed the age of ten or eleven, I began to thrive and grow, and Father says it was much the same with him. I will stay here and ensure Ned enjoys the festivity, and I know that Katherine will stay too, if I ask her. Why don't you go and enjoy yourself with Father? You are the Queen after all, and your place is there. We can join you when the weather improves, and Ned is stronger. Go, Anne, we will look after him and Jayne will too. In fact, we will have such a good time, we won't miss you at all.'

Anne, encouraged by his teasing, felt her reluctance begin to shift as she contemplated travelling to court alone. Both John and Katherine doted on their younger brother, and she had every faith that Jayne would make sure that everything went well. The possibility of joining Richard after all, brought colour to her cheeks. She stifled a growing thrill of excitement.

'Do you know, John, I think maybe I might. If you would be so kind as to forfeit your Christmas at court, I would trust you to ensure Ned enjoys himself. I must speak to him first, but I think it is possible that I shall go to Westminster after all.'

The Palace of Westminster - December 1483

Dusk was falling when Anne's travelling party arrived at Westminster, and she was shown into Richard's presence. When she entered the warm fug of the hall, he held her for a long moment while the fatigue of the journey, and the misery of the last few months melted away. When Richard finally released her, he drew her closer to the hearth, where she removed her gloves and accepted the warm cup of mead.

'Oh Richard, I am so sorry I didn't bring the children with me, but Ned is not yet strong enough for such a rigorous journey, and John and Kathy wanted to stay and keep him company. Once I knew he would be well-cared for, and was happy for me to come, I could not stay away. I have missed you so much.'

She cupped his cheek and, holding her head between his hands, Richard placed his lips on hers.

'Oh, I think I shall do well enough with just you for company, my sweet. Come, come here and let me look at you.'

That first evening, since Anne was not ready to face the frantic festivities in the hall, they dined alone in their chamber, discussing the missed weeks that were now mercifully behind them. Richard sent his attendants away, and locked the chamber door, shutting out the world and all its distractions. Faint strains of music crept up from the hall and the chamber was warm, cushions heaped before the fire. But, despite their hunger, they did not make love straight away but fell instead to discussing the events of the past few months.

Anne listened as Richard agonised over Buckingham's betrayal. He failed to understand how ambition could supersede affection and loyalty and found it impossible to reconcile Harry's 'hail fellow well met' attitude with murder and deceit.

'I cannot comprehend the depths of his duplicity, Anne, and it is impossible to describe. I thought he loved me, but it seems I am gullible.' Richard cleared his throat. 'When Harry discovered the boys had been moved to safety, he lost no time in trying to blacken my name. He let it be known that I had ordered the boys slain.'

Anne dropped her knife.

'What?' she exclaimed. 'And did anyone believe it? Why would you do such a thing? What motive did he put forward?'

'What motive do you think? To secure my position on the throne. He declared my claim was unjust, and to improve my stability Edward and Richard were murdered. Even after everything he has done, this last blow was hard to take. Can he truly have hated me so much? Did he hate me from the beginning, or did it grow on further acquaintance? I don't know what to think, but sometimes I wish I had agreed to see him before his execution, just to force the truth from his God-forsaken mouth.'

Anne placed her hand on his knee.

'Hush Richard, it doesn't matter now. He was a fool and a liar, and you should waste no time on him. Our concern must be the boys; now the rebellion has been put down, we must show them to the people. That will end the stupid rumours.'

Richard rose and fetched a bowl of fruit from the table, rejoining Anne by the fire.

'Is that wise though, Anne? Is that the right thing to do? I have given it a lot of thought and I am still undecided. If I parade them through the streets it will make them a target for Tudor and his adherents. I'm damned if I'll be manipulated into action by Lancastrian lies. I am tempted to leave them where they are. Brampton says they are happy, and we know they are safe; even more so now so many believe them dead. The only drawback in leaving them in hiding, is that their absence adds credence to Buckingham's lies …and marks me as a murderer.'

Anne got up and began to pace about the room. She chewed her lip, frowning in concentration, her loose hair gleaming in the firelight. He watched her until she turned to face him.

'What we must do, is to convince those who matter that the boys are safe but keep the others in the dark. We must prevent the rumour from turning our loyal followers against us.' She paused for a moment, her mouth opening a little as a thought occurred to her. 'Oh, Richard. What about Elizabeth? She must be distraught. I have no love for her, but she is a mother and deserves to know the truth. We do not want to force her into action against us and if she knows they are alive, it may even tempt her and her daughters out of sanctuary... Hmm, I see the predicament though: Henry Tudor will be encouraged to contest your throne if he thinks only you stand in his way. He may even use the lie to his advantage and rally men to his side. No, I think we should ignore the rumours and carry on as usual. Let Tudor go to the devil but, if we can, we must confide in Elizabeth and convince her to keep quiet for the boys' sakes.'

Richard reached for her hand.

'My love, you should have been a politician; your keen mind far outstrips my other advisors. So, do you think we should pay Elizabeth a visit and use the boys to lure her back to court? It's a fine idea, and it may well work. Her lengthy stay in Sanctuary is a continuing embarrassment. We must give it more thought but first ...' He stood up and took her hand, as though in farewell, 'I have a little business which requires the attention of my chief advisory minister.'

Anne's face fell and he smiled, pulling her closer. It was not until he begun to unlace her kirtle that she realised which chief minister he referred to, and they fell laughing on to the bed.

Safe in the knowledge that Ned was enjoying the festivities at Middleham, Anne and Richard celebrated their first Christmas as King and Queen in full measure.

'Richard!' Anne exclaimed, looking up from the list of his preparations. 'Why all the extravagance?'

'Nothing is too good for you, sweeting, and besides, the court expects it. You wouldn't want me labelled as a miser king, would you?'

Anne held up a length of rich brocade that was to be made up into her gown. She owned many fine clothes but none as splendid as this. Richard was pulling out all the stops, raising money from the London merchants to finance the festivities. It was a frivolous side of him she had rarely witnessed. Anne only wished that Ned was there to share it. He would have loved it; all the children would have.

On Christmas morning Richard presented Anne with the finest collection of gems she had ever seen. 'I will be the envy of everyone,' she cried, holding a string of stones against her throat.

'Of course, you will. You are the Queen.' Richard loved to please her. It was well worth the huge debt he'd run up with the mercer to see her joy. With the rebellion quelled, he was determined to fill the period of peace to make it a celebration to remember. That Christmas, the music rang every bit as loudly as it had at the court of the late King Edward. Anne, in order to preserve her strength for the nightly celebrations, found lengthy afternoon naps necessary. Unused to such rich food, and such quantities of wine, she felt queasy and fat, although still as slim as a wand. Over the yuletide both Anne and Richard found themselves the worse for drink and woke with tender heads the following morning.

They woke sluggish, wishing they'd shown more restraint. As the sun rose on the Feast of Stephen they curled together beneath thick blankets and watched the ice on the windows melt as the heat from the fire slowly warmed the room. As they made slow, languid love in the comfort of their royal bed. A few days later, as they broke their fast, news arrived of a ceremony that had taken place on Christmas day in the Cathedral of Rennes.

Across the channel, Henry Tudor, had sworn on oath that when he took possession of the English throne, he would marry the Princess Elizabeth; a marriage that would unite the houses of York and Lancaster and bring an end to civil war in England.

'He really means to invade, doesn't he?' Anne looked up from the letter.

'He will receive a poor welcome.'

'You must marry Elizabeth to somebody else, quickly. That will prevent those who distrust us from flocking to his banner.'

Richard took the letter, tossed it into the flames where they watched the edges curl and shrivel, the scrawled words disappearing.

'Those who do not love me are welcome to join him in exile.'

Anne knelt up on the bed watching as Richard pulled on his boots.

'That is foolish prideful talk.' She said, 'Remember the adage, love thine enemy.'

'Why don't we invite Tudor to court, so I can embrace him publicly.'

'That is ridiculous, Richard, you twist my words.'

Ignoring Anne's advice to marry Elizabeth off quickly, Richard made plans for his first opening of Parliament which was to commence on the twenty-third of January. As a result of the king's continued refusal to assist Brittany in its disputes with France there had been recent conflict at sea, and Richard was seeking to expand his navy to protect the interests of English seaman. It was unusual for a monarch to show concern for the well-being of menials, but he issued a strict warning that made certain that the fishing fleets of East Anglia would be secured.

'for as much as we understand that certain of you intend hastily to depart towards Iceland, not purveyed of wafters for your surety…we…straightly charge…that none of you severally depart out of any of our havens…without our licence first had to do so; and thereupon, that ye gather and assemble yourselves in such one of our havens or ports…as ye shall think most convenient, well harnessed and apparelled for you own surety, and so for to depart all together toward

Humber, to attend there upon our ships of Hull as your wafters, for the surety of you all; and that ye dissever not without tempest of weather compel you…'

Although much beset with the problems of the realm, and attending to matters he wished to raise in Parliament, Richard still avoided coming to a decision about the eldest of the bastard princesses. He did, however, make time to accompany Anne on the difficult visit to Elizabeth Woodville, who still refused to leave the Sanctuary of St Peters.

Although it was early afternoon, the sun was already sinking toward the west. They trod their way through a light powdering of snow that covered the cobbled yard. As they entered the dimly lit hall, they shook flakes from their cloaks and, after removing their hoods and gloves, were ushered into a sparsely furnished room. A fire sulked in the grate and standing close to it, still proudly beautiful despite her sorrow, was Edward's dowager Queen. She did not speak until Richard kissed her hand, as if she was still the Queen.

'Elizabeth,' he said, guardedly 'I hope you are well.'

'Do you indeed? You must have had a change of heart, I heard you wished me and mine dead ...'

Realising she was not going to make things easy; Richard and Anne were immediately on the back foot. The once-merry silver eyes rested coldly on the faces of her enemies. Richard glanced at Anne who squared her shoulders and stepped forward.

'You are looking well, Elizabeth. Where are your daughters? We had hoped to see them too.'

'My daughters are within; their confounded weeping makes my headache. Fools that they are, they cannot overcome their grief for their dead brothers.'

Elizabeth directed this at Richard, leaving no doubt that she had heard, and gave credence to, the rumours. Neither the king nor queen spoke. Elizabeth moved from the fire and began to stalk around the chamber as she let her tirade continue.

'How does it feel, my Lord, to sit on your murdered nephew's throne? I would advise against getting too comfortable, it's a precarious seat.'

Richard, never comfortable with women, least of all this one, fumbled for a response but Anne forestalled him.

'That is unjust, Elizabeth,' she cried. 'Richard has never wished you or yours any harm. We came here today to extend our friendship. Whatever has happened in the past is done. Can we not look forward to a more positive future?'

Elizabeth curled her lip, noting Anne's queenly garb and new assurance. She laughed harshly,

'Oh, how the little Neville mouse roars. Emboldened by your stolen status, no doubt. Do not presume to speak to me of friendship. Do you not comprehend what this Herod … this murderer of babes has done?'

Elizabeth had more to say but a quaver in her voice gave her pause; she swallowed her weakness and glared at Anne.

'Richard is no Herod, Elizabeth; you know that really, don't you? Surely you recall his love and loyalty for Edward and see the rumours for what they are. Richard would never harm his brother's children, or any child. It was always you who sought the enmity between us, Elizabeth, not the other way round. Your children are safe; you have my word.'

The dowager queen raised her wretched head, searching Anne's face for the truth. Then she switched her gaze to Richard and, shaking off Anne's hand, approached the king and stared into his eyes. When she finally spoke, it was with clenched teeth, as if she were a woman of ice.

'Then show them to me. Prove to me that you have not had them butchered. Let me see their faces and hear their voices. Let me embrace them and feel their warm breath on my cheek.'

Richard flinched from the foul breath of her destroyed hopes and threw his gauntlets onto the table.

'I can show them to you, Elizabeth. I can take you to them, and you can remain with them if you wish; but first I must have some assurances. I will not make a move to assist you if you refuse to help me in return. Come, let us sit down and discuss this in a civil manner. Summon your woman to bring refreshment while I tell you of the Lord Bastards' health and whereabouts.'

And so, in the dim, ill-heated chamber at St Peter's, Richard and Anne feasted with their enemy.

Gipping, Suffolk - February 15th, 1484

Every jolt of the horse litter on the journey into Suffolk intensified the ache in Anne's bones. She had been reluctant to join the small entourage that accompanied the king and Elizabeth, but Richard had personally requested that she be present. Unable to deny him, she reluctantly agreed to act as a buffer between him and Elizabeth.

Intrepid on the battlefield, Richard lacked the weapons to deal with an embittered woman. Elizabeth, reluctant to relinquish her conviction that Richard was her enemy, had at least relented slightly in her attitude toward Anne. In truth, the close confines of the horse litter made it difficult to ignore one another, but horseback was not an option.

Richard insisted that Elizabeth remain concealed behind the heavy leather curtains, unwilling that any should see her and question the reason for the journey. Anne, of course, was still too unwell to negotiate the mired roads on horseback but she managed to suffer both the discomfort of the journey, and proximity to Elizabeth.

They conversed on neutral subjects and Anne learned a little more of Elizabeth. Her love for her daughters was outstripped by that for her sons. Anne, who would have defied Heaven for such a family, could not understand the ease with which Elizabeth bartered her girls for knowledge of the boys. It had been a simple matter for Richard to secure her agreement to the exchange. Her daughters would return to court and Elizabeth would be allowed to see her sons and remain with them for a time at the home of Sir James Tyrell in Suffolk.

Tyrell was one of Richard's most trusted Knights, and had willingly agreed to allow Brampton, the Dowager Queen and the Lords Bastard to reside at his manor until such time as permanent arrangement could be made for their safety. As the king, queen and the dowager passed beneath the mighty oaks that marked the boundaries of his small estate, Tyrell appeared in the courtyard to greet them. Sir James was a small man, quick of movement and earnest of nature; he could not do enough for his King and had welcomed Brampton and his charges regardless of the danger to himself. He waited as Richard dismounted, then he kneeled in the drizzling rain.

'Get up Man' ordered Richard. 'I am here as your friend, not your King.'

Turning to assist Anne and Elizabeth, from the litter, he made the formal introductions. Anne smiled her usual sweet smile, remarking what a particularly lovely house he had, while Elizabeth paid him little heed. Still unsure that she hadn't walked into a trap, she scanned the bailey which was more or less deserted.

'I gave the household a day off as you requested,' Tyrell explained as he led them toward the house. 'Refreshments are waiting inside.'

Richard laid his hand on Tyrell's arm.

'I think, my friend, we should not keep the dowager queen waiting. Where are the boys? Can you take us to them now? We can refresh ourselves later.'

Sir James bowed and swept his arm wide.

'I believe they are in the orchard with Brampton, Your Grace. They spend most mornings there, practising their aim. Would you be so gracious as to follow me?'

He led them through a stone archway, taking a gravelled path to the rear of the property and through the gardens where a bent old man filled a wheeled barrow with sticks and leaves. Another gate took them from the formal gardens to a sodden orchard, where two boys were shooting at the butts, their bright garments splashing colour onto the chilly, damp day.

Elizabeth drew in her breath and halted, a hand to her mouth.

Edward was the first to turn. He stopped, stock still but did not approach; it was as if he was unable to believe she was there.

Young Richard had just drawn his bow and, as they watched, let lose an arrow which sailed out of sight, missing the target by a mile.

'Oh Bugger,' he exclaimed cheerfully. 'I missed.'

Then he turned, noticed his brother staring and followed the line of vision to where his mother stood like a statue at the orchard gate.

'Mother!' he cried, his joy enough to break the harshest heart. The sound of his voice seemed to release Elizabeth from a spell and she all but flew across the grass to meet him, sinking to her knees in the February mud. Her scarlet skirts splashed against the winter meadow as, abandoning her ambition, she grabbed and held on tightly to her sons.

March 1484

Edward's daughters burst from Sanctuary like unleashed larks, filling the court with song and laughter. The seamstresses were set to work fashioning new gowns for the girls whose old clothes were bursting at the seams. As they surged about the familiar halls, the younger courtiers roused themselves from ennui to welcome them, for even the taint of bastardy could not erase their beauty. Their royal blood showed in their self-assurance, their intellect and bearing, and Elizabeth, the eldest at eighteen, was unmistakably her father's daughter.

Cecily, at fifteen, was more like her mother in appearance but studious of manner and often reprimanded Bess for what she termed her 'hoydenish ways'. But the elder girl, bastard or not, was euphoric to be free and delighted to learn that her brothers lived.

If Elizabeth was aware of Tudor's oath to marry her, she seemed untroubled by it. He was far away and unlikely to triumph over Richard. Besides, life was for dancing and dance she intended to do.

The younger girls, Margaret, who at twelve was almost old enough to attend court formalities, and Anne, who was only nine, emulated their sisters, eager for the day when they'd be old enough to dance before the king and queen. Katherine and Bridget, who were little more than babies, were installed in the royal nursery where Anne visited them often, for, as far as she was concerned, there could never be too many children.

At the end of February, the court began a slow journey to Nottingham, the heart of the kingdom. Although the king refused to discuss it, Tudor posed a continuing threat and, since his most likely point of arrival was Wales, Nottingham was central and the best place from which to deal swiftly with invasion, should it come.

In early March, the court left the creamy cloisters of Cambridge, where Anne and Richard were pleased to bestow a variety of endowments and gifts on the University. Their stay there was so enjoyable that they tarried until mid-March, when they departed for Chancellor Russell's manor at Buckden, before continuing to the towering fortress of Nottingham Castle.

Nottingham Castle - April 1484

Anne had never liked Nottingham. As the cavalcade rode into the shadow of the keep, she could not help but shudder as the oppressive towers stole the Spring sunshine and plunged them into gloom. The castle was situated above the River Leen and was a magnificent monument to the power of the early medieval kings. Until recently, the fortress had entirely lacked home comforts, so Anne was relieved when she saw the sumptuous new royal apartments added by Edward at the end of his reign.

Richard showed Anne the new windows he'd had installed after seeing Francis at Minster Lovell, and together they admired the apartments, now illuminated with daylight from sunrise until sunset.

'It makes such a difference,' she said. 'There's so much light now.' At the back of Anne's mind, lingered the knowledge that Nottingham was much closer to Middleham than Westminster Palace. They had already laid plans for Ned to join them as soon as his health improved, which shouldn't be long now.

Jayne sent almost daily reports of his increasing strength, and he was expected to join the court by midsummer. Anne had selected the perfect apartment for him and within days of their arrival, she and her ladies fell to arranging them, re-hanging tapestries and drapes and ordering new furniture and tableware for the royal quarters. As Queen, Anne was no longer expected to personally control the running of the household, but she missed the domesticated side of her old life. It was dull to have so much leisure time and soon grew bored with her embroidery, reading and indulging in idle chatter with her ladies. Refurbishing the apartments provided a welcomed distraction.

Princess Elizabeth was a great help when it came to design; she had a flair for style and an eye for colour that Anne entirely lacked. She helped Anne select new hangings for the royal bedchamber and co-ordinated the bedding to compliment the wall-hangings. The queen was thrilled with the result and, as a reward Anne ordered a similar refurbishment for the chambers that Elizabeth shared with Cecily.

The ladies were clustered around a large table which was heaped with samples of velvet and silks; their voices growing higher and louder as they became more animated in deciding which material was the most suitable for the chamber in question.

'Look at the embroidery on this linen; I have never seen anything so fine.'

Anne handed the sample to her niece and continued to rummage through the pile.

'And this velvet, have you ever felt any so soft; the nap is so deep and warm. I really think you should have this one, Bess; the range of colours is quite extraordinary. Tell me, Sir, do you have this in blue?'

The draper moved forward and examined the cloth that Anne held out for his inspection.

'We do indeed, Your Grace, it should be here somewhere.'

He sorted through the material and then exclaimed, 'Oh, here it is, your Grace, it has slipped from the table onto the floor.'

Bess took the swatch of cloth, laughing.

'Thank you Sir, we are quite overcome by the choice on offer. It is a lovely blue, Anne, in between turquoise and aqua-marine, I am tempted to choose it. Does it suit my complexion?'

She held it against her face, rubbing it on her cheek, well aware that the hue enhanced her eyes, making them seem bluer and brighter.

Anne was perplexed.

'But Bess, it doesn't have to suit you, it's for bed hangings, not a gown.'

'And why should my bedcovers not suit me as well as a gown should? You never know, I may have a suitor who creeps into my chamber of a night.'

'Bess!' exclaimed the scandalised Cecily. 'Don't say such things. You of all people should know the dangers of gossip. You cannot afford a spot of scandal to be attached to your name if you wish to marry well. She has no such thing, Your Grace. I share her bed and I think I would know.'

Elizabeth put the material down on the pile and pulled a face at her sister.

'It was in jest, Cecily. Anne knows that. For heaven's sake, if I truly had a lover do you think I'd boast about it in front of the queen and the royal draper? I wish you would cultivate a sense of humour, 'there's none so dull as a preacher,' as father used to say.'

Anne never liked to see dissent between the sisters and intervened.

'I'm sure everyone here knew it for a joke, but Bess you must be careful, for your sister is right, people do love to gossip, and things are all too easily misrepresented. Your honour must be sacrosanct.'

'I know, but it is dull to be thought so chaste. Wouldn't you love to be swept off your feet by love?'

Seeing the dreamy expression on Bess' face, Anne smiled at her romantic notions. She had never had time in her own youth to yearn for such things because it had been snatched away. But, after a few moments' consideration, she brightened and patted Elizabeth's hand.

'Love didn't quite pass me by. I was once rescued from danger by a handsome knight … ah, and I believe that very knight is about to join us now.'

When Richard opened the door he was met by a gale of feminine laughter. He stopped abruptly and proceeded cautiously, uncertain what he had done to occasion such mirth. Taking his arm, Anne led him to view the velvets on the table.

'Which hue do you prefer, Richard, the blue or the green?'

After fingering the fabric for a few moments, he held up a swatch of sea green velvet.

'The green. I like the green, it reminds me of my lady's eyes.'

He kissed Anne on the cheek before holding his hands toward the fireplace, turning his head to watch them. After a while, it became plain he wished to speak to his wife in private and at her signal, the ladies scurried away, the draper collected his wares and bowed deeply before taking his leave. Richard looked around, noting the new hangings and re-arranged furniture.

'I like what you've done in here, Anne, it's very homely now, a great improvement.'

'I'm glad you like it, Richard. It has not been easy to make the decisions, but Bess has been a great help, she has an eye for this kind of thing. It has been fun sorting out fabrics and trimmings. I have suggested that we make similar changes to the girls' chamber. Bess liked the blue so I shall order the fabrics and we can occupy ourselves with sewing during the next few weeks. We also need to make sure Ned's chamber is finished, if we are to remain here for a while.'

Richard looked from the window, out across the bailey which bustled with activity; he yawned.

'I feel weary, Anne, I really think I need to rest before tonight's banquet, all the upheaval has sapped my energy.'

Anne knew this was just his way of encouraging her to rest before the evening, and agreeing she was also very tired, she allowed him to lead the way to bed.

Tired after the excesses of the night before, Anne rose late, finding Richard's side of the mattress had cooled long before she opened her eyes. She had a faint recollection of him kissing her and slipping away earlier that morning.

She sat up and broke her fast while Elayne stoked the fire, warmed some water, and laid out her gown for the day. As she worked Elayne chattered about the preparations for Ned's arrival and, as she passed the window, she paused to look out.

'There's a big cart just trundled over the drawbridge. It's piled so high I'm amazed the load haven't toppled off. The driver is climbing down now and looking around scratching his bald pate waiting for someone to tell him where to unload. He's an odd-lookin' sort, I must say. Oh, here comes Jem to tell him where to go. Oh, I had expected them to head for the kitchens, but they are carrying crates into the downstairs hall. Do you think it's that Venetian glassware you ordered for table. Ho! That got you out of bed, didn't it? Come here then, let me help you with your gown.'

Sometime later, Anne and her ladies were in the great hall levering open cases of fine glassware; the castle dogs sniffed around, intrigued by the smells that issued from the packing straw littering the floor. Taking a glass by its delicate stem, Anne held it up to the light and twirled it in her fingers, sending rainbows of colour flitting around the hall. The bowl of the glass was etched with the words, 'Ricardus Rex,' decorated with the blanc sanglier, and Richard and Anne's coats of arms. She laughed, pointing out the fine craftsmanship. The women clustered around, exclaiming as further treasures and finely wrought cutlery was unpacked.

Anne heard his voice the moment Richard and Francis Lovell entered the hall. She nudged Anna to alert her to their presence and was pleased to see Francis make directly for his wife. She hoped her strategy to bring the couple closer was working, she was sure that once they were properly reconciled, children would follow, to strengthen the union further.

It was immensely important to Anne that her friends were as happy as she and Richard. She sat on the dais and surveyed the gathering, listening to the happy hubbub, tired as usual but happy to be there. She raised the glass once more to enjoy the lights playing on the walls and, as she did so, her eye caught that of a stranger entering the great hall. Something in his demeanour made Anne pause. Or did she know him? Elayne went forward to greet him; Anne saw the smile slide from her maid's face, as she clapped a hand across her mouth and scanned the hall in search of her mistress.

A shrim of fear stirred in Anne's belly.

The boy was no stranger; she had seen him often. He was the eldest son of the steward at Middleham, she had known him since he was a boy. A pulse began to thump loudly in her ears as Elayne led him through the throng in the direction of the king. As she watched the silent mummery unfold, she found it difficult to breathe. When the healthy outdoor pallor drained from Richard's face, Anne whimpered. She wanted to run away, run and run.

She could not face this. Not this!

Anne stood up, backed away behind her chair. She shook her head and held out her hands, denying them the right to approach but Elayne snatched her wrist and held it fast.

'Oh, my lady, oh, my lady,' she murmured as Richard, his face parchment white, struggled to find the words to tell her their son was dead. A crescendo exploded in her head, and a fine Venetian glass fell in shards at her feet.

Coverham Church – April 1484

The leaden skies wept, forming puddles on the compacted earth beneath the tree where Anne hid. Her shoes were soaked and muddy, and the bottom of her robe mired with muck. She could feel nothing, neither grief nor pain, nor cold. As the meaningless words of the priest became unbearable, unable to stand the oppressiveness of the church, she had fled. Her departure had been so sudden and so swift she had easily eluded her ladies but once outside, finding nowhere to run to, she had hidden herself beneath the cavernous ancient yews in the church yard. She had played here often as a child with Isabel, Richard and George. Her attendants would never think to seek her there, but Richard would.

The canopy of the yews had grown together to form a womb-like space, a secret, silent place unknown to adults. Anne huddled miserably, the branches encompassing and shielding her from the harshness of the world. The sharp smell of resin evoked memories of Isabel and Richard and she wished they were with her; she craved comfort, anything that would salve the agony in her heart.

If she could just be alone with Richard.

Since the news arrived from Middleham, they had been kept apart by the suffocating presence of well-meaning friends, advisors who urged him he must get another son. If only she could cocoon herself with him, away from the world and have time to heal, but Richard was besieged by matters of state.

War with Scotland was imminent, the threat of invasion intensified by the death of Richard's heir. Richard resisted naming his successor, but Anne knew she would never provide him with a replacement. He would take another wife. Inadequacy increased her grief.

How proud Richard had been as he invested Ned with the title Prince of Wales; how proud she had been but now the memory was a knife in her heart.

The recollection of his beaming face rose before her, intensifying the pain that burned within. She coughed, trying to stifle the sound lest it alert them to her hiding place. Bands of pain threatened to suffocate her as she fought to repress it. In the churchyard, her ladies were calling her name, running back and forth in search of her but, although guilty at the anguish she was causing, she did not answer.

She crouched beneath the Yew, pulling her knees tightly to her chest and resting her cheek on them. Back and forth, she rocked, trying to block out the vision of Ned laid low in his tomb, the suffocating lid shutting him away forever.

After a time, the voices faded, and silence fell. She wiped her eyes with the back of her hand, streaking dirt across her face and then held her breath as the great trees began to stir and rustle. Someone was coming. She lifted her head and glared at the intruder.

'I thought I might find you here.'

Richard ducked beneath the tunnel of branches and brushed twigs and dirt from his fine velvet coat. He looked around. 'It's a while since we've been in here. I don't recall the entrance being so unaccommodating.'

Humour was Richards usual method of defraying Anne's moods but today, it didn't work. She managed a watery smile as he sat beside her, but feigned humour couldn't conceal his grief. She let him take her hand.

'I am so very sorry, Richard but I just couldn't bear another word of condolence or listen to the priest rattling on about God's will. If it is God's will that we must lose our son, then he is no God of mine.'

Richard, startled by her irreverence, refrained from contradicting her. Instead, he kissed the back of her knuckles.

'Your women are worried about you, Anne; it is no small thing to have mislaid the Queen of England. We can rest here for a while, but I think we should put them at their ease soon. Come, let me hold you.'

She laid her head on his shoulder, the closeness relieving the tension but none of the grief.

'If only we could have some time alone.' she complained. 'Can someone else not see to state matters for you? We need to grieve; our sorrow is compounded by their interference.'

She sniffed and wiped her nose on the edge of her velvet sleeve, making Richard smile.

'What no kerchief, Anne? You never change do you,? I think that's why I love you so very much. I know, whatever happens, you will always be the same little Anne.'

'And inside, you are still that frightened little boy I met so long ago … Oh, Richard do you think Ned is frightened? Do you think he grieves for us as we do for him? Can he see us now …in our grief?'

Richard grew very still; the only movement was his hand stroking her back.

'I don't know, Anne. I wish I did, but there is one thing I do know and that is, if he can see our sorrow, it will grieve him. We must try to find a way forward. He would want us to be happy and live as full a life as we can. We should focus on the joy he gave us. I think he would want us to look forward to future...'

She leapt to her feet.

'Sons, Richard? Is that what you were going to say? Future Sons? Well, I think it is evident that I am not going to produce you with an heir and, if that is what you require, then you had better look elsewhere for a wife.'

'Anne!' Richard faced her. 'How can you? I was not going to say 'sons.' I have a wife, and I had a fine son. There is nobody in heaven or earth that could replace either of you. I want no more children if it means parting with you; you are my life, Anne, surely you know that. All this means nothing without you, nothing.'

Anne threw herself at him.

'Forgive me, Richard, I cannot think straight. I know you love me, and I know you will not set me aside. But I've heard them whispering about your lack of an heir, and I can see no possible way of providing you with one.'

Richard kissed the top of her head as she wiped her eyes.

'Silly girl, I have named John as my successor. He is a fine boy and will do well with further instruction. He is even now on his way from Westminster to join us. Come, kiss me and let's hear no more of it. We must return before they call out a full search. Perhaps I should order an entrance to be cut into the tree before we next have occasion to visit. It would save our backs.' Anne laughed shakily and stooped to follow Richard along the dark green tunnel and into the secluded churchyard.

The rain had ceased and as the disarrayed King and Queen brushed at their soiled finery and looked for their attendants, the ominous dark clouds were chased away by the emerging sun.

July 1484

When Anne looked back on other hardships, she scorned at her old naïve self. How ignorant she had been of real pain; her father's betrayal of York had been the worst thing imaginable until she had been forced to marry Edward of Lancaster. Her imprisonment in the stews of London had been torturous until replaced by the horror of losing Isabel. Her separations from Richard were unendurable until she faced the permanent loss of their son. It wasn't altogether comforting to acknowledge present grief would surely be soothed by greater tragedy.

But now, her pain was so consuming a greater was impossible to imagine. In many ways, Richard was luckier than she; he was used to being separated from Ned and he had the demands of the throne to distract him from grief. He healed much faster than Anne, not because he cared less but because he had other things. He began to sleep again and regain his appetite and, although a degree of sadness remained, he was able to look forward, to plan for the future.

But Anne's loss grew keener every day; she didn't even want to look forward because Ned was in the past. The cry of a servant's child in the bailey made her look up, forgetting for a moment that it could not be him; the laughter of the court children caught at her heart. It was impossible to forget. Unable to sleep, she was constantly tired and, as her appetite dwindled, so did her health. In the end, she was not even able to keep down what little food she did manage to swallow.

When Elayne brushed her hair, large clumps came away in her hand, and Anne was forced to use a hairpiece. In Richard's company, she made an effort, and he was unaware how rapidly her health was declining. He knew she was frail and frequently ailing, but he put it down to lack of sprits rather than sickness. In a bid to cheer her, he decided she needed a change of air and when he announced he was going to Scarborough, Anne summoned the strength to accompany him. She even managed to appear enthusiastic even though the visit wasn't to be all pleasure; nothing ever was. While they were there, Richard intended to review his fleet, checking and increasing ship numbers and restocking the equipment.

The port was roughly sixty-five miles from Middleham and, although Anne had travelled much farther in the past, the journey depleted what little strength she had. But it was pleasant though to rest her face on the edge of the horse litter and watch the beautiful countryside of Yorkshire pass by.

The long grass was green and lush, spotted with wildflowers, and irrigated by the furious waters of the River Swale. The moors were wild and windswept, and the curtains of the litter snapped vigorously in the stiff breeze. Richard rode beside Anne's litter, keeping her company and pointing out landmarks for much of the way. But when the movement of the horses lulled her to sleep, Richard spurred his horse and relished the revitalising air of the moor. Once, she would have ridden on the pommel of his saddle, his arms tight around her, embracing the wildness of Yorkshire together, but now, he rode alone.

Scarborough Castle stood on a rocky crag, a guardian of the seas, impervious to wind and weather. Anne's tower apartments provided views of both land and sea that were unsurpassed by any other castle she had visited. Scarborough was untainted by any memory of her son, and the change of scenery was invigorating. She leaned from the high window, inhaling the salty air and feeling the sea breeze whipping blood into her cheeks. While her ladies made final adjustments to the comforts of the room, Elayne set refreshments on the table beside the bed.

'Come along, my lady, let's have that gown off and then you can get some sleep. If you are serious about joining the king for the feast this evening, you'll need all the rest you can get.'

Anne submitted to the removal of her gown and was glad to slip between the cool sheets with the covers pulled up to her chin. She coughed once or twice, prompting Elayne to bring a soothing drink of honey and camomile. Anne sipped the warm liquid and then slid back beneath the blankets; her limbs ached, and her chest hurt but the fresh air had restored her capacity for sleep, and she soon drifted off.

She was dreaming; the garden was beautiful, the grass lush and cool, and the birds that sang in the trees were brighter than any on earth had the right to be. As she wove her way through the slim trunks of young trees, Anne could hear childish laughter far ahead and she hurried toward it, eager to catch a glimpse of the children. At length, she came upon a daisy-starred clearing that thronged with infants; they had no need for playthings for they took pleasure from the beauty around them. Music issued from above and the children sang and laughed together. When they spied Anne peeping from behind a tree they summoned to her to play with them. She ran to join them but, as she drew near, they evaporated like mist, and she could not grasp them. She could not hold them.

She woke suddenly. Elayne was shaking her by the shoulder.

'Your grace, wake up, it's only a dream. Please wake up.'

Anne stirred and coughed.

'It's all right, Elayne, I am awake now. It was just a bad dream, that's all.'

But as the girl poured her another drink, Anne reflected that these days her life was like a bad dream, a dream from which she could not wake.

The summer passed slowly and uneventfully, Anne took less and less interest in the political problems that beset Richard, and her world grew small and self-contained. He insisted that they return to Nottingham which lay at the centre of England and made jurisdiction easier to manage. She did not voice it, but Anne was reluctant to return. She had been so happy there until she learned the news of Ned's death. Richard was almost back to his former self, comforted by his belief that Ned was with God in Heaven. But Anne, unable to rediscover her faith, remained resentful toward the God who had taken her only joy.

She knew she was damned if she did not at least go through the motions of devotion, but she could not reconcile herself to hypocrisy. She flipped through the pages of her book of hours and stared unmoved at the illuminated borders that celebrated God's greatness, but she was not moved to pray. She slammed the book shut when her reverie was interrupted by the entrance of her nieces and her chamber filled with laughter.

The girls were excited because the king had announced he would be spending the Christmas season at Westminster. It was yet only late September and the thought of Christmas reminded Anne of the afternoon in the gardens at Middleham when she and John had discussed the possibility of her attending court for the Christmas. *Was that truly just a year ago?*

She forgot how she'd ached with the longing to be with Richard and could not imagine why she had agreed to leave Ned, especially at Christmas. If that decision were hers to make again, she would decide very differently.

Cecily and Bess cavorted around the room with their skirts hitched, demonstrating the steps of a new dance. Bess spun away and bounced on the bed beside Anne.

'Oh, Aunt Anne, I can't wait. It has been an age since we've been to London, and all my old friends will be there. Can we order new gowns? Those that we have are far too shabby for Westminster.'

'I can't imagine the king denying you new gowns; you can summon the tire women to my chamber later and discuss with them what you should be wearing.'

'And what about you, Anne, surely you will have something new for the occasion. What would you like to wear?'

Anne, disinterested in the coming festivities, only desired peace, to sleep or read or to merely lie quietly and think of Ned.

'I don't know Bess. Why don't you choose something for me? I trust your taste implicitly and know if you make the choice, we will all look very fine.'

Westminster Palace - Christmas 1484

At Christmas 1484, the court took a self-conscious step from mourning into merriment, and the halls were decked with holly and ivy and the kitchens astir early in readiness for the enormous banquet planned for the evening. The courtiers, relieved to see the king's health and spirits restored, felt the need to celebrate. It was comforting that he was once more in full control of the realm and ready to face the future.

The Queen however, had not recovered and, although it was not voiced in the hearing of the king, many believed that she would not live to see another summer. She had made very little progress since her breakdown at the Prince of Wales's funeral; instead, she had plateaued somewhere between grief and despair.

The Christmas masses said, Anne passed the day quietly in her chamber, conserving her strength for the evening festivities. Richard and she exchanged gifts with the family, and, as an extra surprise, Bess presented Anne with a gorgeous gown, made up in the identical material to her own latest ensemble. The Queen pulled it from its wrappings.

'Oh Bess, it is lovely but I'm afraid I won't carry it off as well as you do.'

Bess came to sit beside her.

'You do like it, don't you, Anne? It seemed a good idea after seeing how much you liked mine, to have one made up for you the same. Once it was done, I began to have misgivings, but it will be fun won't it, to appear tonight, dressed like sisters, don't you think?'

Anne kissed her. 'It is perfect, Bess. I have never had a nicer, more thoughtful gift.' Katherine and Bridget were playing under the watchful eye of their elder sisters, Cecily and Margaret, and their chatter imbued the room with merriment. Isabel and George's children, Margaret and Edward, were still in the north but it was lovely to have her family around her. Anne was loath to leave it for the formality of the hall where she would be subjected to the scrutiny of the court.

The English courtiers and foreign ambassadors were always on the lookout for signs of another heir. The importance of the succession was paramount, but Anne resented the label of failure attached to her because she was barren. Sometimes, she imagined people wished her dead to allow the king to remarry and thus secure the Yorkist succession. Some husbands would not hesitate to set her aside in favour of a younger, fertile woman and the knowledge did little to ease her concern, despite the certainty that Richard was not one of them.

Later that evening, when her chamber window threw yellow light onto the snow-covered roofs below, Elayne helped her into the heavy brocade gown. It was a beautiful shade of blue, but it did not suit her. The hue served to deepen the shadows on her face and highlight the fever in her eyes. She neither liked or knew the thin stranger who peered back from her mirror and did not smile at her.

As Elayne slipped matching brocade slippers onto her feet, Richard entered the room.

'Why Anne, you look splendid. I am the luckiest king alive.'

The immovable lump blocking her throat made it difficult to joke but Anne made the effort for Richard's sake. He had no real idea of the extent of her misery, or the severity of the disease eating into her, and she had no wish to enlighten him.

'I think you flatter me, my Lord. Whatever can your motive be?'

They were laughing as they entered the noisy hall and, a moment later, Bess swept into view, sinking into an extravagant curtsey. She was stunning, the peacock blue of her dress brightening her already brilliant eyes and emphasising the clarity of her complexion. In comparison, Anne, in her identical gown, was washed out and tired. It was like seeing a spring morning beside a winter dusk, and the little joy Anne had managed to muster, drained away.

Her humiliation was so complete, she could barely respond. She watched Bess kneel before the king, and envied her youth, her generous bosom and plump shoulders, the unspoiled years that lay before her.

'Will you dance with me, Uncle? There is no-one so light on their feet as you.'

Anne's gut twisted, her throat tightening as Richard replied.

'I shall be delighted. It's a while since I was on the floor but, for your sake, I shall do my best.'

As her husband kissed the girl's hand and led her onto the floor, Anne's heart grew cold. When the music began and they moved together in the complicated steps of the dance, she could watch no longer. Signalling to Cecily, she asked to be helped to her chamber.

With each step along the corridor and up the twisting stairs, the restriction in Anne's throat grew tighter and tighter until, at last, she sprawled over the chamber threshold. Waving Cecily from her presence, she called for Elayne, shrieked for Jayne and tumbled onto the bed, feebly fumbling with the laces that trapped her in the detested gown.

Gasping for breath, she began to cough, barely able to pull herself onto her pillows. Her throat strained, her chest constricted, as she pressed a cushion over her mouth to stifle the sound.

Elayne had been celebrating below stairs and was quite the worse for drink when she staggered into her mistress' bedchamber. But sobering instantly when she saw the state of the queen, she hurried forward, gently lifted her by the shoulders, and saw the blood on the pillow.

Anne lay back, unable to prevent the tears trickling from her eyes to mingle in her hair. The sight of Bess dancing with Richard had shown quite vividly all she stood to lose. For the first time, she acknowledged death was not far away. Her end was close now. She felt it. It was as if a door had been opened and the reaper ushered into her presence. It was just a matter of time before Richard was left to the mercy of his enemies.

Elayne, unaware of the reason for Anne's distress, stroked her brow and murmured comfort as though she were soothing a child.

'Hush, my lover, hush. Don't take on so, the doctor will be here soon and make everything well. I've sent for the king too.'

'No.' Anne tried to struggle upright. 'I don't want him to see me, not like this. I'm old and ugly; how can he love me when I look like death?'

'Don't be silly, my Lady, you are twenty-nine and a little poorly, that's all. How are you supposed to look? Do you not know your lord better than that? He loves you. You will always be beautiful to him.'

Elayne's words did not soothe her, and Anne continued to cry. Elayne's brow furrowed. In all the years she had spent with Anne, she had never known her give into self-pity or wallow in useless tears. She recognised the approaching footsteps as those of the king but, instead of admitting him, she blocked his passage and requested a private audience.

'Now?' Richard frowned. 'But I want to see my wife.'

'I'd like to speak to you first, if you will forgive me for saying, Your Grace.'

Richard allowed her to lead him into an adjoining chamber. She wiped her red hands on her apron and looked him in the eye, her own face crumpled with concern.

'Your Grace, I've wanted to speak to you for a few weeks, but to my shame, I was afraid. There's no easy way to say this, so I'll be brief. The queen is ailing.'

Richard, uncomfortable in the face of the maid's directness, avoided her eye.

'Do you think I don't know that? Do you think I don't pray daily that she find the strength to overcome the burden of grief that rests so heavily on her? I don't know what more I can do. If she would only summon the strength to…'

'It isn't just grief she is suffering, Your Grace. She is sick, mortal sick! When I comb her hair great lumps of it come away in my hand, she orders me to hide it. And her cough, oh lord, how she coughs, and she is feverish all the time. There is no flesh on her bones and, although I've begged her see a doctor, she refuses. She thinks if she ignores it, it will go away. But I don't believe it will, my lord, and just now, when I attended her, there was blood on her face and on her pillow. And now she won't stop crying and …and I don't know what to do …'

The last words came on a sob and, as Richard flew from the room, Elayne scrubbed her eyes with the edge of her apron. The king hurtled into the corridor, and almost collided with the physician just emerging from Anne's chamber.

'Well?' he demanded. 'What is it that ails her?'

The doctor coughed discreetly, and suggested they retire to the privacy of Richard's chamber. He stood back with elegant dignity, waiting for the king to lead the way but Richard did not move.

'To be damned with that. What real privacy do monarchs ever have? Tell me, sir, about my wife. Is it true? Is she mortally sick?'

The doctor cleared his throat and fiddled with the lacing on his sleeve.

'I fear that may be so, Your Grace. I believe her to be suffering from a similar disease to that which took her sister. I believe it may be the consumption, Your Grace.'

A few moments later, when Richard entered his wife's chamber, Anne could not tell the bottom had just fallen from his world.

He sat beside her.

'I am sorry you are ailing but we will soon have you well.'

When she gave no answer, he groped for her hand and curled on the mattress beside her. They lay together for a long time and soon, she drifted off to sleep but Richard did not rest. He did not close his eyes at all but feasted them instead on Anne's flushed cheeks, still silvered with the tracks of tears.

'God forgive me for being so blind.'

The Palace of Westminster - March 1485

Like a plucked flower, Anne dallied on the verge of death. In the dark days of February, Richard's mother fought her way through the frigid English countryside to be with her son during Anne's last days. Together, they kept a vigil, Richard for once neglecting his royal duty to fulfil his more important role.

Ignoring the doctors' warnings of the risk of contagion, he refused to leave her, growing violently angry when they tried to insist, determined that Anne would not die alone.

As soon as Cecily saw her son's face, she feared for his reason, for his health and most of all, for his salvation. She spent long hours on her knees, asking the lord for mercy, both for Anne and for Richard. Why had God heaped such sorrow on him, the most blameless of her sons.

Toward the end, Anne seemed barely conscious but occasionally, she managed to rouse herself, eat a little, and even speak quietly to those the king allowed into her sanctum. Elayne was always present, tending to her needs and maintaining a continuous flow of chatter. But, each time Anne slipped into sleep, the girl escaped into the adjoining chamber and took refuge in anguished sobs.

The castle was consumed by weeping. For much of the time, Anne lay like the dead, but she was conscious of the people creeping around her. She heard their hushed conversations and worried for those she was leaving behind. When her mother came, Anne's heart broke afresh, and she fretted for Isabel's children who would be left without maternal kin. She agonised for the Lords bastard, and for John and Catherine who needed her so.

She tried to smile for Richard when he held her hand; she didn't want him to see her terror. His tension and suppressed desolation made her guilty at her desertion. Sometimes, when he could not hide his feelings and wept over her, she was glad when he left, and it was Cecily's turn to sit. She wanted to thank her for being there for Richard, but she could not find the words.

One afternoon in mid-March when Anne had not opened her eyes or stirred all day, Richard could bear no more. As he wept in his chair, the touch of his mother's hand halted his tears, and he turned toward the burning heat of the fire.

'I don't know what I shall do without her, Mother. I cannot imagine life without Anne.'

'I know, you loved her from the very first.'

'I remember it so clearly. I had just learned that Father and Edmund had been killed, their heads placed above Micklegate bar. I was afraid and alone and when Warwick took me to Middleham Castle it seemed huge and so did Warwick! But suddenly, there was Anne, smiling at me. She was just a little girl but somehow she was strong and so very sensible.' He gave a laugh that owed more to tears than mirth.

'Since those earliest days she has always guided me, and she's stood by me too. She is the one constant thing in my life, like the sunshine. Can you imagine a world without sunshine? That's how life will be without Anne. I nearly went mad when Lancaster took her. It provoked my greatest sin…'

Cecily, ever vigilant for sinners, broke into his reverie.

'Your greatest sin, Richard? How have you sinned?'

He glanced at his mother whom he knew worried for his soul and body in equal proportion and gave a mirthless snort of humourless laughter.

'Tis not so cruel a sin as I have been lately accused of, but it was a sin all the same. At Tewkesbury field, Mother, I took my revenge and slayed Edward of Lancaster because of what he had done to Anne.'

Cecily snorted dismissively.

'Oh Richard, it is no sin to kill in battle. He would not have hesitated to kill you, had he the chance. You should be thankful God saw fit to endow you with superior strength.'

Richard rubbed his eyes and with his voice sounding hollow in his own ears, continued.

'No, you don't understand, Mother. It wasn't during the battle, and Lancaster wasn't even armed. We captured a small gang of them as they tried to escape the field and were on our way to lock them up for the night so they could be executed the next morning. It was coming onto dusk when Lancaster suddenly made a bid to escape. He plunged, his wrists still tightly bound, down a steep embankment into the undergrowth. I followed, caught up with him easily, and soon had him held at the point of my sword. As I urged him back up the hill to join the rest of the prisoners he began to taunt me.'

Richard paused, wiped sweat from his forehead.

'His back was tight against a tree, totally at my mercy yet he taunted me, like a demon. I am only human, Mother, and I loved Anne just as much then as I do now. On that day, I had not even kissed her, and Lancaster began to describe how he'd taken her by force on their wedding night. He said that while he violated her, Anne called my name ...'

Richard ran his hands through his hair, got up and began to pace the chamber floor.

'I've killed many men, Mother, in battle and in the name of York, but I had never killed with hatred in my heart, as I did at that moment. As he stood there gloating, I knew she was lost to me. I hated him and I killed him, in cold blood. He was unarmed and yet I ran him through the heart and watched, with satisfaction as he died.'

Cecily, for once unsure how to comfort him, swallowed.

'What did Edward say?'

'I confessed my crime to him straight away, ready and willing to accept punishment but, typically, Edward just said, 'good riddance,' and treated me as though I'd done him a great favour. But the deed has stayed with me through the years. It is the worst of my crimes.'

Cecily decided, for the sake of his sanity, to make light of it, as Edward had done.

'Well, he asked for it, Richard, and he was due to die on the morrow in any case. It's no worse than any husband, father, or brother would have done. God will judge your actions. Therefore, keep your regrets for your wife, who is stirring even now. Here, take her this drink, and I will leave you both in peace.'

She swept regally from the chamber and Richard approached the bed and sat quietly waiting for Anne to come fully awake. Her face was pale, her lips tinged blue, but her shadowed eyes brightened noticeably when she recognised him. Her gaunt features stretched into the semblance of a smile and, as far as Richard was concerned, even death could not diminish the sunshine of her greeting. He supported her head and helped her to drink, trying not to flinch from the burning heat of her fingers when she clung to his. She attempted to speak, her voice merely a croak.

'Richard?' she swallowed and wet her lips with a tongue that seemed too large for her mouth. 'Was that Cecily?'

Richard nodded and helped her to sip from the cup again, moistening her mouth, wondering if she had heard him make confession.

'I wanted to bid her goodbye. Thank her for me, won't you? And I thank you too, Richard, for everything you have ever done for me. I love you, so very much and …you'll be a great king, I know you will.'

She coughed again, desperately Richard dabbed the blood from her lips before she gripped his hand and pressed it to her burning cheek. 'You have made me so very happy, my love.'

For a long time, Richard remained beside the rumpled bed. As her struggle for breath ceased, the pain that had sat so heavily on him, lifted and, even when she drew her last breath, the terror he had lately suffered did not return.

He lifted a tress of hair and twirled it between his fingers. He was empty, unable to remember any prayers, and so did not ask the angels to watch over her. Richard was only aware of a supreme reluctance to go on. He pulled the covers up to her chin, trying to retain the warmth that had a short time since burned like fire through her veins. As he closed her eyes for the last time, he did not weep but his hands were unsteady as he kissed her goodbye.

King Richard III stood at the chamber window and stared blindly at the cloudless sky as the midday sun was extinguished, and the spirit of his wife slipped slowly away.

The End

When Anne's story ended, Richard's continued for just six more months. The remainder of his reign beset by treason, intrigue and betrayal, culminating at Bosworth field where some of his followers, notably, William Stanley and

Northumberland, both in the pay of Henry Tudor, turned against the king at the last. The Battle of Bosworth saw an end to the Plantagenet dynasty in England and the beginning of the Tudor era but today, the battle continues …

If you have enjoyed this book please consider leaving a review.

Author's note

Since writing *A Daughter of Warwick* in the early noughties (originally published under the author name of J.M Ruddock,) I continue to write Historical Fiction but have moved away from this romantic style. At the time of writing, I wanted to give Anne the chance to tell her own story. Until now she has always appeared as a footnote in Richard's life, or as a minor character in the larger picture of the war of the roses. If I were to rewrite it now, twenty years after writing this novel, I would probably do it very differently. I have considered starting over but I find it difficult to return to a subject I've already covered. Anne and Richard will make an appearance on the novel I have just begun which tells the story of Marguerite of Anjou.

If you enjoyed this you might like my trilogy, *The Beaufort Chronicle*, which is about the life of Lady Margaret Beaufort. I have also written more widely on Elizabeth of York, or Bess as I have called her in this book. *A Song of Sixpence* traces Elizabeth's life after the battle of Bosworth and considers the possibility that at least one of her brothers survived into the Tudor era.

I have written about Henry VIII in the trilogy, *The Henrician Chronicle*, comprising of *A Matter of Conscience, Henry VIII: the Aragon Years; A Matter of Faith: Henry VIII: the Days of the Pheonix* and *A Matter of Time: Henry VIII, the Dying of the Light*. I also have books detailing the experiences of Anne Boleyn in *The Kiss of the Concubine*, Katheryn Parr in *Intractable Heart*, and Anne of Cleves and Katherine Howard feature in *The Winchester Goose: at the Court of Henry VIII*. *Sisters of Arden,* also set in Henry VIII's reign, relates the adventures of a priory of dispossessed nuns during the dissolution of the monasteries.

My earliest work is set much earlier. *Peaceweaver* is the story of Eadgyth, queen to both Gruffydd ap Llewellyn and Harold II in the run up to the Norman Conquest. *The Forest Dwellers* is set after the conquest in the New Forest and addresses the question of who killed Willliam Rufus. My other early medieval book is called *The Song of Heledd*, a heartbreakingly brutal tale set during the 7th century in what is now Wales. *The Book of Thornhold* has recently been rewritten and republished under my *Judith Arnopp* banner. It is the story of an ancient, illuminated book, the narrative traces its journey from the days of the Vikings, through history to the present day, encompassing generations of the Thornbury family who come to own it, and the evolution of the house they live in, Thornhold Manor.

Many of my titles are on Kindle, Paperback and some are on Audible. I hope you enjoy them.

author.to/juditharnoppbooks
www.judithmarnopp.com

Printed in Great Britain
by Amazon